# Bewitched by Bigfoot

Emilia Abraham
The Cryptid Chronicles #1

# Contents

# Copyright

Copyright © 2023 Emilia Abraham

# Dedication

To my husband and his big feet (he made me do this)
And to all my unhinged readers who believe in Bigfoot...and are convinced he's
fuckable.

# Tropes

**SLOW BURN (seriously, I cannot stress this enough)**
Grumpy/Grumpy (yes it's a trope. I'm making it one)
Dude in Distress
Different Worlds
Sworn off Relationships
Dark Secret
Protectiveness
Touch Her & Die (in a romcom context)
Mistaken Identity
Forced Proximity (of their own making)
Fated Mates
One Bed (sort of)
Secret Identity
Fish Outta Water
Brother's Friend (not quite best, but he only has two so it counts)
Fake Relationship (they're not very good at it)
Hurt/Comfort

**Content Warnings:**
Adult Language
Adult Sexual Scenes
Mild Primal Play (in a romcom setting so settle down)

# Let the Moon Guide You

## Gemma

"I'm sorry, Ginger," my supervisor's boss says in a fake tone.

"It's Gemma," I whisper, blinking back tears.

At least Lucinda has the good grace to look ashamed. Doesn't change the fact she's firing me. No, not firing. They were very clear they were "letting me go," as if that makes it any better. This is the fifth job I've lost in the last three years and I'm starting to think the problem is me. Actually, I know the problem is me, even if I don't want to admit it.

"Well, you can work through the end of your shift and then pack up your things. Nigel will help you get everything to the car," she says, turning away to leave my shoebox of an office.

Rage washes over me and my head snaps up. "Excuse me?"

She stutters to a stop, her ankle almost giving out in her impossibly high heels. Why she's wearing them when we work in a warehouse is beyond me. She's usually ensconced in the offices overlooking the open area I'm shoved into, lording her position over us, both physically and mentally.

"Um." Her mouth pinches, bright red lipstick standing out against her pale skin. "Nigel? The security guard? We don't want you to struggle with your things."

She says it as if they're doing me a favor assigning me a bodyguard when we both know she just doesn't want me to steal something on the way out. As if *that's* the reason they're firing me. In fact, she never gave a reason. They never do. These jobs just never seem to work out.

*They can sense you're different. It's why we live in isolated communities, Gemma. You know that.* My mother's voice is harsh as it rings through my head.

She said the same thing when I was ten and said I wanted to be a musician. And again, when I was thirteen and wanted to travel. And then a final time as I was walking out the door to go off to college, though she thought it was a waste of time and I'd be back by the first snowfall. I never went back, but she was right. Everyone can sense that I'm not like them.

"I know who Nigel is. Why am I expected to stay through the end of the day if you're firing me?" I say, pushing to my feet.

She leans back, as if to flee the room. I'm not particularly intimidating. Lucinda actually towers over me, especially in her heels. It must be my eyes, which are probably edging from the light brown they usually are to gold. Shifting in front of her would be catastrophic, and I suck in a deep breath.

"We're letting you go, Ginger, but you still have tasks to complete. Your final paycheck will be deposited into your account minus any"—she clears her throat, glancing down the hall—"deductions that might be needed."

It's the insinuation that pushes me over the edge into not giving a shit. I would have stayed had they asked nicely or hell, even given me an actual reason. Instead, she hid behind her dark blue pencil skirt and crisp white shirt and fucked me over without so much as a thank you for making the warehouse more efficient in my seven months than what she's been able to accomplish in her seven years here.

"No."

Her deer in the headlights look is comical and I almost burst out laughing.

"Excuse me?" she asks, then pinches her bright red lips together again. It must be her default mode.

"I'm sorry you're unfamiliar with the word, but I said, 'no.' I won't be staying until the end of the day. I won't be finishing any tasks. And I certainly won't be allowing you to deduct anything from my paycheck. If I find that you have, I will be contacting my lawyer to sue your ass faster than you can wobble back to the upper offices."

Her mouth drops open and satisfaction flows through me, easing the tension in my muscles. She sputters before spinning around and clicking her way quickly down the hall.

Sighing, I collapse into my chair, wondering what the hell I'm going to do now. I don't have any friends, much less a fucking lawyer. I worked as an assistant to one for all of three months. I'm sure he wouldn't let me back in the office since it's been so many years. He probably won't even remember me.

"Miss Livia?" Nigel says, tapping on my door. "Are you okay?"

I shoot to my feet, smoothing my hands down my sweater, mostly to get rid of the evidence of my stress. Nigel isn't a hugger, but he always goes the extra mile to make others feel comfortable. It's so at odds with his appearance that at first I thought he was a spy for upper management. It didn't take long to figure out that wasn't the case.

"I'm fine, Nigel. Thank you," I say breathlessly.

Swinging the chair around, I shove it into the corner, which is all of two feet away. I huff, pulling open desk drawers and slamming them shut when I realize I don't have anything here. Even if I had the room in this tiny space, I wouldn't have brought anything other than my phone charger.

I snatch up my purse from the bottom drawer and sling it over my shoulder. Glancing around one last time, I grab my copy of the employee handbook and shove it in my bag, hoping I won't need it. My tennis shoes squeak on the tiles as I make my way toward Nigel. He steps aside and I slip out the door, pulling it shut behind me. I didn't even bother logging out of my computer. I'm sure they can take care of it.

Peeking at the massive windows overlooking the large open warehouse space, I find Lucinda tracking my movements. Even from here, I can tell she's pursing her lips. I don't give a shit. An older man joins her and he leans in, saying something to her. She nods and I turn away from the sight. There's no point worrying about them.

"I sure am sorry about this, Miss Livia. You didn't deserve this," Nigel mutters.

"It's fine. Probably time for a change."

He nods, though I'm sure he doesn't agree. He probably has no idea what I'm talking about. Several workers' eyes follow me as Nigel escorts me to the employee entrance. One or two raise their hands, waving to me, but most just watch as I take my walk of shame.

"Don't be a stranger, Gemma."

I let out a humorless laugh. "I doubt I'll be allowed to come back, Nigel. But I appreciate it. I'll be fine. New start and all that."

I'm almost to my car when he calls my name and I turn.

"Let the moon guide you." He disappears back inside before I can respond, not that I would know how to.

It's been years since I've heard that advice, though I heard it enough growing up. It was a staple within our community, along with never leaving for more than a day or two. Whenever there was an issue, "let the moon guide you." Whenever there was a dispute, "let the moon guide you." Whenever someone got the itch to leave, "let the moon guide you." Which ultimately meant, let it force them to stay exactly where they are for the good of the community, because one is not above the whole.

Scoffing, I slide into the seat, slamming the door behind me. Nigel shouldn't know the saying. It's not exactly a cliché used in polite society, which means he knows exactly who I am. He's probably one of them. I hate that my mind immediately settles on him being a spy for my parents. They're halfway across the country, most likely living their life without a second thought for me. No way they'd send someone to keep tabs on me.

I start the car and make my way home, weaving through the city. I'm not surprised Nigel is a shifter of some type. There's a lot more of us than non-shifting humans realize, though usually we don't settle in the city. The bright lights and sometimes spontaneous shifting occurrences don't exactly mesh well. It's why there are communities like the one I grew up in scattered throughout the country.

Most of them are labeled dying towns, fading from everyone's minds except the people who live there. My hometown is different. They thrive off the superstition and lore swirling through the densely forested area. I spent every summer working one festival or tour after another.

Pulling up to my apartment, I find a spot right out front and grin, until I remember that it's the middle of the morning and everyone else is at their jobs, while I am now unemployed. As I glance up at the five-story building, my heart aches. I didn't particularly enjoy what I was doing, but it paid the bills. Now that I'm free of that responsibility, I realize how depressed I was. Maybe I was just apathetic to my lot in life. I'd rather be in nature, doing whatever people who live in the forest do. I'd probably be terrible at being a lumberjack and flannel isn't exactly my style.

My phone rings as I'm opening my apartment door. Kicking off my shoes, I dig in my bag, pulling it out and sighing. Of course it's my mother. She never did understand that I work during the day and can't talk. Apparently today is her lucky day.

"Mother. What can I do for you?" I say dejectedly, dropping my purse on the entry table.

I don't have much in my apartment since I move more often than I originally thought I would. Collapsing on the small couch, I glance around at the bare walls as the sounds of my childhood filter through the phone.

"Gemma, dear. I'm surprised you're not at work." My mother's voice blankets over me, both comforting and suffocating all at the same time.

"I have the day off." *And tomorrow, and the next and the next.*

"Well, I'm wondering if you're coming back for the Samhain festival. We could really use the extra help. A producer for one of those supernatural shows has shown interest, so we're all working double time. We only have a month to get everything together."

Of course, she's calling for help instead of asking how I am. It's the only time she calls these days—to ask if I'm coming back to work some event or another. I understand it's how the town is kept alive, but it'd be nice if she wanted to actually see me. When I was young, the Samhain festival was special. We celebrated as a community without outsider's influence.

"I don't think I'll be able to. I'm real busy here."

"Notably vague," she snaps. "Everyone else is coming, so I'm sure your absence will be noticed."

The words she's not saying float through the air. Others will notice I'm not there to work, but my family will barely bat an eye. Part of that is my fault for staying away for so many years, constantly rejecting my parents' requests for my presence.

"It'll be so busy, no one will notice." Grabbing my laptop from the table in front of me, I search the website for the town. "How's Dad?"

She prattles on about how much my father is doing, then moves on to everything my siblings are engaged in for Moon Cove. My screen fills with images from the end of summer bash that attracted a news station from the city an hour away. Sightings of mythical creatures coupled with carnival games and ending with a massive bonfire on the beach were all included. My heart aches at the memories. I used to love being a part of the events. As a kid, I wasn't expected to work a booth or let people catch a glimpse of me shifting. Once I hit my first shift, everything changed.

My mother clears her throat and I jolt back to the conversation. "Gemma, you know people don't blame you anymore, right?"

"People in the Cove have a long memory, Mom. I'm sure there's more than a couple townsfolk who will be happy I'm not at the Samhain festival," I say, bitterness weaving into my voice.

"The town has recovered. No one talks about it anymore," she states flippantly, though I can hear the lie in her tone.

She means people outside of the Cove don't report on my fuckup anymore. Everyone in town whispers about it still, at least according to my sister, Kira. She only calls to gloat about being the perfect daughter and to remind me what a disappointment I am.

"Mother, we both know if I came back, I would only be a reminder of the incident. I won't be the cause of the family being ostracized again."

"Oh Gemma. You can't keep running. Come home."

An awkward silence fills the line. This is one of her manipulative tactics. No matter what I say, she'll rebut my reasonings with guilt until she gets called away by something more important. So I wait while the quiet settles between us.

Finally, she clears her throat. "Gemma, you know I love you, but you'll regret—dammit. I have to go, dear. Come home." With her last plea swirling through the air, she hangs up.

I let my phone drop to the couch, sighing as I glance around my bare apartment. Maybe she's right and I should just cut my losses. I've spent the last seven years skipping from place to place, trying to find where I belong.

When I left Moon Cove, I had such high hopes. I thought if I wandered enough, I'd run headlong into fate and my perfect life would fall into my lap. Now I'm thinking the goddess forgot about me in her haste to help everyone else.

My phone chimes, indicating an incoming text. I'm sure it's from my mom, but when I pull it up, it's from my brother Slade, asking me to call him. We used to be close, but as the years passed it became harder to keep in touch. It wouldn't surprise me if he was calling on behalf of my mother. She'll use whatever tactics she can to bring me home. They must be really struggling if she's using Slade. I grab my phone and wait for it to connect.

"Gemma? You there?"

I haven't talked to him in at least six months, and my eyes well up with tears, which cascade down my face when I try to blink them away.

Clearing my throat, I answer. "Hey, Slade. How's it going?"

"No word from you in six months and that's all I get? Fucking-A, Gemma."

"Phone works both ways," I mutter.

"Sorry. Things are a little chaotic around here. I shouldn't take it out on you."

I don't want to ask what's happening in Moon Cove. I left for a reason and asking usually leads to questions about when I'm coming back. Even if living in the city sucks and I hate not having a place I belong, I still don't want to go home. I'd suffocate from the judgment and familial responsibility I'm sure my parents would pile on me without even realizing. Still, I crave the connection to the place I thought I'd left behind.

"What's going on?" I ask, laying my head against the back of the couch.

"Typical stuff. Samhain festival is a month away. Mom's freaking out. Dad's been trying to organize shit for the carnival. Oh, and Debra keeps making snide comments about how this whole thing is going to fail because it's our family's turn to run shit."

"Well, that explains why Mom called me in a panic trying to get me to come back. When was the last time you guys ran things?" I ask, rolling my head to scan the bookshelves lining my walls. They're pretty much the only items I lug around from city to city.

"It's been a while," he hedges.

"You mean it's been since I fucked up and almost exposed us to the world?" I say bitterly.

"They made it worse than it actually was. None of that was your fault, Gem." Slade's voice is a warm balm, soothing my wounded pride.

"Still made me more of an outcast."

"Look, I get why you left. You know I'm on your side, but I didn't call to talk about that."

I roll my eyes, even though he can't see me. No one ever wants to discuss what went down. They push it under the rug, assuming if they ignore the problem, eventually it'll go away. I shouldn't hold on to the past. I've mostly let it go. At least that's what I tell myself. But the way my parents dealt with the aftermath still stings.

"Did you call just to bitch? Because I'm not really in the mood to listen to you complaining about how much of a shitshow your life is."

"Well, aren't you a ball of fucking sunshine. Gem, I need a favor."

"I'm not coming back," I snarl.

"Settle down, pup. I'm not about to use my favor for our mom to drag your ass back here. I actually need you to go to Whispering Pines and help out my friend. He's got an issue with his summer camp."

"Except I don't know anything about summer camps. How the hell am I supposed to help? And did you forget I have a job?" The lie burns as it comes out, but I'm not about to admit I was fired only a couple hours ago.

"First of all, it's not like you're going to be running the damn thing. Second, I *may* have heard you lost your job. So, you've got the time. Think of the kids, Gem."

"How the hell did you find out I got fired?" I growl, snapping upright, and then it hits me. "Nigel."

"Bingo. Nigel and I go way back."

"Way back to when I was hired, you mean," I grumble.

"Gem, I didn't want to have to bring this up, but you owe me."

Shit. He's right, I do owe him. He's the one who helped me when I wanted to go to college—even drove my ass halfway across the country. Our parents were not happy with him, and he took a lot of shit for me. I never thought he'd call it in for someone else.

Pulling my computer into my lap, I search the place he's talking about. Their website isn't much different from every other small town. They're not as extreme as Moon Cove is, but they still have festivals. Clicking on the summer camp tab, pictures of laughing kids fill the screen.

"What exactly are you wanting me to do? It's almost winter, so there shouldn't be any more camp sessions. Shit. Do not tell me he needs me to be a den mother or something."

He chuckles. "Nothing like that. Just work the books. You know, what you're good at. He was trying to make it into a legit business, but I'm wondering if there's another way. All you have to do is go help him out for a few weeks. You can take off by Samhain. Maybe a bit later."

Thunder rolls through the air and I whip my head toward the window. Bright autumn sunlight streams into the apartment and a shiver runs down my spine. Nigel's final words flash through my mind. Thunder isn't exactly the moon guiding me, but as I peer at the computer screen, I figured that's as good as it's going to get.

"I'll need a place to stay," I sigh, resigning myself to going if only to see if I can finally find what I've been searching for.

# Well This is Awkward
## Jake

"Jake? You home?" my one and only friend Chase calls from my driveway.

"Out back," I reply, swinging the axe as he comes around the corner of my cabin.

"Don't you think you've got enough wood for the winter?" He laughs, crossing his arms as I toss the pieces onto the pile.

"Never enough." I grunt, lining up another log.

He glances around the woods. "You ever think this place is a little...isolating?"

"We really going to have this conversation again, Chase? I like being alone. You're the only one who can't take the hint."

Chase's boisterous laugh echoes through the trees and a flock of birds takes flight. I swing the axe again, splitting the wood with one stroke. He whistles, as if this is the first time he's watched me do this.

Half the time during autumn he comes by, pretending he has nothing better to do, but we both know he's checking up on me. For some reason, he thinks I need saving, no matter how many times I tell him I'm happy being left alone. It's just the way my kind is. I was built to be by myself. I've accepted that, even if in the dead of night I wish there was someone next to me.

"Kind of hypocritical to say you wanna be left alone when you run an entire kids' survival camp all fucking summer."

"Kids are different. They don't ask questions."

He bursts out laughing again, sending more creatures skittering through the brush. He doesn't understand the difference. Sure, the kids who come here ask a lot of questions, but I don't mind those ones. When adults ask questions, they don't care about the answer unless it reinforces their judgments. It's fucking annoying. I'll stick to the kids' inquiries into what happens if they eat a random mushroom in the woods.

The blaring of my landline interrupts whatever bullshit he's about to spout, and I dash up the stairs of the back porch. The screen door slams behind me, and I grab the receiver hanging on the wall of my office. Most people don't have these types of phones anymore, but the cell reception here is spotty at best. Perks of living on the side of a mountain.

"Yeah?" I grunt, peering out the back door to spy on Chase. The last time I left him alone with an axe, he nearly chopped his foot off from messing around.

"Jake? It's Slade. How ya been?"

"Slade? Shit, what's wrong?" I haven't spoken to Slade in over a year.

"Nothing. Well, I mean, nothing really. It's not like someone died or something." His usually deep voice squeaks, and I narrow my eyes as I settle in the seat behind my desk.

I don't have a lot of friends, but it's hard not to like a guy like Slade. He's easy-going and persistent, much like Chase. We met years ago when he was driving back from across the country. Something about bringing his younger sister to college. We ended up camping at the same site. Neither of us were in a hurry to get back anywhere, not that I had a place to go at the time. We ended up spending a week drinking and fishing and drinking some more. Over the years we've kept in touch, though since I moved to Whispering Pines, it's been harder. Chase and Slade are some of the few people I actually don't mind hanging out with.

"What's the problem, Slade?" I grunt, resting my elbows on my desk.

"So, I've got a family member that needs a little bit of help. I know it's kind of shitty to call you out of the blue, but they're in a jam, and I thought with that summer camp of yours winding down, you could put them to work. Just for a few weeks."

I sigh, cracking my neck as I try to find a way out of this. "I don't know, Slade."

"I didn't want to bring this up..."

"Then don't," I growl, even though I know he won't listen.

"You owe me, Jake. I could have left you there and I didn't. I saved your ass from that cougar."

"She was like five years older than us. That doesn't make her a cougar."

"Doesn't matter. She would have eaten you alive and we both know it. You said you owe me and I'm cashing in."

Grunting, I shove out of the chair. "Fine. But I don't know what the hell you're expecting me to do with them."

"They can help with the Halloween party you guys put on. Or help winterize the place. It'll just be for a couple weeks." I can hear the grin in his voice as the words rush out, and I scowl.

I could use the help, though I'd rather not accept it from some stranger, no matter if they're related to Slade or not. The townsfolk badgered me into creating a whole haunted house for the kids, as well as a haunted trail for adults at the site. Dealing with the set-up of not one but two of these things isn't something I can pull off by myself. I should have said no, but when the kids got involved, there was no way I could disappoint them.

"What's their name?" I ask, shuffling an order form for a survival kit to the side.

"Gem," he says. "I really appreciate this, Jake."

"Well, hopefully this Jim doesn't mind hard labor and being stuck in a small-ass town."

"One last thing..."

I wait, but he doesn't finish his sentence. I have a feeling whatever else he needs is going to put me over the edge. A soft knock at the door has my head snapping up and Chase raises his eyebrow. I forgot he was here.

"Spit it out, Slade. I've got shit to do."

"You got some extra space at the camp? I tried to book them at the hotel, but it's filled for months."

"It's fine. I'll figure something out. We're done with the sleepaway camp part, so there are cabins open, though if it snows, they're shit outta luck. There's no insulation or heat in those things." No way am I inviting some random dude to stay at my place. I enjoy my solitude and I don't plan on sharing.

"No problem. I'm sure the weather will hold."

"Email me when they'll be here."

"Actually, they're coming today. Like, right now."

"You've got to be fucking kidding me," I grumble, regretting this already.

A woman giggles on the other end of the line and Slade shushes them. "Don't fucking start. We both know you would say yes. I'll email you where to meet up. But I really do appreciate this, Jake. You're really helping me out."

"Slade?" I grunt, breaking into what I'm sure will be at least five minutes of him thanking me.

"Yeah?"

"This makes us fucking even."

His laughter is the only response before he hangs up. Chase gives me a look and I wave him away. The last thing I want to do is explain what the hell I just got myself into. He'll take the piss out of me, and I don't have the energy to deal with it. This whole situation will just be one more thing to add to my list of shit to get through before the snow flies and then I'll be free.

"What the hell do you want, Chase?" I slam the phone back on the receiver and push past him, heading out the back door.

"I actually came for a reason, you know. Paul wanted to know when you were coming to get your supplies. Told him I'd come up and ask." He follows me.

I hate going into town. Usually I have everything I need at my cabin, but once a month I'm forced to interact with people to get supplies. My phone has been ringing off the hook for the past week. It's a miracle I answered Slade's call. I've been putting off heading down the mountain, if only so I don't have to talk to anyone.

"Why didn't you just bring the supplies with you? Paul could have charged my account." I grab one of the logs and toss it onto the pile before picking up the axe, intending to keep working.

"Maybe because he wants to make sure you're still alive. Besides, Paul owns the place. He's got enough to worry about without the added stress." He sighs when I glare at him. "Just get in the damn truck, Jake." Chase turns away, expecting me to follow.

"We might need to deal with some other shit while we're there," I mutter.

He waves a hand over his shoulder, and I slam the blade into the stump. The last thing I want to do is meet up with Slade's family. The more I think about it, the more I realize he didn't give me any information, really. I have no idea if this is his brother or cousin. I don't know what they look like. Fuck, I should have said no.

Dusting off my clothes, I walk back inside to check my email. Sure enough, Slade's message is sitting in my inbox with just a time and description of a car. I glance at the clock and sigh. If I leave now, I'll kill two birds with one stone at least.

Chase honks the horn and I roll my eyes. It took him four years of bothering me for me to even consider him a friend. After almost a decade, he's the only one I'd allow to come here, much less hurry me along. None of the other townspeople would bother putting in that much work, but Chase is cut from a different cloth.

"Would you hurry the hell up?" Chase calls as I round the porch.

I don't even bother to lock the front door. There's no point since no one comes up this way. He starts bumping down the gravel driveway before I've even shut the door. Grumbling, I put on my seatbelt as we enter the trees, dousing the entire area in shadows. It's not until we're halfway down the mountain that he clears his throat.

"The festival is coming up. Marcy keeps asking if you're planning on coming by. Thinks you could help her before your haunted house thing," he says, clearing his throat again.

"Doubt it. And why you been talking to Marcy Higgins about me anyways?"

I love the solitude of living in the forest. The small town at the base of the mountain is pretty nice too, except it comes with small-town people. They get in everyone's business. No one's got any secrets and they sure as hell can't keep anything to themselves—especially Marcy Higgins. Chase is convinced she wants to tie me down, though I don't see how that's true since I barely say more than a dozen words to her in a year.

"You know how she is. Won't leave well enough alone. At some point you're going to have to put her in her place, tell her you're not interested," he mutters.

"The last time I told her I wasn't interested in settling down, she told me she likes the strong, silent type. Whatever the hell that means."

He chuckles, veering right at the fork in the road. The other path loops around to the summer camp I set up five years ago. It's a lot better use of my time than selling survival kits online. When I first started putting them together, I had to go to town at least once a week. Now, Chase picks up the packages and takes care of it for me, thank the goddess, otherwise I would have quit a long time ago. I don't exactly need the money, but I'd get pretty bored if I didn't have anything else to occupy my time other than bumbling around my cabin and chopping wood.

"You could just tell her you're still nursing a broken heart."

"For ten fucking years? I doubt she'd buy that. Besides, I'd rather not lie."

"Well, maybe someone will come through on Samhain and scoop her up."

"One can only hope."

He slows as houses pop up, then give way to stores and a little hotel. The diner comes into view, and I duck down in my seat.

Chance snorts. "She's not going to be waiting outside to jump you through the window."

"If she sees me, she'll come to the general store and accost me."

"Accost you? What the hell are you talking about?" Chance grunts as he pulls into the parking spot.

"Every time I come here, someone scuttles off and spreads it around town. One of the local gossips comes along and then I'm stuck here listening to them prattle on about the latest news going around dealing with shit I don't care about. It's annoying." I run my hand through my long hair. "By the way, I got someone coming to stay in the cabins at the camp."

Pushing from the truck, I slam the door behind me, cutting off his burst of laughter. There's only one rundown car out front, which doesn't say much. Most folks around here tend to walk to work. More will come with the festival. I'm guessing more people drive as soon as the snow flies, but autumn still has a hold on us. I can't wait for winter to bury me in my cabin, exactly where I want to be.

The bell jingles above the door and Adam, Paul's son, looks up from behind the counter, lifting a hand to us. I'm surprised Paul isn't hovering to make sure his kid isn't messing anything up despite the fact Adam is well into his twenties now.

"So your buddy Slade convinced you to let someone stay at the camp? For what?"

"Apparently they need something to do, and Slade offered me up on a silver fucking platter."

I prowl for the back, hoping I can get the rest of the things I need quickly. Chase laughs again and I scowl back at him, though I can't see him as I round the corner.

I slam into someone and grunt. Instinctively, I reach out the grab them, but they slip from my fingers, letting out an oof as they crash to the floor.

"Shit. Dammit," I mutter, leaning down to help the woman up, but I freeze when our eyes meet.

I have no idea how long we sit there with her on the ground and my hand reaching for her. She blinks, breaking whatever hold she had over me. Wide brown eyes gaze up at me, but I could have sworn they were edged with gold only a moment before. Shaking my head, I hold out my hand and she takes it hesitantly.

"Sorry," I grunt, tugging her a little too hard, and she stumbles into me.

She jumps back, hand still wrapped in mine and practically knocks over a display of jams Marcy supplies the store with. Yanking her toward me again, she squeaks and steps on the toe of my boot. They're steel-toed, so I don't feel a thing, but she gasps. As if she'd be able to actually hurt me. Even if she stomped on my foot I wouldn't feel it. I tower over her, but that's nothing new. She barely comes up to my chest, though she's probably average height.

"You alright?" I ask as her eyes dart down.

"I'm fine." She glances up at me again. "You can let go of my hand. Promise I won't plow into you again."

I drop my grip on her, tucking my hand in my pocket. "Pretty sure I'm the one who ran into you."

"It's fine. I'm fine. Sorry."

Narrowing my eyes, I scan her from the tips of her worn tennis shoes over her supple hips and topping out at her russet hair. She's panting, as if she just ran a mile instead of just got knocked to the ground.

I step back, hoping to ease the tension in the air. It does nothing but tighten the pull I feel toward her. I'm used to making people nervous, though they don't usually have such an obvious reaction.

"You hiding, Jake?" Chase bellows, clapping me on the back as he comes up behind me. "Oh, hello there."

He shoots her a dazzling smile and I scowl. With Chase's mussed blond hair and brilliant blue eyes, most women melt into a puddle at his feet. I usually don't care. I shouldn't now either, but as Chase continues to grin at her, my heart twists. I take another step back, letting Chase take over the situation. The woman's eyes never leave mine. Ducking my head, I pull in a deep breath.

Chase sticks his hand out and she flinches, finally looking at him. "I'm Chase. And you are?"

She clears her throat as she shakes his hand. "Gemma."

"What brings you to Whispering Pines, Gemma?"

All I want to do is get my stuff and get the hell out of here. Gemma's attention is fully on Chase now, and it'll most likely stay there for a while if past experiences are any indication. I take yet another step back and her brown eyes shoot to mine. I'm caught in her gaze again, the intensity on her face keeping my feet rooted to the ground.

"Just visiting," she mumbles to Chase before biting her lip. "I'm sorry I ran into you."

"You didn't. I wasn't looking," I say.

Chase groans, running his hands through his hair. "You knocked her over, didn't you? Sorry, he doesn't get out much."

Glaring at Chase, I'm overwhelmed with the urge to wring his neck. To hell with our friendship, he'll survive. Probably. If he keeps talking shit, though, I might just take him for a walk in the woods and leave his ass there. When I peer at Gemma from the corner of my eye, a blush crawls up her neck, staining her cheeks a pretty pink.

"Um, actually, I need some help. I'm looking for a friend of my brothers. A Jake Silvius?" Her eyes bounce from Chase's to mine, and her bottom lip slips between her teeth.

Chase flashes her another grin. "You're in luck then."

He smacks me in the chest, and I glare at him before turning back to Gemma. She stares at me, waiting for a response I don't have. Could this really be the family Slade was talking about?

"I thought you were a guy," I blurt out, instantly regretting the words.

Her eyes widen. "Is that what Slade said?"

I open my mouth to confirm, but snap it shut when I think back. Slade never specifically said, well, anything. "Thought he said your name was Jim, but I suppose he actually said Gem."

"Oh, uh, well. Is that going to be a problem?"

I scan her again, trying to assess whether she'll actually be able to help me with setting up an entire haunted house and a hayrack ride. Assuming that she can't because she's a woman would be a dick move.

"Nope. Just threw me a bit," I mumble, tucking my hands back in my pockets.

"Okay."

She bites her lip again, and I clear my throat, trying to force my body not to react to the move. It doesn't work.

"You got a place to stay, Gemma?" Chase asks, and I shoot him another glare.

"Slade said I could probably find a place in town, but the hotel said they're full."

"You can stay with me," I interrupt.

I snap my mouth shut as Chase turns to me, glee dancing in his eyes. I don't know what came over me, but now the words are out there, floating between us and tinging the air with awkwardness. There's no stuffing *that* cat back in the bag, that's for sure. Shuffling back another step, I run into a clothes rack filled with winter coats. It skitters across the floor, screeching into the space.

"Easy there," Chase mutters as his fingers wrap around my arm and yanks me forward.

I can't stick her in one of the cabins all alone. Gemma might be able to take care of herself, but I wasn't raised that way. How I'm going to find room for her in my one-bedroom cabin is something I'll figure out later.

"Are you sure? I wouldn't be putting you out?" she says, hope shining in her eyes.

I nod, then shake my head, not sure which question I'm answering. "I have the room. It's a little out of the way, though."

"A little?" Chase snorts.

"It's up the mountain," I say, throwing my thumb over my shoulder.

"Mountain? I thought it was just a big hill with trees." Her cheeks flame and the corner of my mouth twitches.

"Used to be, but apparently it shrunk. You don't have to stay with me. I'm sure there's somewhere else you could go." I rub the back of my neck.

"Oh, I don't want to put you out," she whispers, averting her eyes.

Chase's head swivels back and forth and then he smirks, turning to Gemma. "Honey, Jake's got a better setup than anything else you'll find. Wouldn't be bad for him to have someone around to make sure he stays out of trouble."

Scowling, I open my mouth to refute him, but nothing comes out. Normally, I'd prefer to be alone, but for some reason I don't want Gemma to be anywhere else other than with me. A throb in my chest almost sends me to my knees when she twists her hands in front of her. She's going to say no, and I'll be left alone.

Which is exactly how I like it. I shouldn't care either way. I *don't* care either way.

She smirks, glancing at me from under her lashes. "I'm sure I could keep you out of trouble."

# Library boner—Oh and There's Only One Bed

## Gemma

I track Chase and Jake from my car as they load the back of Chase's truck. I'm not entirely sure how I got into this situation. One minute I was searching for a warm jacket and now I'm moving in with a man I'd like to climb like a tree.

Temporarily moving in with him. Because it's only for now, not forever. In fact, I don't even know if I'll make it through the month without having to skip town, consequences be damned.

Gripping the wheel tightly, I track Jake's large frame as he drops another box into the bed of the truck. I didn't think muscles actually rippled, but the evidence is right in front of me. He may be glaring at Chase, but it doesn't hide how striking his eyes are. And his beard does nothing to distract from his sharp cheekbones or his full lips.

I drop my forehead to the steering wheel before I start salivating over a lumberjack in the middle of Main Street. My attempt at hiding doesn't last long, and I peek at the pair. Jake's hair is tied back, but I bet it reaches his shoulders. My fingers flex, itching to run through the dark golden strands. Shit. This is not what I thought would happen when I agreed to come here. I should have told Jake I'd figure out where to stay on my own.

I have no idea what came over me at that moment. When Jake offered me a place to stay at his house, the words just flew out of my mouth without warning. Then my chest throbbed and I couldn't breathe. It was like something was physically stopping me from refusing him. And telling him I'd keep him out of trouble? I am not a flirt.

A knock on the window has me jumping in my seat. Chase ducks down, smiling as he gestures for me to follow them. Jake doesn't even glance my way as they pull out of the spot. He's probably regretting offering up his place.

I don't have another option though, even though it's still early in the day. No matter how awkward it is, I can handle sleeping at his place for one night. I'll just stay out of his way. Hopefully, the hotel will call me tomorrow and tell me a room opened up. Then I can leave without seeming rude.

I'll still have to help him with the summer camp, but I can run the numbers from anywhere. We can meet in town to review his finances. As soon as I've fulfilled my promise to Slade, I can get back to my life. It might be a bleak wasteland of nothingness right now, but I'll bounce back. I always do.

The drive up the mountain, as they call it, is bumpier than I expected. My car bottoms out more than once, and I cringe every time it happens. We come to a fork in the road and veer left. There's a sign pointing the other way, but I've passed it before I can read what it says. When the trees finally give way to a small clearing, sunlight temporarily blinds me and I slam on my brakes, afraid I'm about to rear-end them.

Black spots clear from my vision, revealing a log cabin complete with a wraparound porch. It's fucking adorable and seems to be handmade. Can log cabins be handmade? I don't know, but it's still adorable.

The pang in my chest is back and I swing open my door, only to dive back in when the car rolls forward. I'm not a particularly clumsy person, but this town is doing something to me. Or maybe it's the ginormous lumberjack who's exiting the truck parked in front of the porch.

"You okay there?" Chase calls, laughter tinging his voice. I wonder if he ever frowns. Based on the grooves around his eyes, I doubt it.

"Fine. Sorry," I call back as I throw the car into park. "Is this a good place, or should I move?"

Chase glances at Jake's retreating back as he climbs the porch stairs before turning back to me. "There is good for now. I can get by when I leave."

"Leave?" I squeak, still half in my car, so I'm pretty sure he didn't hear me.

"I'm going to get this shit inside. Why don't you look around out here for a bit, yeah?" He doesn't wait for an answer as he grabs several wooden boxes from the bed of his truck.

"Of course he doesn't fucking live here, Gemma," I mutter under my breath, tucking my foot back inside. "It's only for one night. Then you can scurry back to wherever the hell you're going to end up and pretend you didn't just make an ass of yourself."

"You're going to have to speak up if you need help," Jake grunts, and I jolt as the car door swings toward me.

I don't have time to pull my leg in and I brace myself for it to squish me, but Jake's hand shoots out, stopping it right before I end up limping my way through the next week. Tucking my foot inside, I rest my head on the steering wheel as my cheeks burn.

"You're a skittish thing, aren't you?" His tone is accusatory, but that may just be me projecting.

"No, actually, I'm not. Nor am I particularly clumsy, but this town must bring out some long-dormant trait in me. I'm sure as soon as I leave, I'll go back to being sensible and even-keeled," I say, still hiding my face behind my reddish hair. It's lighter now at the end of the summer, but the strands will darken as winter descends.

"The town?" he growls, and I peek at his scowling face.

"Or the moon. Or something I ate. Or you." I bite my lip as he raises an eyebrow.

I can't read him and it's freaking me out. Usually, I'm able to tell what people's motives are or, at the very least, decipher their body language. My father always said it was instinctual—part of who we are beneath the skin.

Most shifters have some innate ability to anticipate those around us. It was something to do with defenses and mates, but I usually stopped listening by that point. Staring at Jake as he glares down at me, I wish I would have paid more attention to my father's lessons. Maybe I'd be able to figure out why this man is a mystery to me.

"Are you getting out of the car, or do you need more time to figure out if you're running?"

"Jake, don't be an ass," Chase bellows from the porch and Jake's brows pull low over his deep green eyes.

"I wasn't going to run. Clearly, you're having second thoughts about your offer, and I'd rather not force you to house me. It's not exactly a normal thing for people to do," I snarl, grabbing my phone from the center console if only to have something to occupy my hands.

I grit my teeth when the screen flashes no bars. Great, not only will I be stuck sleeping in my car, but the hotel won't be able to call me if they have a room available.

Closing my eyes, I pull in a deep breath, letting the scent of pine and autumn leaves fill my lungs and calm my racing heart. No matter how strange these circumstances are, being able to spend even this sliver of time in the forest is worth it.

A low growl rumbles in Jake's chest, and my eyes fly open. His head is tipped back, long lashes brushing his cheeks. When he exhales, a purr reverberates through him, and I swear it resonates through my body.

"Uh, everything okay over here?" Chase asks, leaning against the hood of my car.

Both of us snap back to the reality and I drop my keys between my legs.

"Sorry, I should get going," I mutter, hands fluttering around my lap. I'd rather not go digging into my crotch when he's standing right there.

"Like hell you will," Jake growls. "Get out of the car, Gemma."

I slide from the seat before I've even fully accepted that I'm moving. Once he slams the door behind me, I blink rapidly, spinning around to figure out what the hell just happened. This town isn't like normal ones. It's more like my hometown, where shit happens that only seems normal to the locals.

Narrowing my eyes at Chase and then Jake, I try to figure out what they're hiding, but it's useless. I don't have the ability to find other shifters. Though Slade does, I doubt he'd fly halfway across the country to investigate a random town in the middle of nowhere for me, even if it is his friend. I make a mental note to call Slade as soon as I'm alone to ask him what he knows.

"You got bags to unload?" Chase asks, leaning to peek at my backseat stuffed with boxes.

If I popped the trunk, it would be mostly the same, but I won't be doing that anytime soon. I packed up my entire apartment since my lease was up. No use renewing it if I wasn't staying in the city. I don't fancy living out of my car for the next several weeks, but it can't be helped at this point. I don't know where I'll end up after I assist Jake with his summer camp.

"Just my suitcase. I can get it." I start for the passenger door.

"Stop," Jake commands and my feet slide on the gravel, refusing to move. "I'll get them."

"What the fuck," I say under my breath.

Chase grins at me as Jake yanks open the car door and grabs both suitcases and the duffel bag sitting on top. He stacks them in one arm and hauls them off to his cabin. I don't know what the hell is going on, but I'm pretty sure I've stepped straight into another shifter community without realizing.

Before I met up with these two, nothing seemed out of the ordinary. Whispering Pines appeared to be like every other small town. I certainly didn't feel like I was being controlled with only a word from anyone other than Jake.

"You coming or what?" Jake calls and I huff.

"Well, that's my cue. You two have fun," Chase says, winking at me before marching to his truck.

In seconds, he's speeding past me as if hellhounds are on his heels, leaving a cloud of dust in his wake. Jake disappears inside the dark interior of his house, and I slowly make my way across the driveway.

As the rumble of Chase's truck fades, the sounds of the forest take over, filling the air with a cacophony of noises I haven't heard in years. When I shift every month, I only go so far into the forest—never enough to experience the woods like the one surrounding Jake's cabin.

Stepping through the door, I ease it shut, waiting for my eyes to adjust to the muted light. Jake clomps down the stairs, his arms devoid of my bags. Peering behind him, I realize there must be a loft, though I can't see anything up there.

"I can see why you like it here," I murmur, stepping out of the small entryway.

The kitchen to the left is larger than I expected, and it has actual appliances. I thought he'd have an icebox or wood stove, but they're modern and look brand new, as if he's never used them.

I can feel his eyes on me as I take in the cozy space. Everything is a lot bigger than I expected, but cozy is the only way to describe it, with the overstuffed furniture flanking the fireplace off to the left. The logs making up the walls are inset, and my mouth drops open as I spy shelf after shelf stuffed full of books. My palms tingle with the need to touch them, read them, smell them.

"Do you want to see the rest?" Jake asks, his voice shaking slightly.

"No," I blurt out, eyes still fixed on the books.

He lets out a low chuckle and then he's next to me, hand on my back as he guides me closer. As the heat from his palm seeps through my shirt, I suck in a deep breath.

"They won't bite," he murmurs, and a shiver snakes down my spine.

"There's so many. Have you read them all?" I ask, stepping away from him, if only to get my breathing under control.

I spin in the middle of the room, eyes jumping from one wall to the next. The shelves are stacked all the way up to the ceiling, though how he reaches them, I have no clue. It's then that I spot the rolling ladder and I groan.

"What's wrong?"

"Absolutely nothing," I whisper, tears filling my eyes. "Have you read them all?"

"Not all, but most of them. Winters are long here, especially when the road becomes impassable. If I run out, I'll just start at the beginning again."

"Wait, you get snowed in every winter. So, you pass the time hanging out in front of your massive fireplace and reading?" I gape at him. "Like all damn winter?"

"Uh, yes? Not much else to do," he says, a blush staining his cheeks. "Seems boring—"

"Boring? Are you freaking kidding me? That sounds like the best freaking thing in the world. No one to bother you or interrupt you when you're in the middle of a really good part? Seriously, I would give anything to have that."

It hits me that maybe I shouldn't have said any of that. Just because I would rather be alone all the time doesn't mean that other people feel the same way. My mother always said we were pack animals, meant to find where we belong among others like us. It wasn't until I was a teenager that I realized how different I was from my family. My siblings were all popular, pulling pranks and getting into mischief, but all I ever wanted to do was read. Sure, I wanted to travel and see the world, but after spending so long in the city, I miss the quiet.

"Anything?" he asks, and my mind blanks.

I glance over my shoulder at him. "Huh?"

"Nothing. I'll show you where you can sleep."

He turns toward the stairs, and I glance once more at the space, wondering if I'll be able to leave tomorrow morning. I may have just fallen in love. Sure, it's not with a person, but this might be better. I've never seen anything like this place before, even in my hometown. Shaking my head, I follow Jake, hoping I can get my head on straight.

The stairs creak slightly as I climb them. I expect the loft to be open to the second floor, but the back half is closed off, creating a bedroom and a small bathroom. The bed is probably made of the same logs as the walls and banister. Asking him if he made all this himself seems like a question he'd brush off, but I don't know how I know that. He's a stranger, no matter how much my mind is trying to convince me otherwise.

Jake wanders to the other side of the bed, leaning down and then hiding something behind his back. He shuffles to the side and tosses what looks like a pair of underwear into the closet before slamming the door shut. Hiding my grin behind my hand, it hits me that this might be the only bedroom.

"Question."

"Answer," he says, crossing his arms and trying to lean back. He jolts upright when he realizes there's a window behind him.

"What's downstairs? In the back?" It's the only way to figure out if he's planning on giving me the only bed in this place.

"Oh, there's another bathroom and an office. I can show you."

He skirts around the bed, his arm brushing mine as he passes, and I shiver. Whatever the hell is going on, I need to get my shit together. His heavy boots mark his way down the stairs, and I hurry to catch up. Swinging off the banister when I reach the bottom, I almost run into Jake's back, but I stop myself at the last second.

"Don't fall over again," he grunts.

Staring at his broad back, I wonder what I did now. I've only been here a half hour and yet he's skipped between wanting me to stay and seeming like he regrets offering at all. As he steps through a doorway, I stutter to a stop. I should turn around and walk away. Coming to this town was a mistake.

He leans around the doorjamb. "You coming?"

"Of course. Sorry, I was just admiring the"—I glance next to me—"walls."

I wince as I turn back to him, but he's already ducked back inside. Sighing, I step into the room and find it stuffed full, but unlike the living room, there aren't any books. First aid kits, ropes in various sizes, and even small shovels are organized on the shelves lining the walls. Jake leans against the small desk filled with papers and a laptop.

"Wow, you really take survival seriously, huh?"

He chuckles, glancing around. "I sell survival kits online. But business slows down during the winter, obviously. I'm trying to get it all done before the snow flies. That's why it's messy."

We sit in silence, dutifully avoiding eye contact for a good five minutes as I drift around the room, scanning all the items.

When I can't take it anymore, I blurt out, "There's only one bed."

"That won't be a problem."

Whatever the hell that means. If I shared a bed with him, I'd either end up on the floor from my attempt to keep as much distance between us, or I'd end up jumping his bones. Neither one of those options is ideal.

He settles into the chair, and I half expect him to dismiss me. I shake my head, wondering what the hell I've gotten myself into.

# Who the Hell Says Icky?

## Jake

Gemma fixes wide brown eyes on me. She opens her mouth again and then snaps it shut, as if she wants to take back the words she blurted out. I wasn't thinking about the fact I only have one bedroom when I offered her a place to stay. I wasn't thinking about the fact that I'm too tall to fit on the couch. I wasn't thinking about anything other than I couldn't leave her alone at the campground. Leaving her to flounder around town or stay with someone else wasn't acceptable, either.

The ache in my chest returns, trying to suffocate me when I think about her being anywhere else. When she stepped through my front door, it was as if something slotted into place, brightening the cabin in a way I'd never felt before. At this point, I'm just glad I got her inside, even if I had to use my skills to get her here. I usually don't use mind control on anyone, but when I saw she was about to run, I couldn't help it. I didn't even know if it would work until she obeyed me without hesitation.

"I don't see how that's *not* a problem. There's only one bed." Her lip slips between her teeth again.

I lean my elbows on the desk to hide my hardening cock. "I'm aware of what's in my house."

Her cheeks flush and she shakes her head, letting out a nervous laugh. "Of course you are."

I'm fucking this up. Admitting my gruffness is because she makes me nervous and I've had a semi since I picked her up off the floor won't help my cause. She'll tell me she should stay somewhere else and then she'll be gone. Swallowing hard, I lean back in my chair.

"It won't be a problem. You can stay here"—*forever*—"for as long as you need."

She blinks and I swear her eyes glow gold, but she ducks her head, hiding from my gaze. Flexing my hand, I try to erase the urge to pull her to me. Fuck. This is out of control and completely irrational.

"The hotel said they'd call me if something became available. The man wasn't very helpful though," she murmurs.

"Rick? He's an asshole. I'll deal with it."

"Oh, that's not what I meant. It wasn't that bad. I'm used to it." She waves my words away, as if Rick's actions aren't any concern.

I've had more than a couple run-ins with him. Gemma isn't the first person who's had a problem. Rick seems to think because his mother owns the hotel, he can treat people however he wants. Unfortunately, I know exactly why he was an asshole to Gemma. Not only is she an outsider with no connections to the town, she's also not tall, skinny, and blonde. Rick would have found her a place or, hell, offered his own bed if she looked like that.

"What do you mean, you're used to it?" I growl, pushing from the chair and leaning my fists on the desk.

She shoots me another wide-eyed look. "Nothing. Humans aren't always nice, is all. I'm sure you know how it is."

Narrowing my eyes, I want to question her about her choice of words, but she rushes from the room, mumbling something about her bags. When I don't hear her footsteps above me, though, I stomp from the office and down the hall.

I'm about to charge up the stairs when I find her wringing her hands in front of my books. I should back away and leave her be. She's clearly not rushing off without her bags. Instead, I watch her for a minute, waiting for my heart to settle.

"You like to read?" I ask.

She jumps but doesn't turn around. "It's pretty much the only thing I like."

"You don't like your job?"

"Nope. Went off to college and thought I'd find whatever I loved, but ended up picking something that would support me financially. Zero out of ten, do not recommend. So, you just do the kits and live here?" She spins to face me.

The throbbing in my chest returns when she fixes her gaze on me. Something is happening and I don't think I can stop it. Not that I want to. Gemma's beauty isn't something I'm used to encountering around here. I keep to myself mostly, but I notice people, especially with all the festivals this town puts on. I swear every other week there's some celebration or another. Yet I've never felt like this with anyone else.

The front door swings open, revealing Chase. I scowl, not that he notices. Usually, I wouldn't care that he's dropping by, but with Gemma here, today is different. When Gemma's face tightens the slightest bit, I wish I could kick him off my mountain. It's like every few minutes she's reminded that she's standing in the middle of a stranger's house and should run for the hills. Chase's reappearance isn't helping to put her at ease.

"He runs the summer camp, too. Obviously, that's done with for the season," he says, dropping a box I must have missed on the floor. I wonder how long he's been standing outside listening.

"How did you..." Her head whips back and forth.

"He was eavesdropping," I grumble, retreating to the kitchen.

I can't watch while he schmoozes her. He'll charm her into some semblance of comfortability. Or he'll scare her off. Or he'll convince her she's better off somewhere else. Or...I shake my head to stop the thoughts rolling around in my mind. Chase isn't one of those guys. He won't swoop in and steal her away. I don't own her, anyway. She can do whatever the hell she wants.

"What the hell is wrong with you?" Chase hisses, following me.

"No fucking clue," I mutter, bracing my hands on the sink to stare out the window.

"Seriously? Listen, Jake, I realize this isn't the typical way to meet someone. You've essentially been set up by her brother. And you kind of went off the rails inviting her to stay with you like ten seconds after you met her when she was supposed to stay at the camp. But you're not going to get anywhere if you keep walking out of the room every time she says something that makes you feel icky."

"Who the hell says the word icky?"

"Apparently me. Now, what the hell is going on with you?" He leans against the counter, crossing his arms and craning his neck toward the living room.

How am I supposed to have answers for him when I don't even have them for myself? He stares at me expectantly, but I have nothing left. He's right on all levels. Gemma and I don't have anything to base a relationship on. I don't know her and she doesn't know me.

My lungs seize, my chest seeming to cave in on itself. When I blink, black spots dance in my vision. The vise around my heart squeezes tighter. My soul is dying, bit by bit, with only the thought of her leaving.

"Must be because I feel some sort of obligation to her, being Slade's sister and all," I mumble. There's no way there's anything else going on. I'm attracted to her, and the nausea is merely guilt eating away at me.

"Well, you better get your shit together or you're going to lose your chance before you even had one," he mutters.

"I can't. Slade would fucking kill me. I just have to get through this, and then she can leave."

He shakes his head. We both know I'm totally fucked.

Chase left quickly after our conversation, dropping off the box we missed in the back of his truck. He doesn't understand why it would be a terrible idea to have anything more than a professional relationship with Gemma. He may not know exactly what type of shifter I am, but he understands the superstition and lore surrounding my kind.

In the ten years I've lived here, I've never revealed to him where I came from or who I really am beneath the skin. It has nothing to do with my friend and everything to do with me. My father instilled in me a strong sense of survival, which hinges on secrecy.

After I mumbled something to Gemma, who was still mesmerized by my living room, I retreated to the backyard. The wood pile is almost double what it was this morning. Glancing at the house for the hundredth time, I wonder if I should check on her. I shake my head, lifting the hem of my shirt to wipe the sweat from my forehead. I lean my axe against the stump and strip the fabric from my body.

"Oh. Oh, shit. Sorry," Gemma stutters.

I glance up, smirking when I find her hand clapped over her eyes. "I don't look that bad, do I?"

Her hand drops along with her mouth, but then she immediately covers her eyes again.

"I didn't mean to sneak up on you."

"I doubt you were sneaking. You can look, sweetheart." *You can touch too.*

The thought skitters through my mind before I can even process it. Just because I'm attracted to her doesn't mean there's any future for us. Stopping this before it even starts would be best for us both. Especially with what I am. I can't imagine living with someone and constantly lying to her. Every time it crosses my mind though, it's as if I'm dying a slow death. Which is entirely skipping the fact that she might not even want anything to do with me.

"Are you decent?" she asks, peeking from between her fingers and I grin.

"Depends on your definition of decent, but I have pants on."

She huffs, dropping her hand, eyes fixed on the trees behind me. "I was wondering if you wanted me to make dinner."

"Dinner?"

"Yes. It's typically the meal you eat at the end of the day." Her eyes dart down and then straight over my shoulder again.

"I know what dinner is. I just didn't realize it was so late."

"Actually, I have no idea what time it is. You don't have any clocks, and my phone went dead an hour ago."

She slips her phone from her pocket and presses the buttons as if it'll magically start working. The sun is below the tops of the trees, but it's autumn now. I grab my own phone, seeing it's just past three.

"Gemma, when was the last time you ate?" As soon as the words leave me, her stomach grumbles and I grin.

"Sorry," she whispers, pressing her hand to her middle.

"No reason to apologize. Just tell me when." I tuck my hands in the pockets of my jeans along with my phone.

"Last night? You don't have to feed me. I can go into town, but I thought I could make dinner as a thank you for letting me stay here."

"You don't need to thank me. This is your house." I clear my throat. "I mean, I want you to feel comfortable here. I'll make something."

I swipe my shirt from the ground, wiping my forehead again. We're having one last blast of summer, giving everyone a false sense of security. They think they have all the time in the world to get ready for winter, but the weather around here can change within the hour. Not such a terrible thing for the residents in town. Up here is a different story. If I wait, the house doesn't get heated, and I'll end up hunting for food. Game is scarce when the snow flies and I'd rather not spend those months shifted.

"You don't have to wait on me hand and foot."

She moves to block me, as if I couldn't pick her up and move her. Or throw her over my shoulder and haul her inside. My cock hardens as I imagine my hands wrapped around her thighs, smacking her round ass, having my way with her. Stopping in front of her, I swallow hard as I struggle to focus on the issue at hand.

"It's my responsibility to take care of you, which includes making sure you don't starve," I say.

"In what world are you responsible for taking care of me?" She plants her fists on her hips, glaring.

"Because I offered you a place to stay. You're my guest. How shitty would I be if I didn't make sure you were taken care of as well?"

Her lips part, tongue darting out, and I'm trapped—mesmerized by her. She does it again and I'm lost. Lifting my hand, I drop it before I can touch her. Her eyes tighten and she steps back, tucking her chin to her chest.

"I'll just go into town. It's no big deal," she murmurs.

"Come on," I say, skirting around her. "You're not going to win this fight, so might as well follow me."

# I'm a Vegetarian
## Gemma

The audacity of the man sitting across from me is beyond anything I've encountered. And yet any time a command drops from his luscious lips, my body moves to obey with no direction from me. Not that I'm staring at his lips or think they're luscious. They're normal man lips. A giggle gets caught in my throat and I end up coughing.

His chair almost tips back as he launches up and I wave him off. He slowly sinks back down, narrowing his eyes. Dropping my gaze to my plate, I stab my fork into another piece of carrot. Of course they're cooked perfectly, along with the roasted potatoes and steak.

He points at my food with his fork. "Are you going to eat your steak?"

"Oh, I'm a vegetarian," I mumble, peeking from under my lashes as his eyes widen. "Just kidding."

"What?"

"I was just joking. Not that there's anything wrong with vegetarians. I just can't...Sorry, I'm not very funny."

I probably look like I have a sunburn with how red my cheeks have been since I quite literally ran into this man. At some point, I should just stop. I should have stopped six hours ago. Hell, I should have stopped when Slade called me, but I couldn't say no.

"I'll figure out for myself if you're funny or not. Though based on that last one, I'm not holding my breath."

Whipping my head up, I'm about to blast him, but a grin stretches across his face, laughter dancing in his green eyes. I scoff, shaking my head as a small smile slips through.

My mouth waters as I cut into the steak. It's hard to cook for one person, so it's been a while since I had a home-cooked meal. It hits me then that maybe I took half of Jake's meal. He's a big guy, even with the rippling abs he's hiding under his shirt. My eyes dart down to his stomach and then I avert my eyes.

"This was all for you, wasn't it?" I set my fork down.

"What do you mean?"

"There's no way you randomly had two steaks sitting around, along with all the extras," I explain, then bite the inside of my cheek.

"Actually, you're eating Chase's portion. He bailed as soon as you said you'd stay."

"So, I mucked up all your plans."

"Course not." He sighs, resting his elbows on the table and hanging his head. "Listen, Gemma. We both know this is a little different."

I snort, stuffing another piece of steak in my mouth. What an understatement. This entire trip has been a whirlwind of random events stacking on top of one another. I can't even count the number of times I almost turned around and went back to the city. Every time I had made up my mind to do just that, the promise to my brother kept me going. Plus, the lack of places to turn around.

He lifts his head. "Okay, it's extremely different. I don't know how you grew up, but where I'm from, this isn't all that strange. I was taught to help people when they need it. Usually people in Whispering Pines are overly friendly. If you would have come a couple weeks from now, they might not have been, though."

"What do you mean? Is there something else happening?"

I'm sure they have some Halloween parade or trunk or treat thing planned. As long as it isn't an entire town festival. I don't know if I can handle going through another one. I've successfully avoided them since I left home.

"Just the festival," he says, and my hope that I've avoided another one dies a slow death. "We get a lot of people coming through. Makes shit a little more complicated."

I nod as my heart jumps into my throat. I know exactly what he's talking about. Back in Moon Cove, the number of strangers that flood into town during any of the festivals is out of control. I hated every minute of it. Coming to Whispering Pines during this time of year should have been the first red flag. Apparently, I'm good at ignoring them.

Getting out of town before the festival shouldn't be that hard, but Jake hasn't brought up anything to do with the summer camp. I might have to force the issue if he doesn't say something soon.

"So, if I would have come four weeks from now, you wouldn't have knocked me over in the general store? And I wouldn't be eating Chase's steak?" I shoot him a grin.

"Chase wouldn't have appreciated the food, anyway. And you would have found your way here regardless of whether I ran into you or not." His gruff voice rolls over me.

I pull in a deep breath to settle my heart that's going a million miles a minute. Jake looks at me like I'm a meal he can't wait to devour. Those actions have been followed by him scowling and stomping off, but it doesn't erase the desire that courses through me. I squeeze my legs together and his nostrils flare. Tilting my head, I wonder if he knows the effect he has on me, but dismiss the idea.

"What's your last name?" I blurt out.

He sits back, folding his hands over his stomach. "Silvius. Yours the same as Slade's?"

I nod, the desire from a minute before blinking out at the mention of my brother. Surest fucking way to kill my libido.

He glances away and I'm pretty sure mutters, "Of course it is." I don't know what's wrong with my last name. It's not a typical one, but neither is his. I've never been good at small talk and this conversation feels like an intense getting to know one another session, even if the questions aren't all that deep.

"Are we going to talk about our favorite colors next?" I ask.

He barks out a laugh and then picks up his fork again. A few minutes pass as we eat in silence, glancing covertly at each other. We both pretend we're not avoiding the conversation.

"Green," he grunts. "Darker, not light."

It takes me a minute to realize he's talking about his favorite color. "Like your eyes?"

"Suppose so, but more like the trees deep in the forest. You going to tell me yours?"

It's silver, but everyone always gives me a strange look when I tell them. I don't have it in me to deal with the passive aggressiveness or the judgment or a snide comment.

"Blue."

"So, we're lying now. Good to know."

He pushes from his chair, gathering his plate before grabbing mine. Opening my mouth, I snap it shut when the plates clatter in the farmhouse sink. I tilt my head, tracking his movements as he stomps to the fridge and yanks the door open.

When he slams it shut again, I bite the inside of my cheek to keep the words I want to spew at him at bay. Jake stalks back to the sink and flips on the water before bracing his hands on the counter.

"Seems like an extreme reaction to what my favorite color is." I stand and make my way around the table. "It's silver, by the way. But I am partial to blue as well."

Slipping my hand under his arm, I grab the dishrag. I pull back quickly when he stiffens. This is ridiculous, and I'm about to lose my shit on him. Screw the favor I owe my brother. Technically, I can't break my promise unless I want to spend the next year shifted. I never should have accepted in the first place.

"What are you doing?" he asks, turning to lean against the sink.

I don't bother to answer as I wipe off the table, but I can feel his eyes on me. The sun brushes the horizon, spiking my nerves. It's one thing to be stuck in a house with a stranger during the day, but when night falls, it's an entirely different story.

Going to bed at six in the evening is pushing it, which means I have at least a couple hours to kill. I can think of a few things to pass the time, but I doubt Jake would be up for me climbing him like a tree. He'd probably shoot me a horrified look and I'd end up sleeping in my car.

I realize I've been scrubbing at a permanent dark spot in the wood for way too long and I straighten. Biting my lip, I toss the rag toward the sink. As it sails through the air, time slows. I trip over the chair in my ridiculous attempt to grab it, but I'll never make it in time. The wet fabric slaps into his chest, then splats on the floor and his head drops.

"Sorry," I whisper, half hoping he doesn't hear me.

I wait for him to explode. I wait for him to kick me out. I wait for him to do exactly what the people from my past have done. Like my ex-boyfriend, who told me I was a crazy, cheating whore, even though he was the one who was sleeping around. Like my sister, Kira, who said I wasn't good enough to be part of the family. Like Lucinda, who thought she could fuck me over time after time because I never fought back. Nausea bubbles in my stomach, but I push it down.

He sighs, bending to grab the dishcloth. "Gemma, why don't you go do whatever you usually do after dinner, and I'll finish up here."

"You know it was an accident, but sure. I'll just go," I snap.

Less than twenty-four hours and I'm already annoyed. I never should have come and yet the thought of leaving turns my stomach. I make it halfway up the stairs before it hits me that maybe I need to shift and that's why I'm so frazzled.

As I continue on, I mentally calculate when the last time I shifted was. If I leave it too long, my body will be forced into the transformation no matter where I am. The last thing I want is to shift in front of Jake. He'll freak out and probably shoot me or something. It wouldn't be the first time something like that happened.

My bags are still packed, sitting at the end of the bed. I grab the two suitcases and move them closer to the door. All I need is the duffel bag, anyway. Slinging it over my shoulder, I stop short when Jake frames the doorway.

"Running away?" he asks, eyeing the suitcases.

"What's that supposed to mean?" I plant my fists on my hips, narrowing my eyes.

He shakes his head. "Didn't even have time to unpack before you're ready to leave. All because of a dirty rag."

"You know what?" I say, then freeze when he leans against the door frame.

"What's that, sweetheart?" He smirks and my heart skips a beat.

"Why would you offer me a place to stay and then act like you don't want me here?"

He rolls his eyes and I get the feeling that I won't get an answer. Crinkling my nose, I drop my bag on the bed and unzip it. I rummage around until I find my toiletry bag.

"Can I shower?" I hug my things to my chest.

"Slade didn't mention you were his sister. He said it was a family member, and I thought he said your name was Jim. I was going to set you up in a cabin at the camp, but when I saw you, I couldn't stick you out there."

"Because I'm a woman?" I ask, raising an eyebrow.

"Wouldn't give up my bed for a man," he says, smirking.

I roll my eyes, glancing around the room if only to escape his intensity. Staying at the camp wouldn't be that big of a deal. I have no problem staying at a deserted cabin alone, and I can certainly defend myself. The fact he thinks I need to be protected like a little lamb is insulting.

"I'm capable of taking care of myself. I realize you don't know me, but if you'd rather I be there, then by all means, get the fuck out of the way."

He straightens, dropping the dopey grin. "There isn't any heat out there. If a snowstorm blows in, you're fucked. I'd rather not have to go out and save your ass from freezing to death."

"It's not that cold out now. I could stay there until the weather turns. *If* the weather turns, that is. So, I'll go there."

"The hell you will. You stay here or you don't stay at all."

He stomps off, leaving me to wonder what the hell I'm supposed to do.

# Sweetheart is a Perfectly Good Pet Name

## Jake

Night has finally fallen and the sounds of the forest ring through the air. I wish I would have kept my mouth shut. I don't want Gemma to go anywhere. I offered her a place to stay, but Chase was right. Every time she says something that freaks me out, I run away, a lot like what I was accusing her of doing. I'm clearly projecting, but whatever is happening between us is too fast.

"Get your shit together," I mumble to myself as I bend over and grab my axe.

Is it smart to chop wood after sunset? No. Am I capable of it? Only if I partially shift. I run the risk of Gemma discovering my secret if I pull that move. What I really want to do is spend some time in the woods without interruptions. The new moon is only a couple weeks away. I'll be forced into it then since my body, or the magic, will insist on it. I was so busy closing up the summer camp and getting ready for winter I haven't had time in the last few weeks.

Gazing longingly at the ever-darkening forest, I resign myself to finishing up with the wood. Then I'll have to go back inside and face the consequences of my words. I'll need to hurry. Gemma is probably hauling her suitcases to her car, ready to fly out of here like a bat out of hell. She won't be able to get into any of the cabins, and the hotel doesn't have any rooms, so she'll be forced to sleep in her vehicle. Like hell will I let that happen.

I set another piece of wood onto the stump, then lean against the axe handle. Sighing, I drop my chin to my chest.

"You shouldn't chop wood at night." Gemma's voice washes over me, and I close my eyes. "Jake? Are you okay?"

I chuckle, glancing up and meeting her concerned eyes. "I'm fine. This needs to get done."

"You looked like you were frozen." She twists her fingers together but drops them when she notices my gaze on them.

Her body tilts as if she's trying to find her center. It's possible she feels as off-kilter as I have since she showed up. Shaking my head, I dismiss the idea. There's no way Gemma could sense the magic flowing between us. Unless she's a shifter too. I doubt that's the case. Slade and I spent a week together and there wasn't any indication he could shift. Not that I revealed what lurked beneath my skin.

Gemma sets her feet, crossing her arms as if she's channeling some inner resolve. I can't keep the small smile from my face, and she scowls.

"Here's the deal. I don't know what the hell is happening, but I'm sick of acting like I'm some meek mouse when I'm really not. So, we're going to set some things straight." She tips her chin up, challenging me to object.

"I'm all ears, sweetheart."

She snorts at my nickname for her, rolling her eyes. "First of all—"

"How many things will you be setting me straight on, exactly?" I ask, wondering if we should move inside instead of having this conversation in the dark.

"Three. Now stop interrupting." She pulls in a deep breath. "First, you're the one who invited me to stay here. So, either tell me to get the hell out or stop acting like you didn't have a hand in this whole thing. Second, I'd really like a shower."

I wait for her to continue, but she stares at me expectantly. Gemma probably thinks calling me out on my shit is going to piss me off, but all it does is send a bolt of desire through me. Shuffling the axe in front of me, I use it to hide the bulge in my pants. The light is almost gone now, but knowing my luck, she'd still spot how hard I am.

"What's the third thing?"

"Huh? Oh, um." She glances around, as if she'll find her final point scattered at her feet.

"You forgot, didn't you?"

"No," she cries. "Third of all...I...we...Oh! Third, I need to know what we're actually doing here."

I raise an eyebrow. "Don't know what you're talking about, sweetheart. Right now, we're talking, or rather, you're putting me in my place."

I grin as she scowls again. Her nose crinkles, and I swear she's blushing. All I want to do is strip her down and see how far that pink travels down her soft body. I clench my jaw, tipping my head back. If I don't look at her, maybe my cock will calm down and my mind will stop imagining all the ways I could bring her pleasure.

Her lip ends up between her teeth again, and I wonder if it's an unconscious move on her part. How often has she had to hide her true feelings? How many times has she had to bite her words back, for fear of someone's response? Once is too much, in my opinion.

"Spit it out, Gemma," I say gruffly.

"The job. Slade said you needed help with the summer camp. I'd like to discuss that."

A rustling behind me has me stiffening and I whip around. Suddenly, Gemma's hand lands on my lower back, and she leans around me to follow my gaze. I'm not entirely concerned, since I'm the deadliest thing for miles around. With Gemma here, though, I might not be able to protect her if there's a beast prowling through the underbrush.

When a roar echoes from deep within the forest, I spin around. Gemma shrieks as I tip her over my shoulder, and I hustle for the back door. No way am I putting her at risk. I can't afford to shift in front of her. That would probably terrify her just as much as a wild animal appearing.

I set her on her feet when we make it to the kitchen before racing for the back again. Slamming the heavy door shut, I brace my forehead against the wood. When my heart calms, I move toward Gemma, who's peeking around the corner.

"You realize I could have just run on my own, right? There was no reason to throw me over your shoulder," she says as she fidgets with the fridge magnets. "Although, I am duly impressed that you did so without much effort."

"Without *any* effort," I correct her, and she glances over her shoulder.

I step closer, invading her space. Her breath hitches and I wonder if she's just as affected by me as I am by her. I drop my head as my palms itch to grab her again. Adrenaline might have fueled me to throw her over my shoulder, but it didn't distract me enough. The feel of her in my arms invades my senses.

My lips brush the shell of her ear, and she shudders. A crack of thunder echoes through the cabin and I jump back. Magnets scatter to the floor and Gemma drops to her knees. She slaps them back on the fridge before scrambling to her feet. I'm too busy staring out the window, searching for clouds in the night sky. There's not a fucking one.

"Well, while I appreciate you trying to protect me, I am capable of saving myself, like I said before. And we still need to discuss the job."

"Not tonight. There's been enough drama today." I sigh, running my hand through my hair then pull it back and secure it with the hair tie around my wrist.

She sniffs, shoulders tensing, and I wonder if I made her cry. Maybe it's just everything piling on. Inwardly scolding myself, I step toward her, but she twirls around and pokes me in the chest. I gape at her. She opens her mouth, then snaps it shut again when nothing comes out.

I smirk as she frowns. "Cat got your tongue?"

"I have nothing further to say to you," she says haughtily.

She stomps from the room, and I track her until she settles on the couch. It takes her a good thirty seconds to realize she has nothing to occupy her time, and she jumps up again. She examines my bookshelves, and I breathe a sigh of relief, secure in the fact that she's not going to blast out the front door.

Once I'm in my office, I peer out the window behind my desk at the dark yard. Other than the slight breeze fluttering the remaining leaves on the trees, nothing moves. Whatever was disturbing the night seems to have moved on. If I didn't know any better, I'd think the roar was a sasquatch roaming the mountain. I snicker, imagining what that meet and greet might entail.

As I turn away, I catch sight of something bright fluttering to the ground by my abandoned axe. Shaking my head, I squint, but I can't make out what it is. I glance behind me to ensure Gemma isn't lurking behind me. She seems to have the uncanny ability to move without me noticing, which isn't something she should be able to do.

Blinking, I partially shift and the glow from my eyes reflects off the glass. The night recedes, the back yard coming into focus. Whatever rests on the stump vanishes in a flash of pure-white, blinding me and I blink away the dark spots in my vision.

"Did you find anything?"

I jolt back, when Gemma whispers from directly behind me. She stumbles into the desk, sending order forms floating to the floor. I almost forget to adjust my eyes, but thankfully keep enough sense in my head to do so before I reach behind and grab her hip. Dropping my hand, I turn. There isn't much space between us now and my cock hardens again, my desire coming back full force in a matter of seconds.

Her nostrils flare and I wonder if she feels it too, this connection between us. Or maybe it's just attraction. That's more likely, since I doubt I'm fated mates with a human. I've never heard of my kind being fated to someone like her. Even if she was a shifter, the chances of us being soul mates are slim at best. There aren't a lot of my kind running around.

"For someone who spouts they can take care of themselves, you sure do fall down a lot," I mutter as I grab onto her waist and set her on her feet.

"Most of the time, it's your fault, anyway." She glares, and I'm caught in her eyes. "You can let go of me now."

I jerk back, dropping my hands from her hips. My palms itch, begging me to snatch her up, throw her on the desk, and have my way with her. It's too much. One of these times, I'll lose my resolve and end up acting impulsively. Gemma's allure has ensnared me completely, to the point where I don't know if I'll be able to control myself even if she let me worship her body.

Sliding between the desk and the wall, I'm careful not to brush up against her and she snorts under her breath. I need to focus and get my shit together. And I need to figure out what the hell was in the backyard. Stalking from the room, I rip open the back door, Gemma's mutters chasing after me.

I slow when I approach the stump. The wood glows, the light receding quickly in the darkness. It reeks of magic, drawing me in and whispering for me to listen. I glance at the moon, feeling the pull of its fullness and I shudder as a crackling races beneath my skin. Sucking in a deep breath, I push the shift down deep, praying to the goddess my resolve stays firm until Gemma is gone. An ache rips through me again at the thought of her leaving.

"You're doing it again," she yells from the back porch.

"Doing what?" I call, not bothering to turn around.

"Walking away. I'd appreciate if you'd stop being an a-hole and running every time something strange pops into your head."

"What exactly do you think pops into my head? I doubt you'll be able to guess."

"I imagine it's you wanting to control everything and have things your way."

"If I had it my way, sweetheart, you'd be bent over my desk with me deep inside your pussy."

# You Maimed My Shower

## Gemma

My mouth drops open at his admission and heat pools between my legs. He whispered it, but shifter hearing and all that. Even in the moonlight, I can see that he's blushing when he faces me. He isn't stomping into the forest to get away at least. He's blurred the lines of what this trip is, and I have no idea what to do with that.

Would I like him to reenact the image he's put in my head? Absolutely. Would it be a good idea? Probably not. We have to work together for the next couple of weeks. Although, going over his next business steps during the day and sleeping with him while tucked away in his cabin at night doesn't seem so bad right about now.

"Obviously, I'm not going to tell you," he murmurs, dropping his hands and tucking them in his pockets.

"Why not?" I whisper so he doesn't hear the trembling in my voice.

"Doesn't matter. Don't go wandering into the woods."

I open my mouth for some snappy retort I haven't figured out yet, but he glares at me.

I cross my arms, more to protect myself from his words than the wind. "We should talk about what happened in the kitchen."

Panic flashes in his eyes. He blinks and it's gone, replaced with a blankness I'm not entirely fond of.

His brows pull low, and he can't meet my eyes. "I shouldn't have done that."

I bite the inside of my cheek, distracting myself from the pain shooting through my chest. "Why not?"

"Your brother."

That's right. This isn't just a random person I found in town. This is my brother's friend. Clearly, they're close since Slade called in a favor for him. I can't even imagine the fallout if my brother found out I spent three weeks messing around with his buddy. Once I started seeing boys as something other than stinky hot messes, Slade told me his buddies were off-limits. They'd never be into someone like me anyway, so I should save myself the trouble.

Also, I may not have a vast amount of experience with men, but I've had enough to know the no-strings-attached thing never works out. Someone always falls and the other one is blindsided. Jake doesn't seem like the kind of guy who would be good at breaking a girl's heart. And I would totally be the one who would fall head-over-heels for him. He'd walk away with memories and I'd be left with a broken heart.

"Right. It would be a terrible idea." I swallow hard.

"You can use the shower across the hall from my bedroom. It's not ginormous, but the water gets hot." He retreats around the house.

Shuffling back through the door, I pause, peering into his office to catch a glimpse of him in the window. He strides past, thankfully not catching me spying, and I sigh. Following him into the yard and jumping his bones would be...not great. Doesn't mean I can't have some quality time in his shower while I imagine it's his hands touching me.

The small bathroom upstairs has barely enough room for the sink and toilet. I find extra towels in a built-in cupboard and hang it on the hook next to the shower with a bathtub. Tiptoeing into his bedroom, I grab my toiletry bag and scurry back, shutting the door quietly behind me.

The pipes clank as I twist the knob, then undress, dropping my clothes on the toilet. Bouncing from one foot to the other, I wait for the water to heat up. Steam billows over the top of the curtain, and I step into the bathtub.

Jake may have said the bathroom wasn't huge, but clearly he built it with himself in mind. I can barely reach the shower head to adjust the spray. My muscles ease as the hot water flows over my body. Grabbing my soap, I squeeze some into my hand before lathering it up and skimming my palms across my skin.

I close my eyes and Jake's image ripples through my mind. He's shirtless and yummy, of course, just like he was when he was splitting wood. I glide my hand across my stomach and my fingers find my clit. Even with the water, I can tell I'm wet. Circling the nub, I brace my other hand against the wall and moan.

Knocking at the door has my eyes flying open, and I yank my hand away from my pussy.

"Yes?" I call, then clear my throat.

"Are you okay?" Jake's muffled voice rings through the small space.

"I'm fine."

I spin, intent on washing my hair instead of touching myself, and my feet slip across the tub. Grabbing the shower curtain, I let out a yelp as it twists around my body. The door bursts open, and Jake's arms catch me before I tumble onto the tiles.

Trembling, I peek up at him and he pulls me closer, the thin plastic the only thing covering my body from his wandering eyes. And wander they do, but concern splashes across his face. He's assessing for injuries. Glancing up at the ceiling, I cringe. I ripped the curtain straight off the rings. At least the rod is still in place. It probably would have hit me in the head and then I'd end up with amnesia or something.

"Are you hurt?" he demands.

He sets me on my feet, and I grip the edges of the curtain. Dropping to his knees, he runs his hands over my legs, dipping under the plastic. I shudder and my legs turn to jelly. I latch onto his shoulder, and he gazes up at me. Even with him kneeling, we're almost eye to eye.

He drops his hands, the corner of his mouth twitching. "You maimed my shower."

My cheeks flush, both from the steam still billowing around us and my embarrassment. All the reasons he should walk away swirl through the air, wrapping around me and stealing the breath from my lungs.

"It's your fault," I breathe, entranced by his stare.

The corner of his mouth tips up. "Is that so?"

"Well, if you wouldn't have busted in..."

"Then you'd be bleeding all over my bathroom right now," he growls.

He lumbers to his feet, reaching past me to shut off the water. When he steps back, planting his hands on his hips and dropping his head, I hold my breath. All I want to do is make a move by dropping the curtain and hoping he takes the bait. A fling wouldn't be so bad. A few weeks of getting dicked down would be glorious. It's not like we'd have to tell Slade. I doubt we'd ever see each other again, anyway.

A pang shoots through me at the thought, which doesn't make much sense, but I'm getting used to it by now. Instead of acting on the fantasy living in my head, I sweep the bottom of the curtain away from my feet. I'm about to step out of the tub when he dips down, wrapping his arm around my thighs and tips me over his shoulder. Again.

I let out a shriek, latching onto his waist while staring at his back upside down. His other hand gathers the excess plastic and throws it over his shoulder too, and a cold draft wafts over my backside. He's already plodding from the room before I've caught my breath to protest.

"What the hell are you doing?" I ask when I find my voice.

"I let you step out of that tub and you'd probably slip again. I'm merely saving you from yourself."

I don't have a defense, since it seems like all the worst possible outcomes have visited me since I crossed the boundary of Whispering Pines. I hate feeling like I'm not in control of my own body. It's as if some outside force is wreaking havoc on me, battering against my senses and disorienting me until I no longer know what I want. It has to be something supernatural with this town. Something no one else notices.

Striding into the bedroom, he tosses me onto the bed, and I bounce. I scramble to pull the curtain over my naked body, but he grabs the end and yanks it away. My cry of protest is lost on him since he's already stomping back into the bathroom, slamming the door behind him.

Grabbing the blanket from the end of the bed, I drape it over myself and sit up. The door swings open again, and my clothes fly toward my face. By the time they land next to me, the wood is separating us again. I wiggle forward and snatch my duffel bag from the floor.

He might have run away again, but I'm not about to lie here and wait for more rejection. I pull my shorts and tank top from the luggage, then freeze. I could dig through the large suitcases by the door for the flannel set my mother sent me for solstice, but that seems like a lot of work. I'd end up sweltering in the warm cabin. The last few days have been exhausting. Throw in a ridiculously hot stranger who offered me a place to stay, and my body is ready to shut down.

I don't bother with underwear, sliding the shorts on, then yanking the top over my wet hair. I wish I would have grabbed the towel so I could wrap it up, but there's no way I'm going to knock on the door to get it. Zipping up the bag, I toss it next to the suitcases, vowing to take the ones I don't need to the car in the morning.

Leaning against the headboard, I spy a book on the nightstand and pick it up. I expected it to be some survival story or something. As I read the back, I realize it's a romance. Flipping it open, I settle further into the comforter. I'm thoroughly engrossed in the story when the bathroom door opens again.

Jake's legs appear in the corner of my eye, and he clears his throat. I hold up a finger, finishing the paragraph, then gaze up at him expectantly. He scowls, brows pulling low as he crosses his arms.

"What are you doing?" he huffs, narrowing his eyes.

"Baking a cake." I raise an eyebrow, silently asking him what the hell he wants.

He rolls his eyes. "I fixed the curtain. You can finish your shower now."

Tipping my head back, I gaze at the ceiling, contemplating whether I actually want to get up again. Going through all the motions would be even more tiring and I'd rather keep reading about the woman who doesn't realize the villain in her story is actually the love of her life.

"I'm good. Thank you, though," I murmur, returning my gaze to the book.

He harrumphs and I swallow the giggle begging to escape. I didn't think people actually made those types of noises. Whatever is happening between us needs to stop. If I have to deal with this emotional roller coaster any more than I already have, I might just disappear into the woods to get away from it all.

"That's my book," he grumbles.

Before I can respond, he spins, vanishing down the hall. There aren't many places he can go, so he must be retreating downstairs. Sighing, I try to get back into the story, but thoughts of Jake intrude every few sentences. I finally turn the rest of my brain off when he swings through the doorway again.

My huff at the interruption turns into a cry of outrage when he snatches the book from my hands. He slides another one in front of me.

"Page seven," he says, rounding the bed and collapsing next to me.

I gape at him as he finds his place further along his own copy. It's pointless to ask him why he has two copies of the same book. I have no room to criticize. The several boxes I have in my trunk with multiple special editions tucked within them would mock me if I did. Turning to page seven, I start reading again.

I don't know how long we sit in silence, the flipping of pages the only sound filling the room. My lids droop and I wonder if this is what it would be like if I stayed forever.

It's the last thought I have before sleep overtakes me.

# Eyes Can't Hear
## Jake

Two days. Two fucking days and I'm pretty sure my cock is about to explode. I've been constantly hard the entire time Gemma has been in my house. She fell asleep, book spread across her chest. All I could think about was her thighs spread over my face.

It was hell to get to sleep that night. Last night was even worse, mostly because she came down an hour after she shut my bedroom door. She stole my breath away when I caught sight of her tiny shorts and slinky tank top. I ended up running laps around the house to blow off some steam. I was too afraid if I went into the woods she'd wake up and I wouldn't be there.

Now I'm back to chopping more wood in the hot autumn sun, even though the pile is almost as tall as I am. I have enough to last me at least two winters. Still, I set another log on the stump and swing my axe. If I'm exhausted and sore, maybe I won't have the energy to lust after my unexpected roommate.

"Jake? I'm going to go into town," Gemma calls from the back porch.

She waves when I look up, disappearing back into the house before I can answer. Muttering a curse under my breath, I slam the axe into the stump and take off after her. I snatch my shirt off the railing, using it to mop my face as I go. Adrenaline blasts through my body, instantly putting me on edge. Usually, I'm glad when instinct takes over, but lately it's like I'm constantly riding the crest of a wave, waiting for the water to close over my head and suck me down into the shadowy depths below. The feeling swamped me as soon as the words left her mouth.

"You're not going alone," I growl as I catch up to her in the entryway.

She laughs lightly, slipping on her shoe. "I'll be fine going into town by myself. I'm a big girl, ya know."

"Well aware of that, sweetheart. Still going with you."

My hand falls on her lower back and I grab my keys from the hook. She stumbles on the doorjamb, and I slide my hand around her waist to steady her. I should let her go. My cock is screaming at me to bend her over the railing and flip her dress up, sinking into her. Not only would that be an incredibly bad idea, but I have no idea whether she would even want me to do something like that. I just need to get myself under control.

"Why aren't we taking my car?" she asks as I steer her toward my truck.

"I'm slightly terrified it won't make it down the mountain."

"My car is perfectly drivable. It got me here, didn't it?" she grumbles even as she slides into the passenger seat.

"Barely," I mutter, and shut her door.

The ride down is silent, though I desperately want to say something—anything. My mind blanks every time I open my mouth. As I pull onto Main Street, I realize I've been wasting valuable time we could have been discussing all the shit with the haunted house. I clear my throat, glancing at her from the corner of my eye.

"I need some supplies for the camp. I'll need some help picking shit out, loading it up, things like that."

"Are you going to call Chase?" she asks, glancing around the town. "Where do you think they sell clocks in this town?"

"Probably the general store. Wait, why are you buying a clock?" I call after her as she hops down.

She slams the door and marches into the general store. I have no idea why she thinks I'm calling Chase instead of helping me herself since that's the reason she's here in the first place. I should go on to the pop-up party store and get the things I need.

As I glance toward the business, I find Marcy Higgins hurrying toward my truck. There's no way I can handle having a conversation with her. She'll try to rope me into something or trying to insert herself into the events at the camp.

I push from the truck and hurry after through the door. Maybe if Marcy "catches" me with Gemma, she'll back off. Even if I wasn't currently obsessed with the woman staring at the pens like they'll save her soul, I still wouldn't be interested in Marcy. She's fine, but she doesn't hold a candle to someone like Gemma.

"Jake!" Marcy calls, and I stumble forward.

I wrap an arm around Gemma's waist, and she jolts, blinking wide eyes at me. A small smile plays on her lips, and my heart jumps. Marcy's heels click across the floor, making me tense.

Leaning down, I whisper in her ear, "Play along. Please."

"Jake Silvius, don't tell me you're ignoring me," Marcy's laughing voice booms throughout the space.

I spin us around, keeping my grip on Gemma. She lets out a soft "Oh," but doesn't say anything else, thank the goddess.

"Marcy. What can I do for you?"

"Oh, and who is this?" Marcy asks, the skin around her eyes tightening when she spies my arm around Gemma.

"This is Gemma."

I really don't want to say anything else. I don't like talking to people, anyway. Add in Marcy's persistence, and this is not the thing I want to do on a Tuesday afternoon. Hopefully I won't have to fake a relationship just to get out of this situation. Although, if Marcy thinks I'm taken, she'll back off.

"Gemma, so nice to meet you. I'm Marcy. What brings you to Whispering Pines? Just visiting your...brother?"

Closing my eyes, I realize Marcy is going to make this more complicated than it needs to be. Gemma's fingers dig into the back of my leg. Hopefully, she'll play along, and we can get back to the cabin before I land myself in a fucking hole I'll never get out of.

"Not my sister. This is my..." I take a deep breath and take the plunge. "Girlfriend."

Marcy's jaw drops, eyes flitting between us, and Gemma's pinches my thigh. Gritting my teeth, I hold my breath and wait for Gemma to deny my declaration.

"Girlfriend? I didn't even realize you were seeing someone," Marcy murmurs.

Gemma chuckles, and I glance down at her. "Oh, you know how Jake is. He's a private guy, doesn't like to spread his business everywhere." A smirk plays on her mouth, as if this is completely normal or she's going to make me pay for this later. Probably the latter, to be honest.

"Well, isn't that nice. Are you staying in town then?"

Gemma laughs lightly. "Actually—"

"We have to get going," I interject. "Lots to do before Samhain."

As soon as the words are out, I wince. I don't know if Gemma even knows what Samhain is. Usually, the townspeople advertise it as a Halloween event. No one here other than Chase knows I'm a shifter. My slip doesn't seem to faze Gemma, although Marcy gives me a strange look.

"Let's go run your errands. We can come back here when we're done," Gemma says, and smiles at Marcy. "So good to meet you, Macy."

I grab her hand, tugging her around the other woman, and practically drag her out the door. We're halfway down the street before she starts muttering under her breath. I've still got a hold of her, but I don't want to let go. This may be the last time she allows me within ten feet of her after the stunt I pulled.

"You want to explain what that was?" she hisses.

"Yes," I whisper, pulling her through the door to the party store.

I nod to Noah, who's stuck behind the counter looking ridiculously bored. His dad owns the feed store in town, but every year they open this place. Noah usually gets roped into manning it. Making my way to the back wall, I stare at the decorations.

"Well?"

"I'd rather not do it here. People talk," I grumble, grabbing a bag of fake spiderwebs and scowl.

"No one is around."

"There are eyes everywhere."

"Eyes can't hear. Also, why are you looking at spiderwebs?"

I sigh as I grab another bag. "I need something to make the haunted house feel creepy but not scary."

"They're terrible for the environment. Not to mention cheesy as hell."

I put them back, not wanting to argue. "Well, I need to set up a haunted house for the kids. You got any better ideas?"

"I don't know. All the ones I've been to were...different," she hedges as she tugs her hand from mine.

My palm itches to grab her again, but I'm not going to push anything. At least not yet.

"Thought you'd actually have some ideas," I mutter, stepping around the corner.

She follows, planting her hands on her hips, and tilting her head. She raises an eyebrow, but I don't know what she's expecting me to say. When Slade said she could help, I thought that meant she'd done this before. Apparently not.

"What?"

"Why would I have ideas for a kid's haunted house?"

"That's why you're here, isn't it? It's fine. I'll figure it out and you can help set it up."

I stare at the decorations, not really seeing any of the displays. The last few days have been a roller coaster I'm not entirely sure I'll survive. I've never been on one, but Chase described them, and they sound like a deathtrap. I spot Gemma scowling from the corner of my eye.

"What do you mean, 'that's why I'm here'?" she asks, eyes narrowing.

"Slade said you were going to help with the camp," I mutter, not exactly wanting to get into this here either.

"Yeah, with the camp books, dealing with expansion, things like that. Did he tell you I was going to help with the haunted house?"

I spin toward her, mouth dropping open, and her eyes widen. Then she tips back her head and laughs. It's as if her entire body is alight with mirth, joy radiating out of her. I'm captivated—completely enthralled. Though I still have no idea what is happening between us, maybe I can stop holding back now that Marcy thinks we're dating. I'm sure it'll spread like wildfire before we even get out of town.

"So, Slade played us both then," I mutter when she calms down, hiccupping every once in a while.

"I guess so. I don't know what you did to deserve it, but I know exactly why he bamboozled me into this." She shakes her head.

"Why?" I ask, mostly because I can't understand his reasoning with me, unless it was only to help his sister.

She waves her hand around, scanning the items to her side. "Oh, I lost my job."

"You...what?"

I don't mean to sound so aghast, but I can't imagine why someone would fire her. Although, to be fair, I don't really know her, no matter that my mind is trying to convince me otherwise.

"I, uh...well, I was fired. Sorry, let go." Her hands shoot up, using air quotes as her mouth twists in disgust.

"What for?"

She waves her hands again, and I wonder how long she's going to sidestep the explanation. The more she tries to downplay it, the more my mind runs rampant. What could she possibly be hiding?

"Hell if I know. It's all bullshit, and I had nothing keeping me in the city, so when Slade told me you needed help, I just went with it. I think he's worried I'll go off the deep end. I think they're going to try to say I was embezzling or stealing or something." Her words trail off, and she sighs, shaking her head.

"Were you?" The words pop out before I can stop them, and I cringe.

"What?" she shrieks. "Of course not! Why the hell would you—"

"I didn't mean anything. Shit."

"No, you know what? It's a valid question. You don't—"

I stride forward and cover her mouth. I wasn't joking when I said there were eyes—ears—everywhere. It's bad enough that I haven't talked to Chase about this little deception. No one will believe Gemma and I are dating if Chase can't back us up.

"Let's just get your stuff and then we'll come back for the haunted house things. We'll talk more when we're back at the cabin," I whisper, subtly trying to check around us for anyone else.

My hand tingles and I'm suddenly caught in her eyes. Her mouth opens under my palm and a thrill goes through me. Then she licks me, and I jump back, a disgusted noise falling from my lips.

"What the hell was that?"

Her eyebrow pops up. "Maybe you'll think twice about silencing me like that. Don't manhandle me and we'll be just fine."

She pivots and marches for the door. I have no choice but to follow, but a grin overtakes my face. Maybe Gemma isn't a wilting flower like I thought.

# Trouble is Afoot

## Gemma

I swear everyone is watching me as I make my way back down the street to the general store. Every time I look, even if it's subtly, no one is. Still, the hair on the back of my neck stands up and I feel like a thin sheen of oil covers my skin. I'm so lost in my surveillance of the townsfolk, I practically jump out of my skin when Jake's massive hand engulfs my own.

He squeezes my fingers, almost cutting off my circulation, and I huff, tugging until he stops with a muttered apology. The panic on his face when he found me in the general store was almost comical. He clearly needed my help, but I didn't expect him to tell that woman we were dating.

How he's going to convince the town we're together when we met each other mere days ago, I'm not entirely sure. I sure as hell won't stage some public breakup. I've read about that shit, and it never works. Actually, fake dating never works either, unless they fall in love, and I doubt that's what Jake has in mind for us.

"So, how is this going to work?" I mutter from the corner of my mouth.

"How is what going to work?" His head swivels back and forth.

"You realize you look guilty."

He whips his head toward me, tripping over a lip on the concrete walk, almost taking me down with him. I sigh as he rights himself.

"I'd rather not get ambushed."

"I doubt anyone will do that. And if they do, I'll just do the talking. But we need to get our stories straight in case someone catches me when you're not around."

He tugs me to a stop, crowding me against the wall of the general store. "You won't be going anywhere without me."

"Possessive much? I'm capable of coming to town on my own." I narrow my eyes even while a thrill runs through me. What the hell is wrong with me?

"And what happens when you get lost? Or some asshole decides he'd like to badger you? No, I'll be around for as long as you are."

He pushes back from the stone, then runs his fingers through his hair as he gazes out on Main Street. My mouth waters as I watch him execute a perfect man bun. I open my mouth to point out that there's only one way in and out of his property, or that I've been dealing with overly persistent assholes most of my life. I snap it shut when I spot Chase hopping out of his truck and making his way over to us. Jake abandons me, meeting Chase halfway.

The two have a heated conversation all while Chase keeps glancing at me, and I roll my eyes. I'm sure they're coming up with some sort of plan that I *should* be a part of, but they won't include me. I'm used to it. Slade in particular used to invent elaborate ruses I was just supposed to go along with, much like the one I'm currently embroiled in with my mountain man.

The thought pulls me up short. He's not mine, even if he is the closest I've ever seen to a lumberjack who lives on the side of a mountain. Even if my lady bits go crazy whenever he's within a ten-foot orbit of me. Even if his cabin is exactly like the one I always dreamed I'd live in when I was a kid. Jake telling people we're dating doesn't mean he's mine.

"So glad you were finally able to come visit Jake." Chase throws me a cheeky grin as he shouts from at least ten feet away.

Several heads swivel toward me, and another blush stains my cheeks. I swear I'm going to have a permanent sunburn by the time I leave Whispering Pines. Shushing him probably wouldn't do anything, so I don't even bother. I stomp toward them, jolting when Jake's fingers intertwine with mine. I momentarily forget what I was going to say, then shake my head.

"That wasn't very subtle, Chase."

He shrugs, waving wildly at someone across the street who hurries into the diner. My stomach chooses that exact moment to rumble, and I close my eyes as I heave out a sigh. I count down from three, then turn my expectant gaze to Jake.

"You're hungry. Let's go."

Just as expected, he drags me across the street, barely glancing around for traffic. Not that there's many cars rolling by. I think the speed limit is fifteen, so they'd have plenty of time to stop.

"I can wait to eat."

Chase trails after us and I glance over my shoulder, sending him a pleading look. He pretends he doesn't see, waving to another person who lifts their hand in return. Obviously, I'm not going to get any help from him.

"You don't take very good care of yourself, Gemma. I'm not going to have you passing out because I didn't feed you."

"I take care of myself perfectly well, thank you very much. Just because I skip a meal every once in a while..."

He stops short and I almost run into him, skipping back at the last second. He glares at me, lips pressed in a thin line, though it does nothing to detract from his appeal.

"Skipping meals is not an option as long as you're with me."

The bell over the door jingles as he rips it open, tugging me after him. Chase jumps forward to catch the handle before it swings shut. I wonder how often they come into town for food. Jake made it seem like he sequesters himself in his cabin most of the time, avoiding all manner of people. I don't think Chase is included in that, though.

Jake slides into a booth, yanking me next to him as he ignores the waitress who tries to wave him toward a table in the middle of the space. I glance around, taking in the stark white and reflective chrome splashed over everything. It's jarring and I squint.

"I feel like we just stepped back into the fifties." I'm trying to keep my voice down, but a man sitting at the counter on a stool bolted to the floor snorts.

"I think this place was built in the fifties, so that tracks," Jake mutters.

"You're going to break your neck, craning your head like that."

"He's looking for Marcy," Chase says, sliding in across from us.

"Is she always like that?" I scoot closer to the edge of the booth, trying to put more distance between Jake and me. His hand lands on my thigh, fingers digging in as he pulls me back.

Chase's elbows land on the table and he leans closer. "She's...persistent."

"Praying mantis, more like," Jake grumbles.

Menus land in front of me before I can respond. The server is already striding away on her wedge heels.

"What's her problem?" I raise my eyebrow at Chase. He's more likely to give me information than Jake, except he ducks his head.

Jake leans in, his breath ghosting across the shell of my ear. "She asked Chase on a date, and he turned her down. She's been a bit salty ever since."

"She's pretty." I peek at the tall brunette as she chatters with another customer.

"Found out the only reason she wanted to go out with me is because I dated her sister in high school. Her sister said Tess could never land someone like me. It was a whole thing."

I wish I wouldn't have brought it up. "So, you grew up here?"

Relief floods Chase's face, and he seizes the opportunity to change the subject. He prattles on for at least ten minutes about people I don't know and events long since passed. Jake's thumb brushes against my knee. I swallow hard, my mind zeroing in on the movement. Concentrating on what Chase is saying isn't a priority anymore. I snap out of whatever horniness spell Jake's put me under and cover his hand with mine. As I dig my nails into his skin, he tenses, then snorts.

"But you probably don't want to hear anything about me. Jake, on the other hand..." He wiggles his eyebrows, a smirk playing on his face.

I purse my lips, my concentration still split between the conversation and Jake's fingers. "We're not allowed to talk about him."

"Wait, what?" Chase glances at Jake.

"We need to discuss things first. Not here," Jake mutters.

"Holy shit, you're blushing," Chase hisses at Jake, attempting to keep his booming voice to a minimum. It doesn't work.

"Chase, do you have a volume button?" I ask, tilting my head.

Jake busts into laughter, covering his face as Chase gapes at him. My eyes dart between the two men. Chase widens his eyes as he gestures to Jake. I have no idea what he's wanting me to do.

"What's so funny?" Tess asks from right next to me, and I practically jump into Jake's lap.

Chase covers his face and Jake's shoulders are still shaking, so I won't get any help from him. I feel like I've stepped into another world I don't entirely understand.

"Nothing really." I smile at her, but she rolls her eyes.

*Oookay then.*

"What do you want to eat?"

"We haven't really looked at the menu yet. Can you give us a few minutes?" I keep my smile in place as she huffs, then stalks away.

I lean over the table. "There's more to that story than you're telling me, isn't there?"

Chase peeks at me, grimacing. "I may have fucked up."

I open my mouth to demand answers, then press my lips together. He doesn't owe me anything. In the last hour, I went from having one foot out the door to imagining that we're best friends who share secrets and braid each other's hair. I blame Jake. He's entirely at fault that I'm off-kilter. As soon as the word "girlfriend" left his mouth, he flipped my world upside down.

I pull in a deep breath, centering myself as much as possible while being three inches from my mountain man. No, not mine. *The* mountain man.

"So, what's good to eat here?" I flash what I hope is a serene smile at them each in turn, though neither will meet my gaze.

Jake scowls out the window. I wonder what crawled up his butt and died. Chase shoves the menu across the table and it slides into my lap.

"It's all good. Just pick something. And tell me if she tries to sneak up again." Chase slides down in his seat as he fiddles with his phone.

"Jake? What are you going to get?"

He grunts, crossing his arms. For all my faults, I can certainly take a hint. Perusing the menu, I find mostly breakfast items along with the normal fare found in a small-town diner. Burgers, meatloaf, and fried chicken are all listed along with a mess of sides at the bottom, but nothing jumps out at me. None of it will compete with Jake's cooking. If I hadn't fallen in love with his library, his cooking would have tipped me over the edge.

"We should go. I'm not that hungry," I mumble.

Neither of them react, though I'm not even sure they heard me. I hate being in the position where I'm the only one who's eating. People tend to stare and silently judge. They pretend like they're not watching me, but they're not exactly subtle. And I have a feeling in a town like this, rumors would fly faster than my feet, even while shifted.

"Pick something or I will, Gemma." Jake's voice rumbles over me and I swallow.

Clutching the menu tighter, I glance around for Tess. She's disappeared into the kitchen. I can see her chatting with the cook, who looks like Santa Claus with a full white beard. I swear I catch his eyes twinkling from here.

"I'd rather just get something from the general store and make it at ho—" I choke on the word, my body reacting to my almost-slip.

Chase's wide blue eyes find mine. Jake squirms, his arm brushing me, and goosebumps erupt along my skin. Glancing down, I find I'm not the only one affected. I jerk my head up before he catches me staring at his crotch. This whole fucking day is out of control, and I just want to admit defeat. Retreating to the cabin sounds perfect until I realize I'll still be stuck with Jake. Or rather, he'll be stuck with me.

I slide from the booth. They can stay here, awkwardly avoiding shit and never ordering anything. I'm sure Tess will just love that. The pens I was going to buy aren't that important. I'll just dig through my boxes and find the ones I packed. Jake's growl rumbles through the air, but this time I ignore it. He doesn't control me. I just need my body to remember that.

# Tall, Dark, and Hairy

## Jake

"Go after her," Chase hisses, his eyes a glacial blue as they spear into me.

"I can't," I grunt.

"Why not? She's going to get away. And if you treat her like this while you're supposedly dating, people are going to talk."

I grit my teeth, tracking Gemma's movements as she stops in front of the diner and glances around. She doesn't have a ride home, so I don't know what she plans on doing. It's another hot day and my truck will be sweltering. An image of her stripping out of her shirt, sweat making her skin glisten dances through my brain.

"Because walking right now wouldn't be easy," I growl, waving Tess away when she starts toward us. She throws up her hands and stomps off again.

Chase chuckles, setting his elbows on the table. "Are you telling me you have a hard-on from just sitting next to her?"

"We're not fucking talking about my dick. Just drop it and go after her."

He sits back, crossing his arms. "Why the fuck would I do that? She's not my woman. You go after her."

"She's not mine either." The words send a searing pain through my chest, and I curl into myself, forehead practically touching the table.

"Is this a...thing?"

"No," I gasp. It most certainly is not a shifter thing.

I refuse to believe my physical reaction to her has anything to do with being a shifter. It took me years to face the fact that I would never find someone. Hiding who I truly am for fear of the repercussions soured any previous relationships until I gave up completely. Gemma wouldn't be any different. I can't even imagine what it'd be like to admit to someone what I am.

*Listen, I know you say you love me, but there's something you need to know. I'm a shifter. No, like I shift into an animal. No, I'm not a werewolf. They don't actually exist. Wolf shifters exist, but they're not like what Hollywood portrays. No, I'm not going to rip your throat out. I'm actually a sasquatch. I know it doesn't make sense. No, I'm not particularly hairy other than my beard, but wait until it gets closer to the new moon. I know I look like a human most of the time. Let me just show you... And now she's running.*

"Shit. Where'd she go?" Chase's frazzled response pulls me from my imagined conversation.

I whip my head up, searching the sidewalk, but he's right—she's gone. I shove from the booth, almost upending the table in my haste. Chase hustles after me, then runs into my back when I skid to a stop right outside the door. She's disappeared. Panic crawls up my throat, threatening to send me spiraling.

"Check the general store." I take off before he can respond.

Main Street isn't busy in the middle of the day, and there aren't many places to search. I lean my head into several businesses, glancing around the small spaces before retreating. I startle more than one person in my quest.

When I end up back in front of the diner, I look for Gemma's reddish-brown hair. I've spent enough time studying her over the last several days I could pick her out of a crowd. My eyes alight on the hotel and anger bubbles in my gut.

I stomp toward the two-story building that's seen better days and rip open the door. It creaks, the wood groaning under my hand. Gemma's familiar form tenses, refusing to face me. Rick's ruddy face glares at her and I see red. Instinctively, I prowl forward, wrapping an arm around her waist and pulling her back into my chest.

"There a problem, Rick?" I growl, giving away how pissed I am.

"Mr. Silvius, can I help you?" His lip curls as he stares at my hold on Gemma.

I'm barely holding on to my sanity, both from her being pressed against me and Rick's asshole attitude. Gemma will surely feel the effect she's having on me if she pays even the slightest bit of attention. I concentrate on my anger for Rick instead of my cock stabbing into her back.

"I'd like to know what the hell you're telling my girlfriend."

"She wants a room. We don't have one. You have a problem with that?"

I lean until my lips brush the shell of her ear and she shudders. "Was he being an asshole?"

"I can take care of myself," she hisses.

"Tell me." I weave my words with a little coercion. Her eyes flash in the light as she tries to hide behind her hair.

Her bottom lip slips between her teeth and I dig my fingers into her hip. My mouth waters, wondering what she tastes like. My palms sweat just imagining her soft skin and the marks I'm probably leaving behind. I could soothe away the redness with my mouth.

"He explained how I wouldn't be getting a room. Ever." She gives me a tight-lipped smile.

I straighten, shoving the images of bending her over the front desk while Rick convulses on the floor with a bloody nose.

I fix my eyes on Rick, and he swallows, fear flashing across his face. "And did he do it politely? Did he give you a reason?"

Rick sputters, never quite forming a full sentence. I nod once, a cruel smile spreading across my lips. His reign of terror is quickly coming to an end. His mother might have retired, but she still owns this place. She won't be happy to hear how he's been turning guests away and treating everyone like he's better than them.

"Expect a visit, Dick."

I drop my hand to Gemma's, then tug her to the door. As it shuts, Rick finally finds his voice, correcting me on his actual name.

"You didn't have to do that," Gemma huffs, nostrils flaring as she tries to pull away from me.

"He didn't have to be an asshole."

I don't need to explain myself. In fact, I couldn't even if I wanted to. Letting her be harassed isn't something I'll allow from anyone. The need to shelter her from Rick was overwhelming—almost debilitating. Her stomach grumbles again and I drop my chin to my chest as I pull her to a stop in front of the general store. Chase runs from across the street, wiping sweat from his forehead.

"Gemma, I'm gonna need you to stay within sight while you're here." His hand lands on her shoulder and a growl erupts from my throat without warning. Two pairs of startled eyes swing to me, and I drop Gemma's hand.

"Shit," I breathe, staring at her. "Sorry."

"What the hell was that?" Chase laughs, but his eyes are tinged with warning.

"Richard was being a dick. I'm still pissed at him."

I can only hope they buy my excuse. I have no idea why I'm reacting like a feral beast. Blaming it on Richard being an ass might not be entirely truthful, but it's the only explanation. Gemma doesn't have anyone to protect her, and my instinct takes over. That's all this is, my true nature coming out at a very inopportune time.

Gemma rolls her eyes. "He was just being a guy. No offense."

"None taken," I grunt, glaring at Chase.

He grimaces, glancing around as he grips the back of his neck. "So, anything else you two need? Gem, you didn't even eat. You wanna go back? Tess might serve us."

"Can we just go back to the cabin?" she whispers.

I nod, pulling her toward the truck. This whole trip was a fucking waste. Not only did we end up not buying any supplies, but I'm also bringing her home with a brand-new title of fake girlfriend. As I pull open the passenger door, I catch Marcy staring at us from across the street.

Plastering on a smile, I wrap my arm around Gemma's back. She shoots me a confused look, then lets out a yelp as I pick her up. She clings to my shoulder, fingers twisting into my shirt. I have to pry them off one by one once I've set her inside.

"What is wrong with you?" she hisses through clenched teeth.

"People are watching, sweetheart. Try not to look like you're about to bite my head off, hmm?" I subtly glance through the back window at Marcy.

She lifts a hand to someone in front of the general store, and I follow her gaze. Beth, Marcy's best friend, is posted up on the bench next to the door, eyes darting between Marcy and us. When she zeros in on Gemma, I swoop down, brushing my lips across her rosy cheek.

Gemma whips her head toward me, and I freeze. It's as if time slows, each second stretching until it's heavy in the air. My gaze fixes on her lips as they inch for mine. A horn blares and the spell is broken. Time resumes as I jerk away, smacking the back of my head into the ceiling.

"Shit. Are you okay?" Gemma's hands reach for me, and my brain short-circuits.

"I'm fine," I sputter, spinning and slam my face into the open door.

Pain radiates from my nose, spreading across my cheeks and making my eyes water. Shaking my head, I rub my nose, hoping it helps ease the throbbing. It doesn't. Thankfully, my bones are made differently than a regular human's, so I doubt I broke anything.

Chase's laugh follows me as I round the hood to slide into the driver's seat. I'm going to ban him from coming to the cabin if he keeps it up.

"Hey, Jake," Beth calls.

I lift my hand without looking at her. The last thing I need is to give them more fodder for the gossip mill. Then again, I'm pretty sure Beth saw the whole damn thing. This is why I don't come to town. I never should have told Marcy who Gemma was. I should have just sucked it up and dealt with Marcy's advances instead of coming up with the asinine idea of Gemma being my girlfriend.

I swing open my door, ready to climb in, when Beth leans against the fender. Beth isn't as pushy as Marcy, but she likes knowing everything about everyone. It's not easy to keep shit private in a small town, but Beth takes it to a whole new level. From what I've seen, she doesn't actually *do* anything with the information. Honestly, she's a nice girl if I was looking for friends. Which I'm not.

"How's the haunted house coming?" She smiles sweetly.

"We're fine. Coming along just fucking fine." I hop into the truck, slamming the door behind me.

Unfortunately, the window is still down, and Beth takes full advantage. She's just tall enough to rest her arms on the frame. I glance in the rearview mirror, keeping an eye on Marcy. I'd rather not have them gang up on me with their questions, especially since Gemma and I haven't come up with a plan.

"You're Gemma, right?" Beth leans around me to eye Gemma. I expected her to know who Gemma is, but I'm still irritated by it.

"Yes. How are you?" Gemma scoots closer on the bench seat to lean over me.

She extends her hand for Beth to shake, her arm brushing my chest, and my heart skips a beat. Fuck, just her nearness sends me into palpitations. I need to get my shit under control before I have a repeat of my reaction to Chase.

"I'm good. Getting geared up for the Halloween fest. Will you be around to see the decorations? Or do you have to leave before then?" Beth raises an eyebrow.

Gemma sends her a dazzling smile. "I'll be around for a bit. Anything to help Jake."

I wonder what it would be like if she turned that smile on me. I'd probably pass out. Shaking my head, I frown. This woman is turning my life upside down and I'm only making it worse

I like being alone, secluded in my mountain retreat. No one bothering me is exactly how I like things, but the minute Gemma crashed into me, she knocked me off-kilter. Getting back on track should be my priority. I peek at Beth from the corner of my eye. Determination settles on her face, and I tense, waiting for the inevitable deluge of questions.

"Sorry, Beth, but we have to get going. Lots to do and all that." Gemma's hand lands on my thigh and her tits press into my arm.

I grip the steering wheel, eyes fixed out the windshield. Chase tilts his head, a slow grin spreading across his lips. My knuckles turn white as I glare at him. Punching my best friend would not go over well. Gemma would be upset. Beth would spread it around town. And I'd eventually feel bad. Chase would probably laugh it off. He nods slowly as if he can read my mind and I bare my teeth at him.

"Jake, start driving," Gemma hisses, waving at Beth, who's already halfway across the street.

I didn't even notice her leaving. Somehow, Gemma knew I needed to be saved and she slid right in. I pinch the bridge of my nose, wondering what alternative universe I've fallen into.

"Yes, ma'am."

She pats my arm. "Good boy."

She slides away, then pulls on her seatbelt. I gape at her as she smirks, waving to Chase. If we keep up this charade, I'm completely fucked.

# Step on me Daddy. Shit. Sorry.

## Gemma

"No, Slade. There's something different about this place," I mumble as I dig in my trunk.

Miraculously I was able to find a spot on the mountain where my phone actually connects. It's spotty and Slade's voice is tinny, but I'm not going to complain. Too bad I can't just camp right here, waiting for a call from the hotel. I'm essentially stuck at the cabin. No, I'm *literally* stuck here with the promise I made and nowhere else to stay. Unless I want to spend a ridiculous amount of time shifted.

Pawing through the contents of my entire life isn't what I planned on doing today, yet here I am. Sweat pools on my upper lip and I lick it away, saltiness hitting my tongue. It shouldn't be this hot in October. Glancing over my shoulder, I wonder if anyone will sneak up on me.

Jake disappeared a half hour ago, mumbling something about checking on the summer camp. And he walked there. I still haven't been there, haven't seen the books, haven't worked on the haunted house. Jake has made no attempt to involve me in anything. Chase dropped off a bunch of packages two days ago, and Jake took them straight to the camp.

I jolt when Slade sighs. I forgot he was still on the line. If I can get Slade to reveal something, anything really, about this place, I might be able to handle being here for another couple weeks.

"Gem, you're just not used to being in a small town anymore. Of course it's going to feel off, because it feels like home."

"No, that's not it, but whatever. Your friend isn't acting right, either." I don't know how else to word it without being a bitch.

"Well, he's the closest thing to a recluse as I've ever seen. He doesn't like people."

I haven't bothered to tell Slade that I've been staying with Jake at his insistence. Or that there's a tension between us, both sexual and otherwise. My brother doesn't need to know about my dreams of jumping Jake's bones. That's something I'd save for my sisters if I still talked to them or my friends if I had any.

"Well, everything was fine and then he growled at Chase before running off to the summer camp, so..." I'm hoping Slade has another explanation other than the ones my brain has come up with.

"He growled? Like a man or..."

I slam the lid and glance around. I shouldn't be this paranoid, but Jake seems to have the ability to walk without making a sound. There are only a few explanations for such a large man to be able to do that.

"Like an animal," I whisper.

"Why are we whispering?" he murmurs. I can barely make out his hushed voice.

"Because I don't want to be overheard. Duh."

"I thought you said he ran off?"

I huff as his rumbling laugh rings down the line. I hate when he tries to distract me from the actual issues at hand. He never did take anything seriously, especially when it came to me. I was too uptight, too concerned, too worried. I haven't felt like this in years—afraid of being too much, just like Kira told me so many years ago.

"Alright, Gem, you just have to hunker down a couple more weeks. I've spent enough time with Jake to know he's not like us, so it was probably just a guy thing."

"You can't honestly expect me to stay here when he doesn't even want my help."

Slade's sigh is tinged with frustration. I'm ready to reach through the phone and strangle him. I already know what he's going to say—a deal is a deal. I have to stay here until I've fulfilled my end of the bargain. And Slade knows it.

"Never mind. I'll figure it out." I hang up before he can respond.

I don't need to hear his excuses for why he lied about why I'm here. Each one will be well thought out and completely reasonable. I'll end up agreeing that Slade never had a choice other than to mislead me. He'll hang up and I'll wonder what the hell just happened. It's the same thing every time, which is part of the reason I stopped calling him as much. He's a great brother, but a master manipulator. Our mother was convinced he was blessed twice by the goddess. As if that made up for the shit he pulled.

If Jake won't let me help him, I need something else to do other than read. I love getting lost in a good book, but the itch to shift is steadily scratching at my psyche. I could go into the woods right now and get it over with. Running through the trees, connecting with nature would be a balm to my soul.

The leaves wave lazily in the wind, their rustling the only sound for at least a mile. I close my eyes, shutting out the voice in my head urging me to go into the house. I turn off the noise from the trees and listen for any sign of other animals.

Sighing, I glance at my palms, then curl my fingers into fists. Of course there are no animals foraging within a half a mile. I'm the only predator in the immediate area.

I resign myself to trudging back inside. Maybe I can clean or organize his office or something. There's no way I'll be able to stay with Jake if he keeps ignoring me. I thought it would be fine, but it's eating away at me. The hotel is a bust, so I'll be sleeping in my car. Unless I can finagle my way into one of the cabins at the summer camp. From the way Jake reacted before, I doubt he'll let me.

The pull toward the wilderness hits me hard, almost bringing me to my knees. I stumble into a tree, the bark biting into my skin. Wrapping my arms around the trunk, my heart races, the shift trying to take over. It's too early for this to be happening. The new moon isn't for a couple weeks, not set to happen until just before Samhain. I push the shift down deep, locking the beast away as it rushes against the bars I've erected inside myself. I have time before I need to let it out.

"Gemma!" Jake's voice echoes through the air, bouncing off the trees and wrapping itself around my body.

I shake my head, dispelling whatever enchantment he's woven into my mind. The more time I spend with him, the more I'm convinced he's a type of shifter I haven't encountered in years. It's the only plausible explanation for everything.

I met a girl when I was a child who reminds me of Jake. She was beautiful beyond words. She attended a festival in Moon Cove, and I followed her around, ignoring the duties my mother had given me. It wasn't long before I realized she was different, even from the rest of us shifters. There was something that pulled me in, blinding me to any logic. It wasn't until she left that Kira told me she was a lorelei, a creature much like Sirens from Greek and Roman mythology. Instead of singing, though, the lorelei merely had to speak. *A unicorn among shifters,* she said. I've never seen or heard of one since.

Until now.

Jake's ability to command me without thought, his self-imposed isolation, the ache in my chest when I imagine leaving him, the pull toward him when he's gone—all of it feels like I'm ten years old again, following around that girl like a puppy begging for attention.

Flakes of moss crumble off the bark under my palms as I slide around the trunk. Two pairs of feet stomp up the dirt road, and I wonder if Chase is one of them. I dismiss the thought as soon as it pops into my head. No way he's anything other than human. I wonder if he knows about Jake or if he's as clueless as I was.

"I know you're here, Gemma. You can stop hiding now," Jake growls.

Peeking around the trunk, I jolt back. Bastard is leaning against the tree I'm hiding behind. No wonder his voice sounded so close. Chase crashes through the brush on the other side of the driveway as if he's still searching for me.

"I'm sorry I startled you," Jake mumbles. "Are you okay?"

I snort, unable to help myself. Of course I'm not okay. I'm actively fighting against my own nature. If Jake is a lorelei then maybe he knows what I'm going through. Maybe he's known the entire time that I'm a shifter and just hasn't said anything. But if that's the case, why not just come out and say something? Why hide that from me?

Doubt weaves its way through me, making me second-guess every conclusion I was sure of not thirty seconds ago.

He sighs, knocking his head against the tree. "Okay, yeah. That wasn't a very good question. You just..."

"We don't have to talk about this. In fact, I think it's best if I go stay at the summer camp. No rogue storms will randomly pop up. We'll figure out your haunted house situation or the camp's books or whatever you need. Then I'll be on my merry way. I'll be a blip on the radar of your life." I'm quite proud of myself for getting through all that without my voice cracking. My heart doesn't fare so well.

He's silent so long, I start counting to see how long it takes for him to give in. He has to know I'm right. It's not just the growling or the ignoring or the running away. It's all of it piling up, and I feel like I'm drowning.

"Why are you still here? Your brother lied to you about why you came, so why stick around?"

I grit my teeth, leaning my head against the tree. "Because I promised."

Even if he's a lorelei, I can't reveal that I'm a shifter. He'll ask questions and I don't know if I can handle answering them. With the way Jake looks, I'm sure he never dealt with the backlash from his peers. No one bullied him for being too big or reading too much. No one set him up to humiliate him, risking exposure of the entire community for "just a prank." He wasn't told to get over it all while dealing with the backlash from everyone around him, including his family. So, I'll keep all my secrets to myself, relying on Jake's propensity to walk away at a moment's notice.

"Promises can be broken." His voice floats along the wind, wrapping around me.

Part of me wishes I could see his face. The other part demands I continue to hide behind this tree. If I'm facing him, I'll be able to read his expressions, ascertain where his head is at. But he'll be able to call me out on shit, too. His power of persuasion will be stronger, and I need to have a clear mind for this conversation.

"Not all promises can be broken. Especially when it comes to Slade. Once you owe him, you'd better pay up or pay out."

"Pay out?"

"Pay the price. One time he..." I let the wind carry the rest of my story away. There's no reason to open up more than I already have.

He sighs and I can almost taste his frustration in the air. "We're never going to get anywhere if you don't open up to me."

"We don't *need* to get anywhere. You need help with your haunted house. I need to fulfill my end of the bargain. End of transaction." My heart cracks, but it needs to be said.

I yelp as his tall frame blocks the sunlight filtering through the trees. Jake glares down at me, invading my space. The pull between us is too tight, too heavy, too potent. I shake my head, trying to shake off whatever spell he's put me under, but it doesn't go away. If anything, it strengthens the closer he gets. Bark digs into my back as I press against the trunk, attempting to put space between us.

"You've been staying in my house, sleeping in my bed, and you're going to continue to do so until—" His teeth snap shut as he tips his head back.

When his nostrils flare, I tilt my head, watching the progression of emotions skip across his face. The thread, the persuasion, the insistence—all of it points to him being a shifter. It also explains why he's been acting so strange. He'll never reveal it to me, assuming I'm a human. Now I really can't tell him I'm a shifter. He clearly is struggling with being around me.

"Okay, so clearly something is going on with you. And I'm sorry for that," I murmur, and his eyes meet mine. "I'll stay at the camp if that helps, but perhaps we should keep this strictly business."

"Strictly business."

I nod slowly, holding my breath. Chase's voice echoes through the air as he calls Jake's name. One of us should answer, but I'm caught in Jake's gaze. I couldn't pull away from him if I wanted to.

Clearing my throat, I dig my nails into my palms, hoping the bite of pain will snap me out of it. His eyes dip and a flush crawls up my neck as I release my lip from between my teeth.

"If you want this to be strictly business, you're going to have to stop doing shit like that," he says gruffly, eyes still fixed on my mouth.

"Like what?" I have a good idea, but he's going to have to spell it out.

He leans in, his lips brushing the shell of my ear, and a shudder rolls through my body. Jake's scent wraps around me, filling my pores and sending fire through my veins. The need to seize him, capture the moment with both hands, overtakes me. I beat it back, like one does with a beast who howls for their mate.

"You're a walking temptation, Gemma Livia. And if you keep it up, I'll chase you, capture you, and claim you for my own."

# The Call of the Wild

## Jake

A week later and I'm still kicking myself for revealing my lust for Gemma. On the surface, it was wildly inappropriate. Dive a little deeper and I realize how much I fucked myself over.

Her gazes when she first got here were wary, tinged with apprehension. Now they're downright lustful. She thinks I don't notice, probably because I've been avoiding her as much as possible. But I do. And every time I catch her, my cock hardens and my blood heats and my head swims. It's getting harder to ignore the tension between us.

Thankfully, we haven't had to go into town again. Gemma demanded my credit card and started buying things for the haunted house. She warned me she wasn't holding back. I didn't argue.

I may be convinced she needs to leave eventually, but I'll give her anything while she's here. It's hardwired in my brain to protect others, which is the excuse I'm using for my possessiveness over her. I'd sooner choose to stop breathing before denying her.

"I'm going into town," she calls from the back door. She tromps back into the house without another word, the screen slamming shut behind her.

"Like hell you are," I mutter.

Rushing around the house, I skid to a stop by her car and lean against the hood. I cross my arms over my bare chest, kicking myself for not putting my shirt on. It's still hanging from my back pocket. I *was* chopping more wood, even though I have enough to last me into the spring—two years from now. It's one of the few things I can do to keep my blood pumping and my hands off her.

My phone buzzes, and I reach for it, then drop my hand to my hip when I catch her coming out. When she spots me, she halts at the top of the steps.

"We talked about this, sweetheart. No going into town alone."

Her eyebrow pops up and I suppress a grin. "And when did I give you permission to control where I go and when?"

"Don't need permission. We're not having this discussion again. Get in the truck."

This is probably the longest conversation we've had in a week. We've been tiptoeing around each other, waiting for one to break. I should talk to her, explain what's happening, but that would require either lying or telling her a lot more shit than she needs to know.

"Seriously, you should see someone about your possessiveness." She huffs as she comes down the stairs.

Her hips sway as if she's purposefully adding sass to her stride just to drive me insane. She hops on one foot before hauling herself into the passenger seat. I slide my shirt on, then stretch my arms over my head, trying to ease the ache in my back. It's not often my body doesn't heal quickly, but sleeping on the couch for almost two weeks is taking its toll on me. I wince as I pull myself into the cab.

"You okay?" she snaps, but concern lines her eyes.

"Fine," I mumble. The last thing I'm going to do is complain.

"No, you're not. What's wrong with your back?" she demands, raising an eyebrow.

Gravel kicks up from the tires as I whip the truck around, pointing it toward town. Every rut in the road sends a shock of pain from my hip to my shoulder, and I grit my teeth. It isn't until we reach the turnoff for the summer camp that she heaves out a sigh.

"You're being ridiculous. Just tell me what happened. Did you pull a muscle? Trip over a log? Shit." She turns wide eyes to me. "You didn't cut yourself with the axe, did you?"

"What?" I shake my head. "There'd be blood then, Gemma. Plus, how would I hit my back with the blade? Have you ever chopped wood before?"

She scoffs, turning to glare out her window. "Maybe it slipped. I'm sure if I chopped wood, I would find a way to stab myself behind the knee or something."

"Thought you weren't that clumsy?" I smirk, though she doesn't see.

"That was under the assumption that I'd be learning to chop wood here. Clearly, this town has some supernatural power over me."

I choke, leaning over the steering wheel as I cough. Gemma's hand lands between my shoulder blades, more than a pat. I swear she's trying to dislodge my lung. I wave her away, still attempting to catch my breath. The burning sensation in my throat eases, but now my back is truly fucked. I groan as she mutters under her breath.

"You pulled a muscle, didn't you? All because you couldn't handle being in the damn house with me."

I slam on the brakes, and she yelps, hands slapping on the dashboard. The tires skid before finally coming to a stop. I throw the truck into park and open my door. Of course, I forgot to unbuckle my seatbelt and end up strangling myself. Thankfully, Gemma is too stunned to laugh at me.

When I make it to the passenger side, her damn lip is back between her teeth. She holds up her hands in surrender as I rip her door open. I *should* calm down. I *should* think about what I'm doing and the consequences barreling toward me. I won't, because I'm sick and tired of doing nothing.

I reach over her, hand sliding along her hip. Her nostrils flare as she pulls in a shaky breath. My fingers brush her bare skin where her shirt rides up, instantly setting my veins on fire. Instead of acting on the images rolling through my mind, I unbuckle her seatbelt.

"Get out," I command, stepping back to give her enough room.

Her mouth falls open as she stares at me. "Are you for fucking real?"

"Get the hell out of the truck, Gemma." I swallow hard and curl my trembling hands into fists.

She slides from the seat, landing on shaky legs, and I step into her space. She freezes, refusing to meet my gaze, opting for staring at my chest. I grab her hip, shuffling her to the side until I can close the door. Her chin quivers and I sigh, knowing I'm doing shit wrong again. Leaning down to her level isn't easy, especially with the twinge in my back, but I do it anyway.

"I'm not making you walk. But I'm done being blamed for shit that's both our faults."

She jerks away, her back hitting the metal as she meets me glare for glare. "*Both* our faults? Oh no, you're not going to blame me for this shit. This is entirely on you, buddy."

She pokes me in the chest, and I capture her finger in my hand. Pink splashes across her cheeks as her mouth parts. I shouldn't be doing this, but I've tried to stay away. I've tried ignoring her. I've tried to act as if she's nothing more than a house guest. None of it has helped my need for her.

"What are you doing?" Her voice trembles.

"Something I probably shouldn't."

I'm not slow and gentle, easing into a kiss to give her enough time to reject me. I should have. It's only been two seconds, but I already know something is wrong. My lips barely brush hers and she jerks away, slamming her head into the truck. I stumble sideways, almost falling on my ass in an attempt to get away from her.

"Dammit!" My shout echoes off the nearby trees.

"I'm sorry," she whispers, and I spin to face her. She clears her throat, tipping her chin up. "Actually, no. I'm not sorry. I didn't do anything wrong."

"No, you didn't. I, fuck, Gemma, I'm the one who should apologize."

She nods, then gives me an expectant look. "Well?"

I rub my neck, not sure how to explain. "I'm sorry. I shouldn't have tried to kiss you."

"You think I'm pissed that you kissed me? No, don't answer that. Just shut up a minute."

I open my mouth, but nothing comes out. I try again and still nothing. No words. Not even a grunt. My jaw flaps open and I run my hand through my hair roughly. Another minute passes while she gradually narrows her eyes. It's not even that I can't find the right words. It's as if I no longer have the ability to speak.

I spin, stomping toward the front of the truck. Leaning against the hood, I scrub the heels of my hands into my eyes. This is my penance. I ambushed her, knowing I couldn't keep her, and the goddess decided that was it. Never speaking to her again will be my punishment. The thought makes me shudder. I'm not one to get overly emotional, but I just might lose it over this.

"Uh, Jake?"

My head snaps up at her tone. It's one I haven't heard before. Glancing over my shoulder, I expect her to be where I left her. Instead, she's staring into the trees. She turns her head the slightest bit. Her eyes are saucers, a warning etched on her face. It's not quite terror, but it's edging into that territory. I follow her line of sight and heave out a sigh.

A large dark eye peeks from behind a tree thirty feet in, shadows dancing along its golden coat. His antlers tip his head to the side, and I realize the poor thing is lopsided. I take a single step toward him, and he spins, taking off for the cover of the forest. A bolt of pain hits me in the chest, making it hard to breathe. Usually, I'm able to help them. With Gemma here, I'm sure the buck was spooked.

"Why'd you scare it away?" she cries, dashing toward the ditch along the road.

I rush forward, wrapping an arm around her waist and pulling her back into my chest. Her feet leave the ground with a squeal.

"Not a good idea, sweetheart," I breathe in her ear, eyes fixed where the buck disappeared. At least I got my voice back.

She freezes, every muscle in her body tensing. Then she melts into me. Her head rests against my chest, soft russet hair tickling my neck. I pull in a deep breath, letting her scent fill my lungs and seep into my pores. All the reasons I should leave her alone run through my mind, the conviction of each one fading away bit by bit.

I set her gently on her feet, making sure she's steady before I step away. These are the reasons I've been staying away from her. It's too hard to control myself when she's around. My instinct to claim her overrides every other thought in my head. Even if I could dismiss her being Slade's sister, I still would have to let her go eventually. My secrets are too deep, too much for humans. I found that out the hard way and I refuse to go through it again.

"We should get going." My steps are heavy as I walk back to the truck.

As I pull open the door, I find her still staring into the forest. Her shoulders droop, along with her head. I wish I could hear what she's thinking, but I'm not that type of shifter. Some of the lorelei, siren-like shifters, have the ability. My kind do not, and I've never envied them until now.

"Gemma?" I call after a few minutes, and she jolts.

"Yeah, okay." Her whispered voice barely carries over the breeze.

She hops a few times before pulling herself into the cab, a despondent look stamped across her face.

"The buck will be fine, Gemma." My reassurances don't seem to register.

The rumble of the engine fills the silence. She cranes her neck as I pull away. I've got to figure out what I'm going to do with her. Maybe sending her to the camp would be for the best. She'd get her space and I wouldn't be the asshole anymore.

The problem with that plan is I'm going to be at the camp more the closer we get to the Halloween festival. Not only do I have to winterize the cabins, but also set up the haunted house and the haunted trail.

"What are we getting in town?" I ask gruffly, trying to get us back on track after my failed seduction and the appearance of the buck.

"Packages," she whispers.

I glance at her, but she's turned her face away. "Gemma?"

She sniffs and the vise around my heart squeezes. I slam on the brakes again, the seat belts locking as we skid to a stop. Fuck me, I made her cry. And now I have to fix it.

# Why Does This Keep Happening?

## Gemma

I shouldn't be crying, but I can't seem to stop the tears from welling in my eyes. I don't even know if I'm crying over Jake's attempt to kiss me or the injured buck taking off into the forest.

It's not often animals approach me, sensing my shifter nature. The only time they seek me out is when they're hurt. My mother always said it was because the goddess guided them to us. I don't know how much I believe that, but this isn't the first time it's happened to me.

The fact Jake was going to run him off broke me. He probably wouldn't have caught the buck. Regardless, I couldn't let him hurt the poor thing. Even with my added strength, I wouldn't be able to fight off Jake. He towers over me and is pure fucking muscle. Not that I'm afraid of him. For all Jake's strange behavior, he would never hurt me. Of that I'm sure, and not only because my brother would murder him if he did.

"I didn't mean to make you cry. I shouldn't have tried to kiss you," he says as his knuckles turn white on the steering wheel.

"I'm not crying." It's ridiculous to lie since even I can hear the tears in my voice.

He snorts, turning to face me. "Prove it."

I huff, glaring at him. "Fine. I'm a little upset, but not because of your failed attempt at seduction. I'm concerned for that deer. He was hurt."

Glancing out the window, I stare into the trees, only half hoping the animal comes back.

"I'm well aware. Which is why I was going to help him, but he took off."

I whip my head around. "What do you mean, help him? I thought you were trying to chase him off."

A soft smile overtakes his face and heat floods my cheeks. The grooves in his forehead disappear. His eyes crinkle around the edges, the green within brightening. It's as if he's affording me a small glimpse into who he is when no one else is around. The true him. I wonder what happened in his life to make him so guarded.

"You have a nice smile." The words pop out before I can stop them. "I uh..."

His smile morphs into a grin. "Did that hurt?"

"What?"

"Complimenting me. Must have hurt to say something nice." He's smiling still, a twinkle in his eyes.

I tip my chin up, sniffing. "It was terribly difficult, what with your grumpy attitude."

His mouth drops open, then he scowls. "I'm not fucking grumpy."

"Sure you're not." Nerves bubble in my stomach. Or maybe it's butterflies. I'm not a doctor.

"Liking solitude does not mean I'm grumpy."

"And yet every time you have to go into town, you grumble. And scowl. And harrumph. In fact, you harrumphed the first night I was here." I smirk, daring him to contradict me.

"Harrumphed isn't a word," he grumbles as he puts the truck in gear.

I wish he wouldn't. I wish we could stay right here on the side of the road, bantering until the stars pop out. After almost a week of basically silence, it's...nice. Telling him to stop, to put it in park, and to just be isn't something I'll do. If he wants to continue our journey into town, effectively cutting off our communication again, so be it. I can't force him to want to talk to me, but I can draw this conversation out a little bit longer.

"It most certainly is a word. It means disgust." I cross my arms, settling back as we crest a hill, the sleepy town spreading out before us.

"Even if it is, I didn't harrumph at you."

I let out a short laugh, leaning forward and scanning him up and down. "Seriously? You caught me with your book and accused me of stealing it. Then harrumphed as you walked away to get another copy."

"Stop saying harrumphed," he snarls, but there's little heat behind the words.

"Why? It's a fun word to say." I sit back, leaning my head against the headrest and closing my eyes.

He sighs and I peek at him to find him pinching the bridge of his nose. It's the same thing my brothers do when I talk too much. The same move my father does when I'm arguing too much for his liking. The same gesture every single one of my past boyfriends—all three of them—did when I'd get excited about something. Realizing I pushed too far, I clamp my lips together. I let too much of myself show. I should have kept my fucking mouth shut.

I refuse to apologize. Every other time I've been in this situation I've said I was sorry. I made myself smaller and more digestible and I refuse to do it anymore. Losing my job did something, woke me up, I suppose. I'm done putting other people at ease because they can't handle someone different from them. Doesn't mean I have to force my presence on Jake. Maybe his plan to avoid me was a solid one after all.

I clear my throat, closing my eyes again. "You can drop me at the general store."

"What?" His voice is jarring after a whole minute of silence.

"I said you can drop me off at the general store. I'll only be a minute. Then we can go back to the cabin."

We hit Main Street and I find new decorations in several storefront windows. The hair salon advertises Halloween cuts and colors. The diner has a special on green eggs and ham, though what connection that has to the holiday is beyond me. New banners grace the light poles, monsters marching down main street as they flap in the breeze.

Jake passes the general store and I glance out the back window as it passes. Biting my lip, I resign myself to going wherever he wants first. He didn't have a problem with us splitting up the last time. Then again, the last time we were here we were suddenly in a fake relationship. I probably should have pushed more for us to get our stories straight, but honestly, I forgot.

When we're at the cabin, he certainly doesn't treat me like his girlfriend. Or maybe this is the way his relationships go, and he just ignores them until they get fed up and leave.

"Have you ever had a girlfriend?" Based on the growl I receive, that probably isn't an appropriate question, but fuck it. He's already pissed at me, so I might as well ask what I want.

We careen around the corner to a dirt side street, a few houses popping up before they give way to trees. Jake leans over the steering wheel, his usual grumpy look plastered on his face.

"Boyfriend?" I ask, hoping he doesn't bite my head off.

"No. I've never had a boyfriend. And yes. I have had girlfriends. Now would you stop prying?"

I hold my hands up in surrender. "Sorry, but if we're supposed to act all lovey-dovey, I figured I should ask."

"Who the hell said we had to act...like *that*?" He pulls onto another street, the houses giving way to the forest.

"I assume you're going to need help running the haunted house. And the trail. I'll be there. You'll be there. You told Marcy, who I get the feeling is a big ole gossip, that we're dating. Suffice it to say, we'll have to pretend to actually like each other," I say matter-of-factly.

"I do like you," he mumbles, probably hoping I didn't catch what he said.

"What was that? I didn't quite hear you." I bite my tongue to keep the giddiness from my face.

"Nothing. We'll be too busy at the festival to do anything like that." He yanks the wheel at the last possible second, turning into a driveway.

I brace myself on the dash, thankful I put on my seatbelt. "Well, you realize you have to get people to actually work the haunted house, right? So we'll have to ask for volunteers. Which might require you to be nice to people."

"That's what I have you for. You'll be nice to them, and I'll guilt them into it."

My mouth drops open, wondering how the hell he's going to pull that off. I don't exactly have sunshine and rainbows shooting from my butt. I'm painfully awkward, occasionally sarcastic, and often described as abrasive, although that's usually from my bosses. No one has ever called me nice. Timid? Sure. Especially when I'm in a new place. But never nice.

He stops in front of a house with a wraparound porch much like his own. A small pond glitters behind the structure as sunlight dances off the water. Brows pulled low, I glance around until I spot Chase's truck parked next to a four-wheeler. For some reason, I assumed Chase lived in town, but this place is at least a good five miles into the woods.

"Stay here," Jake snaps as he pushes from the truck.

"Yeah, okay," I grumble at his retreating back.

Jake doesn't even bother with the front door, instead rounding the house and heading toward the lake. I roll down the window, not because I want to spy on them, of course. It gets stuffy in the truck and for some reason Jake took the keys, almost as if he was afraid I'd run away with his vehicle.

The two-story house needs a new roof, but the rest of it seems well taken care of. I wonder why Chase didn't offer me a place to stay. I shake my head before leaning my head in my hand, elbow propped on the window frame. No use thinking like that. It wasn't either of their responsibilities to help me out. Plus,

Jake was adamant I stay with him. The thought of crashing with Chase in his lake house makes my chest tighten.

"Why the fuck didn't you call me?" Jake's voice echoes around the forest and I swear the orange and red leaves shudder from their branches, floating to the forest floor.

I shouldn't get out of the truck. I shouldn't interfere. I shouldn't eavesdrop. The urge rides me hard. Usually I leave the snooping to my sister Alissa, but I hate being left in the dark. I always feel like they're talking about me.

Nope. This has nothing to fucking do with me. This isn't some secret being kept from me. Or something that will ever affect me, so I'm going to do exactly what Jake said and keep my ass in the truck.

I'm glad I did, too, when Jake stomps around the house again. Chase limps after him, stuttering to a stop when he spots me. I lift my hand, but he's already turned away. He disappears again and a lead weight drops in my stomach. Clearly, something is wrong with him. Or with me being here. Chase obviously didn't want me to see his house or know where he lived. Maybe I said or did something that pissed him off. Even thinking back, I can't figure out what I supposedly did.

Jake swings into the driver's seat again, slamming the truck into drive before the door has even shut. I bite my tongue as the questions bubble up, threatening to pop from my mouth. Repeating over and over in my head that it's none of my business helps. At least, that's what I tell myself as Jake points us back toward town.

The silence is deafening, pressing down on us. I swear it thickens the space between us, pushing us further away from each other. He's not even scowling anymore. Just a blank mask of nothingness. I wish I was one of those people who can handle not talking, but I'm not. It's physically painful for me not to fill the quiet. My mind starts to spin, wondering what I did wrong, even though that's not possible.

"Are you okay?" I kick myself as soon as the words come out.

Of course he's not okay. Something is going on with him and Chase, or just Chase. Or it is really something to do with me. Jake presses his lips into a thin line, the grooves between his eyes deepening. I open my mouth, then snap it shut before I can ask what I did.

*Not everything is about you, Gemma.*

"We don't have to stop by the store," I murmur.

He's barely blinking at this point.

I rub my fist against the ache in my chest. "Or I can just run in while you stay in the truck."

His knuckles whiten as he grips the steering wheel. I should just shut up now, but he doesn't give me any indication that he's heard me, and I can't stop.

"It's just a few packages for the haunted house," I say, and his nostrils flare. "If you want me to stop helping, just say the word."

The tires hit pavement, jostling me into the door. I throw my hand out and my finger bends back a little too far. I suck in a sharp breath as my eyes fill with tears. Pain shoots up my hand, wrapping around my wrist, but I don't make a sound. It's not the first time I've had to keep quiet when I've hurt myself. My finger refuses to bend and I realize it's broken. To a human, it probably would feel wretched. Thankfully, I'm not human.

It'll take a few minutes before it'll stop aching. Once it starts to heal, there's no going back. It'll be crooked forever and I don't want that. I glance at Jake, who is still studiously ignoring me. Slipping my lip between my teeth, I wrap my fingers around the broken one. A bolt of pain shoots up my arm and I bite down harder.

Jake pulls onto Main Street. I don't have much time, so I close my eyes and tug. It's not enough and a single tear tracks down my face. I curl my body around my arms slightly, hoping to keep my injury from Jake. I don't know how he'll react, and I don't want to find out. If he yells at me, I'll cry more. If he ignores me, I'll cry more. If he's gentle, I'll cry more. I'm fucked no matter which way he goes.

"What the fuck are you doing?" Jake's voice travels to me as if through a tunnel.

My lip pops out and I grit my teeth, bracing myself to yank hard. I never make it that far. Jake's large hand wraps around my wrists, stopping me before I can take care of it.

"Stop. Just let me," I pant, attempting to pull away.

"Seriously? You're over here hurt, and you don't say a fucking word? Who does that?" Despite the harshness in his voice, he's surprisingly gentle as he rests my hand in his. He examines it, muttering under his breath.

"It's not that bad. I just need to straighten it out," I whisper, then swallow hard. It doesn't hurt, but I need to fix it now before the bones set.

He turns my hand over, the tip of his finger tracing mine to my palm. I shiver, my breath hitching. I'm sure he hears it, but thankfully doesn't comment. Heat builds in my stomach and settles between my legs.

Before I can even brace myself, he seizes my finger and yanks on it hard. A yelp leaves me, but at least I'm no longer crying. His hands engulf mine, heat seeping into my skin. I tuck my chin to my chest, breathing through the pulsing ache that radiates from the injury. After a minute, I lift my head and our gazes collide.

My lips part and he glances down. When did he get so close? Why doesn't he let go? I lean forward slightly before I can stop myself. Nothing good can come from us kissing, but the tension between us reels me in, threatening to drown me. At this point I'd welcome it with open arms, if only so I could taste him just once.

# I'm an Awkward Sasquatch

## Jake

I can't pull my eyes from her lips. All I want is to lean forward, molding them to my own. I want to taste her, devour her, dominate her. When her body sways toward me, I'm lost. Her eyes flutter closed as she tips her face up.

I jolt back when someone raps on my window, breaking whatever spell we were under. Gemma's head falls forward and she tugs her hand from mine. Instantly I'm cold, shivering without her warmth. The butterflies in my stomach die one by one, their wings fluttering once more, then ceasing to exist.

Glancing from the corner of my eye, I grind my teeth. Fucking Marcy. Every time I give in to my desires for Gemma, something comes between us. Maybe it's the goddess attempting to keep us from one another. It's just one more reason I should leave her be. No good can come from this. Knowing my luck, Gemma would turn out to be another shifter, one incompatible with my own inner beast.

I snort, dismissing the idea. I may not have the ability to sniff out other shifters, but there's no way Gemma is one. She's too...human. Her inability to keep her feet underneath her is only one of the reasons. I'm sure there are many others, though I can't point to any of them right now. If she were a shifter, there's no way she'd stay with something like me. And most humans wouldn't choose to live in a cabin with minimal interaction with others.

Marcy knocks again, tilting her head and pursing her lips. She won't just leave, especially since she probably knows what I was about to do. I don't understand why she's so fixated on me. At first, I figured it was because I was single, but the longer this goes on, the more I wonder if there's something else.

I scoot back to my side, then roll the window down a few inches. "We're kind of in the middle of something, Marcy. Can I help you?"

She raises her eyebrow and glances at Gemma. Sniffing, she tips her chin back and marches to the passenger side. Gemma rolls down her window. All the way. I sigh, shaking my head.

"Hi, Marcy. Are you okay?" Gemma asks, her voice still thick. I'm sure her finger is killing her.

"I'm fine, but you don't seem to be." Marcy leans closer and whispers to Gemma as if I can't overhear. "Did he hurt you? We can help you if he did."

As much as I appreciate Marcy trying to look out for Gemma, an edge of annoyance needles at me. It takes a bit to pinpoint why, but eventually it hits me. I could never hurt Gemma. Not intentionally. I'd lay down my life for her if need be.

The ache is back, weaving its way around my heart. I don't know why it hits me so hard to think about her being in danger. Must be the shifter in me. It's been years since I've spent a significant amount of time with anyone other than Chase and the kids at the camp. I don't have an explanation for the reactions I'm having for Gemma.

At this point, blaming my shifter side has become the excuse I use every time I encounter something unfamiliar. Examining my feelings any closer will only drive me to the brink of despair.

"I really appreciate that, Marcy, but I just hurt my finger. Jake was helping me." Gemma holds up her finger, which happens to be the middle one, and I suppress a snort. "I swear I'm okay."

And she looks it. Even with her face blotchy from tears and the tightness around her lips, she seems fine. The redness has faded from her hand, no bruising to be seen. Marcy says something else, but I don't catch it, I'm so focused on Gemma's supposed injury. It was definitely broken. I could feel the bones shifting as I reset it. The crack as I yanked on it echoed between us. There's no way she healed already.

*Unless she's not human.*

I narrow my eyes, gaze sweeping the length of her body. Shifters have the ability to blend into their surroundings, throwing off humans by adapting to societal norms. It's entirely possible Gemma has gone years without someone finding out what she actually is.

I shake my head to dispel the thoughts swirling in my head. While Gemma might be able to fool others around her, even me, there's no way I could have spent almost two weeks with her brother without finding out. And if Slade isn't a shifter, Gemma isn't either. Maybe the break wasn't as bad as I thought. I was clouded by my fear for her. That's all.

Marcy flounces away, glancing back several times before she slips into the diner. Gemma flexes her fingers, then curls them into a fist.

"Is Slade your full brother?" I didn't mean to sound so accusatory, but the question sits between us as she turns wide eyes to me.

"Uh, yes?" Confusion, or maybe guilt, etches its way into the grooves between her eyes.

"Are you sure?"

I close my eyes, shaking my head. What a ridiculous question, but her answer didn't sound very convincing. I shouldn't even be asking her this shit, but it just popped out. I can't get the idea of her secretly being a shifter out of my head.

"Why would I not be sure about something like that? I don't have any half-siblings. Or stepsiblings."

I nod, pressing my lips together to keep from probing deeper. Adam wanders past the window of the general store, lifting a hand when he spots us. I don't bother waving back, though Gemma does.

"How many?"

She turns her body toward mine. "How many what?"

"Siblings."

"Is this like the first night when you were trying to get to know me, but it sounded like an interrogation instead? Because we both know how that turned out." She spins, reaching for the door handle.

My hand stops her before I register what I'm doing. She glances at my fingers wrapped around her thigh, then slowly up to meet my eyes.

"I wasn't trying to interrogate you. And I wasn't trying to pry." My hand flexes on her leg instinctively. I should let go, but her bare, smooth flesh is heaven under my fingertips.

"Well, then." She huffs, but her breath hitches the slightest bit. "I have a lot siblings. Where I grew up it was pretty common."

This isn't the time or the place to be having this conversation. Still, I can't stop my fucking mouth.

"Where'd you grow up?"

Her hand covers mine, and my heart skips a beat. Until she slowly lifts it away and places it gently on the seat.

"As much as I'd love to continue this interrogation, I need to pick up these packages before Adam comes out wondering why we're just hanging out in the car. I don't want him thinking I'm some pampered princess who needs her shit hauled around for her."

She pops open the door and slides out before I can respond. She's almost to the front of the general store when her words process. Like hell is she going to be hauling shit on her own. Or at all.

Rushing from the truck, I trip over the curb in my haste, almost going ass over end. I stumble to the door, latching onto the wood before it closes in Gemma's wake.

She whips around, her concerned gaze on my face. "What the hell is wrong with you?"

"Sweetheart, I'm going to need you to stop running away from me." My heart races and I run my fingers through my beard. "I'm going back to Chase's. How long do you need?"

Surprise flits across her face. "Ten minutes?"

I raise an eyebrow. "Is that enough?"

"A half hour. Meet me back here to get the packages," she says, then smiles.

Some emotion I can't name floods me, warming me up as if I've slipped under the covers after walking through a rainstorm. I sway, though whether my body wants to step closer or run away, I don't know. And I'm not going to stick around to find out.

I nod sharply, then slam my way out the door, almost plowing into Richard. His face turns red, screwing up to scream at me. Until he realizes who is standing in front of him and he flinches, stumbling back. He spins, practically sprinting back to the hotel. Good riddance. If he stuck around, I'd end up paying Paul for a new window after I put Dickhead Dick through it.

Chase's house comes into view, and I pull around back this time. Chase doesn't move from his chair, opting to continue staring at the sunlight dancing along the water. His text earlier was ambiguous at best, but he wouldn't respond after that.

I collapse into the matching chair, following his gaze. The forest lights up with a chorus of wildlife, a breeze rustling the leaves overhead. It's still out here, much like my place. He has the added benefit of the pond, though. I won't admit I'm jealous since he already knows.

"What do you want, Jake?" Chase asks dejectedly.

"How about some answers? Because 'I feel off' doesn't exactly tell me what the hell is going on." I lay my head against the chair, closing my eyes.

If Chase really doesn't want to tell me, so be it. But I won't let him wallow if he's got a problem I can help with. He's been there for me, pulled me back from the edge, and stood by me when no one else would. Abandoning him to whatever the hell is going on isn't an option.

"I told you I just woke up feeling like shit. Probably the flu," he grunts.

I roll my head, eyeing him. "You didn't say you had the flu. You said you blacked out. Those are two different symptoms."

He sighs, rubbing his chest with his fist. Then he leans forward, resting his elbows on his knees. He's hiding behind his hands, pressing his fingers into his eyes. I don't know what's going through his mind, but he's been avoiding me for days. I thought he didn't want to get me sick, not that I would. Now I'm not so sure.

My hand lands on his shoulder and he jolts. Bursting from his seat, he snarls. My mouth drops open, and I hold my hands up in surrender. I've never seen Chase act like this. When his cabin flooded, he sighed, then grinned, saying shit happens. When his last girlfriend cheated on him, he walked away without a word. He didn't need revenge. There are countless other examples of him being the bigger person, letting shit roll off his back, and always having a smile on his face.

"Chase, what's going on with you?" My attempt to keep calm doesn't help, apparently, since a rumble rolls from deep in his chest.

He deflates, all the fight leaving him, and he crumples to the ground. I freeze, unsure if I should go to him or not. Chase has always been the strong one between the two of us. I'm not equipped to handle a breakdown. Especially since he won't tell me what the hell is going on.

I push from the chair and go into the house to get him water from the kitchen. When I make it back, Chase is settled back in his chair, a blank look in his eyes. Silently, I hand him the bottle before sitting down as well.

"I can't help if you don't talk to me, Chase," I mumble, gripping the wooden arms. I don't want to set him off again.

"I just need a minute. Shit isn't like I thought it would be." He glances around as if just noticing the world around him. "Where's Gemma?"

I sigh, tucking my chin to my chest. "She's in town getting shit."

"Surprised you're not freaking out with her not being attached to your hip."

I scowl, refusing to mention the burning in my chest or the pounding of my head or my itching palms. No good can come from exposing myself. Chase will only use it to push us closer together. Despite my desire for her, eventually I'll have to let her go. No use telling him I'm not sure if I'll survive the aftermath.

# A Hairy Situation
## Gemma

Slipping my phone from my pocket, I check the time again. He's late. Not an "oh I got caught up finishing a conversation" late. He's really late. I've been hiding inside the general store for the past ten minutes, waiting for him to appear. That was after spending ten minutes loitering outside.

I told Jake a half hour was enough time, even though it probably wasn't. But now I'm left worried if I go to the diner or something, he'll be upset I wasn't where I said I'd be. Then again, he's forty minutes late to pick me up. At first, I was pissed. Now I'm just worried. Especially since he's not picking up his phone or answering my texts.

"Gemma, you need something else?" Adam asks me for the fourth time.

My cheeks flush and I shake my head. "No, I'm fine. Sorry."

I push out the door before he can question me some more. I'm not about to ask him for help. Jake has to live in this town and abandoning your supposed girlfriend isn't exactly the story a small town lets die easily. This fake relationship is starting to feel a lot like my real relationships. I've been ghosted more than once, though I always chalked it up to something I did. This relationship may not be real, but I didn't do anything wrong either.

I glance up and down the street once more before setting off to the road Jake took to Chase's earlier. A crisp breeze blasts through me as I round the corner and head for the trees. The farther I walk, the more pissed off I become. He didn't even have the decency to text. It's not like Chase's place is far. If he needed extra time, he could have called. Or he could have picked me up and we could go back to Chase's together. Based on how things went before, they probably don't want me there.

With all the rage flowing through me, I still end up searching the ditch along the side of the road for Jake's truck. Fear grips me, wondering if he's hurt. He could be waiting for me to come find him. He could be scared that no one will save him. He could be dead.

The thought has me stuttering to a stop. I grab my phone again to call him, but it won't connect. I send him a frantic text, yet it fails over and over. My heart skips a beat and I rush onward.

Suddenly, I can't see anything other than his bloody body being cut from his truck while Chase screams at paramedics to save Jake. Reminding myself of all the other possibilities does nothing. I want to believe I'd know if he was gone, if he was hurt, but my mind has latched onto his death and only seeing him in the flesh—whole and well—will erase it.

I stumble down the road, gravel skittering in front of me. As the trees thicken, the shadows lengthen. They swirl through the air, taking on a sentient form as it wraps around my heart and whispers sickening realizations in my ear. I should have told him I wanted him. I should have told him there was something between us. I should have told him who I truly am.

I've spent so long hiding my identity, I feel like I've lost an essential part of my being. I'm loath to admit my mother was right. If I had stayed, surrounded by shifters like me, I never would have lost myself. My career would have suffered, but what good has that done for me? I'm still floundering from job to job, waiting for my life to make sense.

And the one person I've connected with, I've done nothing but push away. I used excuse after excuse to put as much space as possible between us. He clearly wants me. He's literally thrown me over his shoulder. All it would have taken was one conversation and we could have had the last couple weeks together.

Instead, I let fear and insecurities hold me back. And now he's gone. Taken from me in some cruel twist of fate.

Tears drip down my face, but it doesn't matter since the skies open up. Ten feet down the road and I'm soaked. I scowl at the clouds and end up choking on the deluge. The goddess is punishing me for not realizing my own potential. Or maybe it's just a freak storm that blew in out of nowhere. With the way I was raised, it's hard to believe in coincidences.

I'm glad it's a straight shot to Chase's house. I can't imagine having to search a bunch of side streets for wreckage. Confusion swirls within me when I reach the driveway with no sign of Jake's truck. My stomach twists and I swallow hard.

The trees thin to reveal Chase's house and I trip, falling to my knees. Jake's familiar brown truck sits off to the side of the house, practically hidden by the wraparound porch. No damage. No fire. No bodies littered nearby. It's exactly the same as when Jake drove off over an hour ago.

The grief that threatened to drown me washes away, replaced by a burning inferno of rage. The bastard forgot me. Did he drive away and I ceased to exist for him? Did he get here and expect me to just be fine? Did he even notice how late it got? I could forgive him not calling or texting. I could forgive tardiness. But dismissing me completely? Fuck him. And to think I was plagued with guilt and regret over this man.

Pushing my wet hair off my face as I pull myself together. The last thirty minutes have taken its toll on me. All I want to do is run, but my promise to Slade locks my muscles. I can't afford to shift where Jake or Chase could spot me. I've thought about leaving before, but not seriously. If I really wanted to leave, I would have dealt with the all-encompassing pain I'm currently trapped in. My entire body vibrates, and I slam my eyes shut.

I can be upset with Jake and still do what I promised. I can stay in this small-ass town and survive. I can do what needs to be done without breaking down.

I repeat my new mantra until my body relaxes and the rain eases into a light patter on the ground. I can make it another two weeks in Whispering Pines. My next move will be to swing by the hotel and demand a room, though Jake may have burned that bridge. The summer camp is still an option, as well as my car. Either way, I'm done making myself smaller. I'm done letting Jake dictate what I do just because he has an attitude.

Pushing to my feet, I wobble until my head stops spinning. I may need to shift before I leave Whispering Pines. At least there's enough wilderness out here I won't stumble across anyone. Throwing my shoulders back, I stomp toward the porch. Just because I'm staying doesn't mean I'm going to let Jake off the hook. I'm still incredibly pissed. He deserves the tongue-lashing I'm about to visit upon his sorry ass.

I lift my fist to pound on the front door when voices rumble from the back. Sneaking up on them isn't a good idea. As I skirt around the house, thankful for the roof covering the porch, I realize I shouldn't eavesdrop on them either. But when I hear my name, I can't help but inch closer.

"She's fine. Not that kind of woman," Jake says and my heart seizes.

"Then maybe you should stop hitting on her," Chase responds.

"What would be the fun in that?"

I may be incredibly angry with him, but his words still sting. Chase scoffs. At least I think it's Chase. I sag against the wood, wondering what other bullshit Jake will spout behind my back.

"Why don't we focus on your problems rather than mine?" Jake grumbles.

"What do you want me to say? I blacked out and when I woke up, I was three miles away. You want to talk about that? Go right the fuck ahead."

Jake mumbles something I can't hear, and I realize I've overstepped. They might have talked about me behind my back, but that doesn't mean I should be listening in on Chase's problems.

Easing upright, I tiptoe back the way I came. I'm not exactly looking forward to trudging back to town to wait him out. Maybe I can ask someone to drive me back to Jake's. I don't fancy dealing with the fallout from a move like that, but I'm done waiting for him to make up his mind.

I'm so lost in my thoughts, I miss the planter until I'm tumbling over it. I bite my tongue on the way down. Blood seeps into my mouth from the wound, and I curl on my side. Sucking in a deep breath through my nose, I squeeze my eyes tight as pain sweeps up my leg and my tongue slowly stitches itself back together.

"Gemma?" Chase's voice rolls over me and I groan.

I really thought I could sneak away. I forgot I'm clumsier now, either from Jake's presence or just being in this town. Maybe it's because I haven't shifted in so long. Not that I should be worrying about any of that right now. I peek from beneath my lids and Chase's concerned face floats above me. My eyes dart to Jake several paces away.

Shit. He's pissed. I wonder if he knows I was eavesdropping. Maybe he's just mad I showed up. My anger from before comes back full force and I shove to my feet. Stepping away from Chase's outstretched hand, I cross my arms. I don't want his help or sympathy.

I tip my chin up. "Sorry to interrupt. I didn't see the planter. I'll be in the truck."

I pivot, forcing myself not to run. My ankle still throbs slightly, and I attempt to keep from limping. Clearly, I don't do a good enough job.

"She's hurt. Go after her," Chase hisses.

"We're not done talking," Jake grumbles.

"You're such an asshole. No wonder she's ignoring you."

Halfway across the lawn, I spin and plant my fists on my hips. "You know I can hear you, right? I don't need him to come after me. I don't need anyone to take me to town. I don't need to be coddled. And I refuse to be anyone's back-up option. Now, if you'll excuse me."

My pulse pounds in my ears, drowning out whatever asinine comment Jake has as I continue to the truck. I'm done giving him chances to hurt me. He clearly doesn't want me here other than for some eye candy and to play his fake girlfriend. Well, he can plan a fake breakup then, too. To hell with my promise.

I stomp past the truck and keep going. As soon as I clear the bed, I take off for the trees, hoping neither of them notice. Dodging fallen trunks, I push myself to run faster. I need to get away from him. I'll run all the way to the cabin if I need to. Hell, I'll probably make it back before Jake does, even if he leaves Chase's.

"Gemma, stop!" Jake's bellow wraps around me, urging me to listen. "You're going to get yourself killed."

Of course he doesn't trust me to keep myself safe. In his eyes, I'm incapable of doing anything alone. I've been letting him railroad me long enough. I pump my arms, flying through the underbrush. Despite Jake's size, I'll be able to outrun him. My vision blurs and my shoulder clips a tree. Slowing, I glance behind me, finding the forest empty.

I skid to a stop, wrapping my arms around a trunk. My heartbeat hammers in my chest, aching all the while. This isn't my finest moment.

My life has been a series of pathetic missteps. And I keep tripping over the ones I thought I'd dealt with long ago. They're rearing their ugly heads, interfering with my hastily laid plans, and choking the life from me slowly. I hate it. I thought if I pushed my insecurities down deep enough, everything would be fine. How wrong I was.

# Oh Heel No

## Jake

Gemma's sobs lead me straight to her. I would have been able to find her regardless, but her tears made it easier. I don't know what she overheard, which is terrifying. Everything I said to Chase was a deflection. He spent enough time rebuffing my questions about what is wrong with him, I got annoyed. Doesn't excuse what I said. She's more than just someone to toy with.

My heart clenches as I round the tree trunk and find Gemma curled in the fetal position in a shallow dip in the ground. A wave of protectiveness washes over me. I don't know how to protect her from me, though. Crouching, I brush her wet hair from her cheek. Blank eyes stare out into the forest, not even acknowledging my presence. I suppose I deserve that.

"Gemma?"

She blinks slowly, then sniffs. "What do you want, Jake?"

"You can't just take off like that, Gemma." I try to keep my tone gentle, but fire blazes in her dark eyes when she turns to me.

"I can do whatever the fuck I want, thank you very much. I've spent the last two weeks letting you boss me around. You stomp around like a surly bear, expecting me to make myself small." She swats at a branch, sending the yellow leaves fluttering to the ground.

"It's not safe out here." The words come out in a rush.

She shoots upright, then shoves me hard. My foot catches a branch and I tumble back, arms pinwheeling as if I can right myself with willpower alone. I land on my ass, mud seeping into my pants.

"What the hell was that for?" Swiping my dirty hands on my thighs, I glance around for a dry place to set them. Not surprisingly, there is none.

"Don't interrupt me, dammit. I told you that first night if you didn't want me to stay, then just say that. And you *insisted* I stay. You made me think it was all in my head."

She pushes to her feet, but when I go to do the same, she shoves me again.

"Would you stop pushing me?" I growl.

"No. You're going to sit in that mud puddle and think about how you treat other people. You spout ridiculous shit, tell people we're dating, and then....and then..." She swallows hard, shaking her head. "And then you turn around and ignore me. You talk about me behind my back. I can't even imagine what the hell you've been saying to the people in town."

The longer her tirade goes on, the more flushed she becomes. She may be handing my ass to me, but she's intoxicating. Everything she's yelled is true. I'm a walking contradiction when it comes to her. Wanting her and wanting what's best for her is a constant battle within me. The proper response would be to apologize. What comes out of my mouth is anything but that.

"Fuck you're sexy."

Her jaw drops open, and she narrows her eyes at me. "You have got to be fucking kidding me. Seriously? That's what you say?"

I shake my head, planting my hands on the ground to heft myself up. Her booted foot on my shirt tips me back and a rumble starts in my chest. It's involuntary, but she doesn't know that. Digging my nails into the ground, I relax my muscles one by one. I don't want her afraid of me.

"Don't you fucking growl at me," she spits out, and my head snaps up. "I said sit there and I expect you to obey. Now, I want some answers. And so help me, if you lie, I will be gone so fucking fast your head will spin."

She raises an eyebrow as she crosses her arms. Apparently, I didn't need to worry about frightening her. I've caught glimpses of this side of Gemma, but I never thought she'd be so assertive. The thought of her leaving sends another bolt of pain through me, and I rub my chest, smearing mud across my t-shirt.

"Ask away, sweetheart," I mumble as my hands tremble.

Her brows pull low and she purses her lips, probably wondering if I'm going to actually tell the truth. Lying to her outright isn't something I'll do, but I might have to get creative with my answers.

"Why did you ask me to stay with you?"

"Because you needed a place. And Slade is my friend." It's the truth, though not entirely.

"Why did you immediately turn around and act like I was intruding?" Her chin quivers and I lean forward.

"I'm not used to having someone in my space," I mumble. "And because you make me nervous."

Shock spreads across her face. I couldn't let her think it was because of her. She did nothing wrong and seeing her close to tears, wondering if she is the problem, isn't okay. None of what I've done is okay.

I huff out a sigh. "I like having you there. I like being around you. You make my world brighter. It makes it harder to imagine what it'll be like when you leave."

"Which doesn't make a lick of sense. We've barely spent any time together. We barely *know* each other. Are you sure it's not just because you're so isolated up there?" Her lids droop, exhaustion weighing her down, but her jaw still juts out like she doesn't want to let go of her fury.

"I don't know. It's not being alone, though." I hold my breath.

She nods slowly, eyes peering off into the trees. I fight off the urge to glance behind me at what she's searching for. I'm pretty sure she's just lost in her thoughts, but the compulsion sits in my brain.

"Why are you ignoring me? Every time I've tried to help you with the haunted house or talk to you about this whole fake relationship, you walk away." She tips her chin up.

"I shouldn't have told Marcy we were dating. That wasn't fair."

"I don't care, Jake. Don't you get that? I don't fucking care that you told Marcy we were together. In fact, I like—" Her spine snaps straight. "You didn't answer my question. You ignored me long before that."

"I didn't want to put you out. Gemma, we're not getting anywhere with this. I'll stop ignoring you, but it doesn't change the end."

She looks like I've slapped her. "Okay. Why did you leave me?"

"I didn't leave you."

I don't know what she's talking about. We've been staying at the cabin together. I've gone to the summer camp, but it's not that far from my place. And every time she's come into town I've taken her, unable to let her out of my sight.

"Thirty minutes. You were supposed to be back in thirty minutes." She slips her phone from her pocket, then waves it around. "Time was up an hour ago."

Horror floods my body, twisting my stomach into knots, and I push unsteadily to my feet. I grab my own phone and check the time. She's right. I was supposed to be there an hour ago. Which means she was standing around waiting for me to come and I didn't show.

"I lost track of time. I'm sorry, Gemma." I don't know what else to say. I fucked up.

"It's fine. I get it. Let's just go back. I'm sure Chase doesn't want me hanging around."

She walks around me, giving me a wide berth as if I'll snatch her up if she gets too close. I've been in this situation before with someone too afraid to get near me. Sometimes it's that gut instinct humans get.

The one time I told a woman about being a shifter, she did the same thing. She acted as if I was a wild animal set to attack her. I never saw her again. I'm sure she never said anything, assuming I was lying, but clearly she was afraid of me. Other than Chase, I never told anyone again.

Gemma's words finally filter through my memories, and I rush after her.

"Gemma, wait!" I snag her hand, pulling her to a stop. "Why do you think Chase doesn't want you around?"

She shakes her head. "It's not a big deal. I intruded on his space. He's obviously going through something, and I shouldn't have pried."

She continues on, tugging to free herself from my grasp, but I link our fingers together. Our arms brush and a tingle sings down my body, echoing through the air. Several times we have to go single file, but I keep hold of her. Having her here, keeping her close, might not end well. Yet the thought of letting her go right now is physically impossible.

"We need to talk about the haunted house. You talked about getting people involved. What if you had some of the older kids you have at the camp do the trail part?" she says from behind me.

My feet stutter to a stop, and she runs into my back with a muffled cry. I spin, wrapping an arm around her waist. My hand grips the back of her head, holding her close to my chest. She barely comes up to my sternum. I bury my nose in her damp hair. The rain didn't wash away her scent, and it invades my pores, filling me up in a way I've never experienced before.

"I'm sorry," I mumble.

Her fingers grip my shirt, twisting the fabric. "It didn't hurt. I was just startled."

I shake my head. "No, for everything."

I drop my hands and step back. While I might have been an ass, I can change the way I've been treating her. It's not how I was raised. That doesn't mean I have the right to hold her, comfort her, bed her. Our time together isn't going to last forever. If I let her in now, it'll only unravel in a few weeks' time.

She opens her mouth, but I step back again, holding up a hand to stop whatever she's going to say. I don't deserve her forgiveness. At least not yet.

I clear my throat. "I like the idea of having the older kids help. Some of them are from out of town, so they might not be able to participate, but I can talk to their parents."

She nods, her eyes skipping from mine. "Did you get the cabins winterized? Something with the pipes?"

I can't help the smile from blooming on my face. "That's not how it works. There's no air or heat. No water. It's mostly making sure all the holes are plugged and the roof is set for snow."

"Oh, yeah." She forces out a laugh. "I don't really know a lot about camps."

"I'll take you out there tomorrow." The words pop out before I can stop them.

Nerves swirl in my stomach, and part of me hopes she'll decline my invitation. I don't know how I'll spend more time with her, even knowing I have to stop ignoring her. It's a delicate dance, toeing the line between involving her and not ravishing her. The idea of putting her against a tree while sinking into her heat has my cock hardening. This won't be easy at all.

"I'd like that. Maybe I can start figuring out where to have the haunted house."

As she walks past me, she grabs my hand again, pulling me toward the edge of the forest. She mumbles under her breath, coming up with ideas and discarding them just as quickly. I don't bother commenting, content to listen to her brain create a whole world. One centered on making my camp kids happy.

"What if we made the entrance of the haunted trail super barren? Then the little kids wouldn't want to go in, but it also wouldn't scare them?" Her dark eyes meet mine, hope shining from them.

"I think that's a great idea, sweetheart."

It takes longer than I thought it would to get back. When we finally step from the trees, Chase is nowhere to be found. Gemma's hand tugs from mine and she puts distance between us. Her entire demeanor subdues as if the forest brought her to life, yet as soon as she came back to civilization, she left her spirit behind.

I have the urge to scoop her up and dash back for the comfort of the shadows created by the canopy of leaves blazing overhead.

"Do you think he's okay?" Gemma asks, turning to me with her hand resting on my truck.

Glancing around the lake, then back to Chase's empty chair. "I don't know. I'll deal with it, don't worry."

# Big(foot) on the Gas

## Gemma

Jake saying this place was a simple summer camp was an understatement. I thought I'd be walking into something small with a couple shacks, maybe an open fireplace with logs to sit on. Instead, I am met with a massive enterprise with a dozen primitive cabins, a large lodge complete with a kitchen, and a ginormous fire pit with amphitheater seating.

As I round one of the many stations focused on survival skills, I spot Jake at the top of the climbing tower. He's teased me more than once in the last several days about getting me on the zipline. I'm not against the idea, but I'm always blindsided by his newfound sunny disposition. Being out here woke him up. At least that's what I assume it is and not my presence. I've focused on cleaning up the lodge to keep my mind off him.

"Gemmy, come here," Jake calls, and I shake my head. "You're no fun."

Ever since I screamed at him in the woods, our days have been filled with setting up for the festival. Our nights have fallen into a routine of cooking, then reading in the living room until my eyes can't stay open anymore. I blush every morning when I find myself back in his bed with no recollection of how I got there. This new normal is messing with me.

Jake's caught me more than once staring off into space. When he pulls me from my musings, I lie and say I had a new idea for the haunted house. In reality, I'm daydreaming about the future. One that doesn't exist and never will. I've tried pulling away, keeping my heart locked away, but every day I fall under his spell just a little more.

It doesn't help when he retreats to his office or disappears into the woods. Usually, it's after we've flirted a little too close to the line—the one between friends and something more. It's razor thin and could cut us to ribbons, but I'm struggling to remember all the reasons we shouldn't cross it.

"Gemma," Jake calls from several feet away, and I jolt from my thoughts. "Got a list of people coming back to help. Lot of the counselors said they're up for either the trail or the house. I'll set them up where I think they'll do best since I know them, but a few don't have costumes."

"You have counselors?" I plop down on one of the rocking chairs set out on the lodge's wraparound porch.

He settles in the other one and I have another flash of my future. Ten years from now, rocking back and forth while the sun sets behind the trees after another successful summer spent teaching kids to get in touch with nature. I shake my head, focusing on what he's saying.

"Course. You didn't think I ran this place by myself, did you?" He grins, shuffling the papers in his lap.

"Actually, I thought Chase helped you."

He shakes his head, pulling out a sheet and handing it to me. Numbers jump out at me, marching down the spreadsheet tallying up donations and headcounts.

"What's this?" I murmur.

I know what it is, but I don't want to ask why he's giving it to me. Sure, Slade told me Jake wanted help with the books, but that was clearly a lie to get me here. Especially after how things started, I didn't think Jake would want me to have anything to do with his money.

He doesn't look up from his stack. "That's the season end totals for the camp. Figured you'd like to see them."

"You've got a lot of kids coming each year..." My eyes snag on the bottom number. "Holy shit."

He glances up, then leans over my shoulder. "What? Did I do something wrong?"

"You're making *that* much off this place?" The number has so many zeros I have to count them three times since I keep losing count.

"Oh, yeah. It goes back into the camp mostly," he mumbles.

Now I feel like an asshole for bringing it up. "Do you want me to assess where you can save money? Or see if you're balancing everything right?"

He snatches the paper from my hands, and the edge slides along my finger, leaving a sting behind. A single drop of blood seeps from the wound. I stick my finger in my mouth quickly, hoping Jake didn't notice. When I pull it out again, the paper cut is gone. I peek at Jake, but he's too busy scowling.

"I didn't show it to you so you could analyze it, Gemma." He pushes to his feet, and I feel like we're right back where we started.

"I didn't mean to pry," I say, but he's already disappearing into the lodge.

Counting down the minutes, I wait. He'll shuffle out in five minutes, apologizing for overreacting. I'll tell him it's fine, because it's not something I want to fight about, and the next few hours will be okay. I'm getting tired of the cycle. With under two weeks until the festival, I wonder if it would make a difference to call him out on it. He wasn't wrong about this whole thing ending before long.

The door squeaks when Jake pushes through it. "I'm not doing very well at dealing with shit instead of walking away, am I?"

He collapses into the rocking chair, sending it swaying. I bite my lip, weighing the consequences of dealing with this now. I suck in a deep breath and take the plunge.

"Not particularly. There a reason you shut down and run?" I tap my finger on my leggings.

Whatever heat wave was happening finally stopped, making the days cooler and the nights downright chilly. Doesn't stop Jake from stripping off his shirt most days. Not that I'm complaining.

"I don't want to lead you on. We only have a couple weeks left." He sighs, gripping the arms of his chair. I swear the wood groans when he twists his hands around it.

"Okay, well, maybe stop thinking I have an ulterior motive. I'm not going to jump you just because you walk by."

The corner of his mouth tips up. "Been imagining jumping my bones, have you, sweetheart?"

The ever-present butterflies erupt in my stomach. "Comments like that don't exactly help your case."

He sighs again, rubbing his hand along his jaw. "I suppose it doesn't."

We sit in silence for a few minutes while purples and reds splash across the sky. Insects start up their nightly song, creating a symphony of sound that bounces off the trees surrounding us. I close my eyes, enjoying the peace washing over me.

I've studiously ignored what I'm going to do after I leave Whispering Pines. It's not like I have a job to hurry back to. The longer I'm here, the more I realize I skipped from city to city out of spite. Everyone told me I'd fail if I lived in a booming metropolis, and I was determined to prove them wrong.

Being here among nature, I understand why my father told me it was always okay to come home. He might not have pushed as much as my mother, but he made sure I knew returning was an option. Crawling back to Moon Cove isn't what I want to do either, though.

Perhaps what I was missing was this. A place where I can't hear any traffic. Where lights don't drown out the stars. Where I don't have to schedule a camping trip just to shift. I don't have to go home to find all that. Whispering Pines is a prime example that places like that exist outside of the Cove.

This is the closest I'll get to admitting I don't want to leave. Jake made himself perfectly clear—we don't have a future. Staying here would only lead to heartbreak. I wouldn't be able to live in the same small town knowing I could run into him randomly. Constantly crossing paths would chip away at my sanity.

"I need to check on Chase," Jake says, breaking the comfortable silence.

"I can walk back to the cabin." I count to three in my head, then smile when he scoffs.

"I'm not making you walk up the mountain, Gemma. Get in the truck." He shoves from his chair and tromps down the stairs.

I haven't seen Chase since I tripped over his planter almost a week ago. Before, he popped up constantly with a smile and a joke. Now it's like he's dropped off the face of the planet. When I asked Jake about it, he said Chase was sick. There was a shadow in his green eyes when he said it, though. He's worried, but he won't lean on me. Of course he won't—we are temporary friends at best. At worst...

I follow Jake, not willing to analyze our relationship to that extent. It doesn't matter anyway. If I say it enough, maybe my body, particularly my heart, will get on board. Most of my day is spent pretending things don't exist. Like the thrill I get every time Jake's hand lands on my lower back. Or the heat that floods me when he strips his shirt off and wipes his face. Or the burning need between my legs when he walks into his bedroom in only a towel. I swear he's doing it on purpose now.

I climb into the truck, slamming the door. Jake's nostrils flare and his hands grip the steering wheel. I cross my legs, squeezing my thighs together to ease the ache after my chaotic thoughts.

Peeking at him from the corner of my eye, I wonder if he can tell how horny I am. Since he almost caught me paddling my pink canoe, I've been terrified to touch myself. My toys are languishing in the bottom of my suitcase, crying for me after I've slipped between the sheets, his scent clinging to my damp skin. I'm about ready to say "fuck it" and spend some time finger painting whether he can hear me or not.

A low rumble echoes through the air, and I roll down the window and stick my head out. There isn't a cloud in the sky, but that doesn't mean much. Jake said random storms pop up all the time without warning. I leave the window down as he navigates toward the driveway. Even if he can't smell the pheromones dripping from my pores, I'd rather not risk it. If he was a shifter, he'd pick up on it right away. It's the only time I'm thankful he's human.

"Don't go into the forest," he snaps, and I whip my head around. It's a warning he's issued before, but not with so much vitriol.

"There a reason you're being so nasty about it?"

Gritting his teeth, he cracks his neck. "I'm just worried about Chase."

"Bullshit."

He slams on the brakes in front of the cabin, then narrows his eyes. "Excuse me?"

"I'm calling bullshit," I say, crossing my arms and tilting my head.

"Fine. Every time you get in my truck, you're just...there."

My mouth drops open before I can stop myself. Part of me wants to lambaste him. I could stick a skewer in him and roast him over the large fire pit back at camp. The other part wants to jump out the window to get out of this conversation.

"You're the one who insists on driving everywhere."

"As if your car could make it down the mountain," he grumbles.

I snort, shaking my head. "Made it up here, didn't it? I'll refrain from getting in your vehicle from now on."

I tumble from the truck, not bothering to look back. Thankfully, Jake doesn't lock his front door or he'd see the tears forming in my eyes. I'd rather he not catch me crying. I'm not even upset about what he said. Having a stranger dropped in your lap is awkward enough. Jake is used to being alone, so I'm sure it's been an adjustment having me constantly up his ass.

I snort at the thought as I close the door gently behind me. Leaning against the wood, I close my eyes. After a few minutes, an engine revs and gravel skitters across the ground as Jake pulls away.

Did I want him to come after me? Maybe. Every day is still a roller coaster of emotion with him. When he smiles at me, I catch a glimpse of the man I'm sure he hides from others. It's the quiet moments in between his teasing where I question his sincerity.

His face falls and his brows pull low. Once I caught him mumbling to himself, though he was at the top of the tower, so I couldn't make out his words. I'm pretty sure I heard my name. He's fighting some battle within himself and I'm at the heart of it. Maybe he was right to stay away from me. Maybe ignoring each other was exactly what we should have been doing all along.

# Of Forests and Fur

## Jake

Gemma's scent lingers as I drive to Chase's. It's not just her shampoo or soap. It's the overpowering smell of her desire. She's permeated my truck with her lust, and I can't seem to get away from it. She's overwhelmed my senses. Ten minutes later and I'm still fucking hard.

The minute she climbed in, I knew how wet she was. One of the hardest things I've ever done was to keep driving. The two minutes it took to get to the cabin was excruciating. All I wanted to do was pull over and taste her. I wanted to bury my face between her thighs and make her come all over my fingers. I wanted her essence dripping down my cock as I fucked her in the bed of my truck. I wanted to hear her screams of pleasure as I brought her over the edge again and again.

Throwing the truck into park, I slam my forehead on the steering wheel. The horn beeps, but I refuse to move. Panting, my mind flashes images of every fantasy I've ever had of her behind my lids. Reaching down, I squeeze my cock through my jeans, wishing I was home. Then I could fuck my fist or take a cold shower at the very least. But then she'd be there, too—tempting me.

That's what Gemma is—a walking temptation I'm struggling to fend off. The last few days have been both a blessing and a curse. Being around her eases the ache in my chest, but I'm constantly drawn to her. And when I'm violently ripped into the reality of the situation, I turn into an asshole who pushes her away. Keeping her at arm's length isn't working.

Chase knocks on my window, yet I still can't move. As soon as I start walking, he'll know the pain I'm in. He'll comment on it, and I don't have an explanation for him. Though he knows I'm a shifter of some kind, I try to shield him from the finer aspects of what that entails.

"I'm not waiting forever for you, Jake. Either get out of the truck or go the fuck away." Chase stomps to the back of the house.

Huffing, I follow him slowly. Several times, I kick my leg out to adjust myself. My pants are too tight. I wish I was home in sweatpants instead. I could be reading on the couch or cooking Gemma dinner. I could be packaging survival kits. Instead, I'm chasing after my best friend.

"You'd better start talking, Chase. I'm done dancing around whatever this is," I growl as I round the house.

I stop short, my brain refusing to process what I'm seeing. Chase is perched on his porch railing. Not sitting. Not leaning. Crouching on the wood as he stares into the forest. His head turns slowly toward me, and he blinks. I swear his eyes aren't human.

"Chase?"

He shakes his head, confusion flooding his face. He climbs down, running his palms down his chest and legs as if searching for wounds that aren't there.

"What the hell happened?" he cries, clearly disoriented.

"Come sit down." I latch onto his arm and pull him to the chairs overlooking the lake.

He collapses in one as I hover over him. "Chase, you have to tell me what's going on."

Staring at his palms, he mumbles, "I don't know."

"Start at the beginning, then. You said you felt sick last week. What kind of sick?"

He shakes his head as he swipes at his ear over and over. I seize his wrist, forcing his hand away, and he shudders. I don't know whether to call a doctor or send him to bed. The air around us shimmers and a flash above the water draws my eye. Something white floats back and forth, settling on the surface of the calm lake. My muscles clench as my mind rejects the truth.

"What was that?" Chase whispers, fear weaving through his voice. Tendrils of terror thread their way through the air, threatening to strangle the life from me.

"Tell me what you've been experiencing. Even the most mundane things. Now." I keep my eyes fixed on the water, even though I know nothing else will appear.

He rubs his hands over his face, leaning to rest his elbows on his knees. "I was tired. Disoriented. I slept, but every time I woke up, I was in a different place. Then—"

"Wait." I hold up a hand. "What do you mean, a different place?"

"At first I would end up at the foot of the bed. Then the floor. Then—" He clears his throat. "I woke up deep in the woods."

He points across the lake to some far-off area. Out here there's nothing for at least a hundred miles, hills and valleys blanketed in trees with secret lakes hidden within the forest. It's the reason I chose this area to settle down. With fewer people around, I can shift whenever I need. Helps that I've spent my whole life surrounded by nature. I don't know how Gemma survived existing in the city for so long, even as a human.

"Was there blood?" I ask, swallowing around the lump in my throat.

He shakes his head. "No. But I was naked. I don't understand what's happening to me."

"What else? Because perching your ass on the railing isn't exactly normal human behavior."

"You think my brain is short-circuiting? Should I go to a hospital?" His frantic eyes find mine. All he wants is reassurance, but I can't give it to him.

"Did you hit your head? Get in an accident or something?" I ask, and he shakes his head again. "What happened after you got back to the house?"

He pushes up, then paces back and forth as he runs his hand through his blond hair. "I slept for two fucking days. I didn't even wake up to eat. I lost track of time, kept blacking out. Finally took a shower and..."

"Just spit it out, Chase. Not much can shock me."

He stares at me, contemplating his options. I blink, letting enough of my inner beast out to make them glow, and he nods.

"I have...hair." He grips the back of his neck, tipping his head back.

I cover my hand with my mouth, swallowing down my laughter. "That's puberty, man."

He scowls, rubbing his jaw. "Asshole. It's fucking fur. I have fucking fur growing on my—"

"On your dick?" I burst out laughing, doubling over as I clutch my stomach. Chase grimaces and I sober.

"Seriously? Tell me you don't have fur on your dick."

"It's on my ass, okay? Want to tell me what that's about?" He glares, then spins around to stare at the water.

Tipping my head back, I peer at the sky as fluffy clouds pass overhead, dousing the world in shadows. This isn't something I'd choose for him. If I could ignore it, or hell, reverse the process, I would. The goddess doesn't work like that, though.

"Sit down," I grunt, waiting for him to settle next to me. "Listen, you're not going to like this. And it's probably going to freak you out."

He waves me on as he stares at his feet. I wish my father was here. He'd be able to explain better what's happening. He was always the one I turned to when I didn't understand what my body was doing. Never judging, never brushing off my concerns, he always took the time for me. My mother was amazing, but she left most of those talks to my father.

"Just spit it out, Jake," he mumbles bitterly.

"The world used to be a lot less crowded. Shifters could disappear into the wilderness, set up their own communities, and stay away from humans. But the world changed and grew and that meant we had to change and grow. Not everyone adapted, but we made it work for the most part. Then the goddess decided other things needed to evolve too. Do you know about fated mates?" I don't think I've ever mentioned it to him, but I assume he did research after I told him I was a shifter.

"Yeah, something about the moon choosing the one person meant for you or whatever." His dejected voice barely carries to me, though we're only a few feet away from each other.

"Exactly. The goddess chooses your soul mate, and the moon leads you to them. Unfortunately, not everyone finds their mate." My heart clenches, knowing it's even less likely for my kind. "Shifters started choosing humans as their mates, even if they weren't fated, but their offspring don't always become a shifter. Some of them are human and nothing more."

"What does this have to do with me?"

"I'm getting there," I growl. "When shifter numbers started dwindling, the goddess decided to make more."

His head whips to me, narrowing his eyes. "How the fuck do you make more shifters?"

"I don't know. I've never seen it happen before, though my father told me about it. It's supernatural."

"Magic," he spits out, lip curling. I try not to take offense since he's obviously going through some shit, but it still stings.

"Whatever you call it, there's no rhyme or reason to who she picks. No pattern or way to reverse it once it starts. You're over the worst of it—the blackouts—and now you just have to wait for the shift. It probably won't hurt. At least my first time didn't." My words trail off into the darkening twilight.

"So let me get this straight. I've lived my entire life as a human, with no connection to this other world. I meet you and we hang out for *years* and nothing happens. Then suddenly I get violated by some goddamn goddess who thinks it's a great idea to fuck with my entire life and I'm just supposed to be okay with this?" He leaps to his feet to pace again.

I watch him impassively for several minutes while he pulls himself together. Biting my tongue, I keep the words I want to scream at him in check. I'm the only one he can take this out on, and I'll let him. Hopefully, after he's settled into the idea of changing, he won't be such a dickhead about it. It's not my fault he's going through this.

"Is this because we're friends? Did I catch something from you?"

I roll my eyes. "That's not how it fucking works, Chase, and you know it. This isn't a cold. And even if it was, it would have happened years ago. Pull your head out of your ass. I get that this is frustrating and disorienting, but blaming me won't stop it."

Apparently, I'm not that great at keeping shit to myself. The things I've been saying to Gemma are a prime example of that. More often than not, I should just keep my mouth shut. Sometimes it just slips out, though.

He crumples to the ground, legs splayed out in front of him. He looks lost as if the whole world has shifted underneath him. "What do I do now?"

"You'll know when you start to shift, and you can call me. It'll probably happen around the new moon."

His head snaps up, clarity finally coming to his eyes. "That's why you disappear once a month? You're shifting?"

The beast slumbering in my chest perks up. I close my eyes, taking deep, calming breaths. It's hard enough to keep him from waking up this close to the new moon, especially since it's been too long since I've shifted. Having these discussions with Chase isn't going to be easy. The more I talk about shifting, the harder it'll be to resist.

"Yes," I say through gritted teeth. "Don't leave it too long, Chase. Don't fight it. You don't want to be forced into it in the middle of main street."

"I never thought I'd be a werewolf," Chase says miserably.

"Dammit, Chase. You're not a fucking werewolf. They don't exist."

"Wait, you're not a werewolf?"

"Again, werewolves don't exist. There are wolf shifters, but that's not the same thing. You won't be howling at the moon or biting anyone." I huff at his smirk and mumble, "Unless you're into that sort of thing."

Slowly, he pushes to his feet. At least he doesn't look like he's going to fall into a pit of despair anymore. He does look like he's about to pass out.

"What kind am I turning into?" He stares at his palms, curling his fingers until his nails dig into them.

"Won't know until it happens. Probably something common, though."

I slip my phone from my pocket to check the time. It's later than I thought, even with the sun fully set. Gemma is probably wondering if I'm coming home. I wish I had service out here. Then I could text her at the very least.

"How many types of shifters are there?" Chase asks, interrupting my thoughts.

"A lot. And no, I'm not going to name them all. I don't even think I could," I say, staring as the seconds tick by, my mind still halfway up the mountain.

"What's going on with you and Gemma?"

My gaze snaps to his and I put my phone away. "Nothing."

"Doesn't seem like nothing. You ever get out of her why she took off?" He doesn't exactly seem invested in the answer, probably using the conversation to distract him from the other issues overshadowing his life.

"I fucked up."

He lets out a short laugh. "Of course you did."

I scowl as I push to my feet. "I was supposed to pick her up, but you were having a meltdown, so I lost track of time. So actually, it's your fault. But then she got it in her head I was dead in a ditch or something and she lost it."

His eyebrows climb up his forehead. "That escalated quickly."

"I'm working on not being an asshole," I mumble, half hoping he doesn't hear me.

"Good luck with that. Get back to your woman. She probably needs you more than I do." He waves me away and goes back to gazing at the lake.

I don't bother to correct him. If I could make her mine, I would. Too many things stand in the way. As I make my way back to my truck, I can't help but imagine what life would be like if all those obstacles disappeared. If she was mine, I'd spend the rest of my life proving I was worthy of her.

# Edging With Bigfoot

## Gemma

Goddess, I hate being a morose bitch. Most people wouldn't describe me as a sulker, but I am definitely sulking. I've gone through all the stages of grief—denial, bargaining, depression, and finally anger. I haven't gotten to the acceptance part. Honestly, I might leave here always looking over my shoulder wondering what would have happened had I taken a chance.

"Bastard," I mumble around the forkful of pie I've been eating straight out of the pan.

It's apple and delicious and I've now eaten half of it. I spent the first hour after Jake left in denial that he just left after insulting me. Then I took a shower and cried because tears don't show in the shower. Then I spent an hour wandering around the house wondering what I did wrong and how I could fix it. In my rage phase, I thought about trashing his office or messing with his perfectly stacked wood, but that seemed like a lot of work.

Now I'm wallowing in deliciousness and I'm not even able to enjoy it. I sigh, dropping my forehead onto the table. A punch of anger hits me and I fling my fork at the wall. It hits with a thud, quivering as the prongs stick into the log. I didn't think I threw it that hard, but apparently when I sulk, I don't know my own strength.

I shake my head, glaring at the utensil. Now I have to get up and either retrieve it or get a new one. For half a second, I consider just using my hands, but dismiss the idea. Knowing my luck, Jake would bust through the door right as I was shoveling the dessert in my mouth.

As if I've conjured him, the rumble of his truck echoes through the air. I scramble up, covering the pie and shoving it back into the fridge. Grabbing the rag, I wipe the crumbs scattered across the table. I can't help the mess under my chair. The washcloth hits the sink with a splat as his footsteps ring out on the porch.

Dashing to the living room, I jump over the back of the couch, then snatch up the book Jake's been reading. I'm out of breath and probably flushed, but at least I don't look like I've been moping around.

Jake shuts the door quietly and his boots drop one by one with a thud. The urge to glance over my shoulder is overwhelming. The words on the page blur. Thankfully not from tears, but I close my eyes anyway.

Maybe he won't even notice me here. He'll walk on by and...shit. I forgot he sleeps on the couch. Plus, it's like seven at night. Jake doesn't go to bed until at least eleven. I'm getting in too deep if I know his habits so well. I allowed myself to get too comfortable in such a short time.

I can tell the minute he notices me. It's like all the air is sucked from the room, leaving me breathless with nerves inching along my neck. I don't know how long we stay with him boring holes in the back of my head and me pretending I didn't hear him come in. I wonder how long I can last in this bubble of nothingness. Obviously longer than him, as he clears his throat not ten seconds later.

"Have you eaten?" he asks, his voice barely above a whisper.

*No.* "Mhm."

"What'd you eat?"

*Three-fourths of an apple pie.* "Leftovers."

I'm not exactly lying. Technically, there was one sliver of pie eaten before I got a hold of it.

"Are you still hungry?"

My mind spins as my eyes finally focus on the page I've been staring at for the last five minutes. One word pops out at me: cock. Of course I opened the book right at a spicy part.

*Extremely, but not for food, now.* "I'm fine."

"Do you want me to feed you pie while you ride my cock?" His voice growls from right behind me.

I jolt, tossing the book over my shoulder, and Jake grunts. My body attempts to jump and spin at the same time, which only makes me fall onto the couch again until I roll off the edge and end up on the floor. Curling into a ball, I squeeze my eyes shut.

Does he know I was eating pie right before he came in? He definitely knows I was shoveling it into my mouth, imagining it was his cock. No, I was pissed at him, so I definitely wasn't thinking about spreading anything over his body. Especially since food, in my opinion, does *not* belong in the bedroom. There are too many things that can go wrong, and I end up sticky enough by the end. At least if my partner is doing it right, I end up sweaty and in need of a shower.

Rolling onto my back, I throw one arm over my eyes, trying to remember the last time I was properly dicked down. It's been so long I can't even picture the person's face. That seems like something I should know.

"I think you broke my nose," Jake grumbles, his voice muffled.

I peek from under my arm to find him holding his face. No sign of blood seeping out, so I'm sure he's fine. It's not like I hit him with a hardback. He's probably just trying to make me feel bad, but he's the one with the dirty mouth that can't keep shit to himself.

"Maybe if you didn't sneak up behind me and say shit like that, I wouldn't have thrown a paperback at you." I bite my lip, my stomach tightening as I wait for him to admit he's attempting to seduce me.

"I was quoting the book, sweetheart. Maybe if you were actually reading instead of pretending, you wouldn't have been surprised."

He stomps from the room, footsteps pounding on the stairs as he runs from me. Not like I'm not used to it from him. He's constantly running. Say something shitty—run. Throw a heated look my way—run. Regret his decisions when it comes to me—run. It's getting annoying. Throw in his inability to have an honest conversation and I'm back to being pissed.

Scrambling to my feet, I charge after him. No way I'm letting him get away with hiding again. We have two more weeks to put up with each other. Add in the haunted house and we'll need to be able to work together. Clearly, there's some tension—sexual and otherwise—that we need to work through.

I'm only a few steps away from the top of the stairs when I stutter to a stop, contemplating whether I should just proposition him. We could fuck the mad out of each other. I shake my head before continuing slowly. We need an honest conversation first. After that, I can dredge up the courage to ask if he'd like to bang. Or I'll finally take care of my needs myself. If he hears me, so be it. I'll probably never see him again after this.

The thought almost sends me tumbling down the stairs. I rub the ache in my chest, hanging onto the railing with my other hand as I double over. Sinking to my knees, I breathe in through my nose, then exhale through my mouth as the pain slowly recedes. I need a game plan on where I'm going. The inability to see the future is what's making it hard to think about moving on from Whispering Pines. From moving on from him.

"If you want to be on your knees, I can get you a pillow."

I don't bother lifting my head. "There a reason you went from being upset I'm always around to dirty talk?"

He scoffs and his feet come into view. He crouches, then tips my chin up with his knuckle. I attempt to wipe my face of all emotion. My knees are starting to ache just as much as my chest, and I wish he would have brought that pillow with him. I'd probably end up tumbling to the bottom, but at least my muscles wouldn't be seizing.

"I'm not upset you're around. You—" He clears his throat, glancing away as his hand drops from my face. "You smell...good."

I bite my cheek to keep from laughing. I'd think he was lying since he looks so put out, but based on how he randomly hits on me, I'm pretty sure he's just frustrated.

"Don't fucking laugh," he snaps, his green eyes piercing into mine.

"I wasn't going to laugh," I mumble, then bite my lip.

His gaze dips down to my mouth and he scowls. "Do you realize my entire fucking truck smells like you? All the damn time whether you're there or not. Every time I take a shower, the scent of your shampoo or soap or whatever wafts up. And don't get me fucking started on my bed. If you leave, it'll be months before it'll fade. And I can't convince myself that'd be for the best."

"What would be for the best?" I whisper. My brain must not be computing. I blame the fact that his finger is painting lines along my arm. I don't even know when he started touching me.

"If you disappeared," he murmurs, eyes fixing on my mouth again.

His head dips down and I panic. Not because he's about to kiss me. Not because there's so much more I want to talk about. Not because my heart is doing a tap dance in my chest. Nope, it's entirely because I'm terrified I'm about to fall backward and tumble down the stairs.

I won't die, but I'll definitely get injured. Then my shifter body will start to heal long before a normal human's would, and he'll question what the hell is going on. I'll have to lie to him, and I desperately don't want to do that. Plus, it would hurt to go down the stairs the hard way.

My panic over a possibility gives way to reality when my body sways and my center of gravity tips over the edge of no return. My fingers slip from the banister, and I can't get my feet underneath me since I'm on my knees. It's as if time slows, giving me the extra few seconds to register Jake's eyes widening, my bones cracking, and his outstretched hand grasping for me.

I tuck my chin to my chest, hoping I can avoid hitting my head. Time speeds up and Jake yells something unintelligible as his fingers wrap around my arm. They dig into my flesh as he stops my descent. I feel like I'm floating as he reels me back in. When his arm wraps around my back and he hauls me against him, my breath hitches. We tumble back into the hallway and I clutch at his shirt.

As I rest my forehead against his chest, my heartbeat slows to normal, but my mind is still racing. I should get off of him. The lines are blurred enough as it is and straddling him doesn't exactly help. Something pokes at my belly and I squirm. I won't acknowledge it's his cock—his rapidly hardening cock. The minute I do, I'll have to change my underwear.

Jake's hand slides over my hair, fingers combing through the strands. He lifts his head and I wonder if he's smelling my shampoo. Now he'll probably have my scent all over him. It'd be a mark of pride if he was a shifter

I doubt there are any others like me around here to claim him. If there are, at least they'll know he's taken with just a whiff. Not that he's mine. It's only because we're supposed to be fake dating. Possessiveness floods me at the thought of someone else making a move on him.

With that thought, I shuffle to the side, but Jake's eyes tighten as he winces.

"Not yet," he breathes.

"I'm mad at you," I say, my voice muffled by his shirt.

"Every time I make a decision about you, something goes sideways."

"Maybe that's because you're making decisions by yourself. You could involve me since this is my life, too."

He sighs, squeezing me, then his arms fall to his sides. I don't know if he's giving me an out or expecting me to crawl off instead of helping me.

"Gemma, I can't keep you—"

My phone blares from my pocket and both of us jump. My knee pops up, forcing a groan from him. He curls his body and I slide off him as he clutches his crotch.

"Shit. I'm sorry," I cry, hands fluttering over him.

"Don't touch me," he wheezes as a tear leaks from the corner of his eye.

"I really didn't—" My phone blares again and I push myself into the wall. There's no landing to this staircase, so I can't really get farther away without retreating down the hall.

"Answer the damn phone," he moans as it rings again.

Fumbling, I pull it from my pocket. Half the time I don't even carry it around anymore since the line never connects. Slade's name flashes across the screen and I groan, tipping my head back. I swipe at his name, shushing Jake as it connects.

"Please tell me you don't have a baby there you're soothing," Slade says, laughter lining his voice.

"Unless you count Jake, then no."

I wrinkle my nose at Jake's flushed face, wondering how long it takes someone to recover from being kneed in the balls. I've read stories about people losing them after shit like this and I do not want to be the reason this man can't have kids. Unless I did him a favor and he doesn't want them.

I lift the phone from my mouth. "Hey, do you want kids?"

Bewilderment chases exasperation across his face. "What?"

"Sorry, not the time. Go back to writhing around on the ground." I pat his shoulder.

"Uh, is this a bad time, Gem?" Slade's voice pulls me back to him.

"No," I say, scrambling to my feet. "What's up?"

Jake lies on his back, spread-eagle with his legs hanging off the steps. He stares at the ceiling, then his eyes dart to mine.

"Who is it?" he mouths.

My brother hems and haws, clearing his throat several times. "Slade, just spit it out."

"Just wondering how things are going. You're not bugging Jake too much, right?" Slade asks.

And there it is. I knew this phone call was coming sooner or later. I figured it would come from my mother after Slade spilled the beans that I was in

Whispering Pines. Since she still hasn't called, maybe he kept his mouth shut for once. I'm not surprised it's Slade, though. He might have orchestrated this entire situation, but he definitely didn't want me to get involved with his friend. Jake is off-limits.

I shuffle away from Jake as my stomach flips and I hiss, "What's that supposed to mean?"

"Ah, Gem, don't take it the wrong way. Jake's just used to being alone. And once you get comfortable somewhere you tend to..."

"Tend to what?"

"You sometimes blurt out whatever pops in your head. It can be disconcerting," he mumbles.

"Disconcerting," I repeat quietly.

He doesn't respond, but he doesn't need to. He's right, which is why I'm hesitant to actually open up to people. I didn't realize I was doing it with Jake. It's one more example of how far I've fallen in just a couple weeks.

With the number of times I've moved and found myself in a new place with new people, I've never been this comfortable this quickly. I actually don't know if I've ever been this content somewhere, even with Jake's wishy-washy behavior.

Slade sighs. "Listen, Gem. I love you and all your quirks. I just don't want you to ruin anything because you didn't think it through."

I peek behind me, tracking Jake as he stumbles down the stairs. Hopefully he didn't overhear what my brother said. My time here has been filled with enough embarrassment.

"I understand," I whisper.

I end the call, staring at the wall without really seeing it. This was exactly the wake-up call I needed. Slade doesn't want me to fuck up his relationship with Jake by hooking up with him. I don't know why my brother insisted I come here if he was so damn worried, but it doesn't change the fact I'm here now. I'll make the best of it, stay away from his friend, and move on. I'll leave a piece of me behind, but I'll leave, nonetheless.

"Gemma! Why the hell is there a fork in the wall?"

Shit.

# Are You Fur Real?

## Jake

I don't know what Slade said to Gemma, but I'm about ready to call him up and cuss him out. If she was sulking or avoiding me, I could deal with it. If she was on-edge and skittish, we could work through it. But this is something else.

We've gone from some strange dance between flirting and ignoring each other to nothing. When I ask her questions, I get one-word answers. She's floating through our days setting up the camp with a detachment I can't pull her out of. She takes most of her meals on the back porch, staring at the forest. After dinner, she doesn't linger and read in the living room with me anymore. Instead, she retreats to my room, shutting the door softly behind her.

I've started to ask her what's wrong a dozen times over the last four days but bail when I see the emptiness in her eyes. I figured if she had something to say, she'd say it. As she makes her way up the stairs to sequester herself once more, I doubt she'll ever tell me. I should go after her and demand some answers. I make it halfway across the kitchen before I think better of it.

We're not together. She's not mine to comfort or cajole into opening up. Hell, we're barely friends. Our relationship, if you could call it that, is temporary and fraught with pitfalls. I clench my hands by my sides as unease rolls through me. Something isn't right and I need to figure out what.

I stomp out the back door, intent on cleaning up the yard before the sun sets. The cold air hits me, carrying the smell of winter. Hopefully, the snow will hold off until after the festival. Gemma and I have put too much time and effort into the haunted house. We haven't even started the trail for the adults. I've let Gemma take the lead on organizing everything. Now that she's pulling away, I feel like I'm taking advantage of her. I should tell her to just go, regardless of her promise to my friend.

Glancing back at the house, I pull my phone out and call Slade. I've tried to get Gemma to talk to me and she won't. Whatever Slade said affected her and I won't let him get away with hurting her. We could have worked out the problems between us if he wouldn't have interfered.

"What the hell did you say to her?" I hiss. I'd yell at him, but I don't want Gemma overhearing.

"Hello to you too, Jake. How's the haunted house coming?" Slade says as he holds back laughter.

I pinch the bridge of my nose. "I'm not calling you for small talk, Slade. What the fuck did you say to Gemma?"

He sighs, or maybe it's more of a huff. The blood roaring through my ears makes it hard to tell.

"Listen, I appreciate you helping Gemma out. I know she can be a bit much."

I don't know what that means. Gemma may say some off-the-cuff things, but that doesn't bother me. I don't know why it would bother Slade. They don't talk much, according to Gemma. And she hasn't been home in years. Why he thinks he's qualified to judge her is beyond my understanding.

"What do you mean?" He must not hear the warning in my tone as he prattles on about Gemma and her "quirks," as he calls them.

Everything from how she eats muffins to how she randomly blurts out whatever pops into her head. Most of the time, I see those things as endearing. They make her who she is. The longer the list gets, the more annoyed I become.

I clear my throat to stop his tirade. "Seems to me you just don't understand her and that makes you think she's not as good as you."

"What? No. Jake, I love my sister. She just doesn't..." He sighs again. "When she gets comfortable with someone, they don't always accept her for who she is."

"So you told her to hide who she is because *I* might not be able to handle it? Because someone might make fun of her, she's supposed to change how she acts?" I pace along the tree line, the scent of pine invading my nose.

"When you say it like that, it sounds dickish," he mumbles.

"Because it is. How long have you been telling her to hide herself to fit in better? I understand you were trying to protect her from assholes, but that was a cop-out, and you know it. You didn't want to jeopardize your own social standing in your small-ass town, so you threw your own sister to the fucking wolves."

Slade snorts, though nothing about what I said was funny. And the fact he's not taking it seriously makes my blood boil all the more.

"I didn't mean to do that," Slade says after a minute of silence while I contemplate hanging up on him.

"What exactly did you say to her? I want exact quotes."

He mumbles a little before finally huffing. "I told her I didn't want her to ruin anything by not thinking shit through."

His revelation has me slumping against a tree. Slade may have gone about it the wrong way, but his message is loud and clear. He doesn't want Gemma and me getting involved in any way other than business. I knew he wouldn't approve, but I've been fighting with myself ever since she came to Whispering Pines. At least I know why she's pulling away lately.

"Perhaps you should choose your words more wisely in the future," I growl, then hang up on him.

I'm not about to reassure Slade. If he was the only thing standing in the way of me claiming Gemma, I would have pushed more. I would have called him out and told him he doesn't control her. Unfortunately, there are too many other things blocking a future for us. If she was a shifter...

I erase the thought from my mind. There's no reason to imagine what-ifs. Unless the goddess chooses her to change, like Chase, I need to stay away. Even if she was a shifter, there's no way she'd choose someone like me. She'd run, just like the others. I'm different, even in the shifter world.

"Jake, Chase is here to see you," Gemma calls. There's no inflection in her voice. If I didn't know any better, I'd think she was an automated message informing me of the weather.

By the time I turn around, the back door is closing. Shaking my head, I make my way around the house. I doubt Chase went inside. He's been avoiding everyone lately. Not that Gemma would have many opportunities to run into him. She's been keeping to herself, refusing to go into town with me. I've been picking up all the items she's purchased, then dropping them at the camp.

Chase leans against his truck, chin tucked to his chest. He doesn't bother looking up, even when I'm standing directly in front of him.

"What's going on?" I cross my arms and peer at the house, wondering if Gemma is spying from one of the windows.

"Not much. Thought I should get out of my head, so I came here. You need help with shit at the camp?" He finally meets my gaze. His eyes flash, turning into slits, then he blinks and they're his normal blue.

"Could use some. Gemma's got the lodge set up for the kids. All that's left is the haunted trail, unless we add more to the entrance. Gemma thought it might be good to have a clear path on where to go."

The corner of Chase's mouth tips up, though it lacks the usual flare. "Really letting her in then, huh?"

I glare at him as I grit my teeth. "It's what she's here for."

He scoffs, glancing away. "Sure. You could ask her to stay, though. Find some place for her to rent and see where things go."

I'm shaking my head before he's finished. "Slade—"

"Seriously? You two are grown-ass adults. I can't believe you're going to let her older brother dictate your relationship," he scoffs and I have the urge to stuff him back in his truck. Literally.

"Let's say I was willing to jeopardize my friendship with Slade. Then what? You remember how you reacted when I told you I was a shifter. How do you think it would go with someone I wanted to sleep with? Spend my life with? Fall in love with? No, I've been down that road before, Chase. I'm not about to put myself in a position to be rejected again."

Chase's head tilts as he studies me. I don't particularly care if he understands. He might not fully grasp it until he goes through it himself. Then again, maybe he doesn't even want to settle down. We've never talked about it. He's spent most of his personal time with hook-ups and one-night stands. That might be his plan for the rest of his life. I wonder if becoming a shifter will change those feelings for him.

"Don't let the fear of rejection hold you back, Jake. If she's the one, she won't care what you are. You're more than what you turn into once a month." He turns before I can respond, not that I know how to.

Chase climbs into his truck and starts it, then stares at the house. I glance over my shoulder and catch one of the curtains fluttering back into place. We're far enough away she wouldn't be able to overhear our conversation at least. Chase leans out his window, leveling me with a look.

"You're not going to take my advice, are you?" he asks.

"It's not that easy, Chase," I mumble.

He runs his fingers through his hair. "You know, I never asked what kind of shifter you are. And I'm not going to push you into it. But you make it seem like it's bad. I just need to know if I'm going to turn into one and what I'm going to face if I do."

I smirk, rubbing the back of my neck. "Not something you need to worry about. The goddess doesn't choose humans to become sasquatches."

His eyes widen as he looks me up and down. "No shit. Like Bigfoot?"

I chuckle. "We don't really use that word, but yeah."

I didn't expect his reaction. It's so different from the other times I've revealed what lurks beneath the surface. Admiration gleams in his eyes and my chest swells with a pride I haven't felt in years. My father always told me to never be ashamed, but dealing with the fallout of relationships over it when I was younger dampened my enthusiasm to share. I should have known Chase wouldn't care either way.

"So, I don't get to turn into Bigfoot?"

I laugh at his crestfallen expression. "Sorry, Chase. You're going to have to settle for something a little more mundane."

He nods, then glances at the house once more. "We should go out for dinner. I'm getting sick of eating rice."

"I could have dropped some food off if you told me," I grumble.

"Meet me at the diner," he says as he starts the truck, then grimaces. "Hopefully, Tess isn't working."

I roll my eyes. "You could just apologize to her."

"I did. She called me an asshat. Go get Gemma."

My muscles lock and I swallow hard. "I doubt she'll want to eat with us, but I'll ask her."

Chase's brows pull low. "Maybe I'm not the only one who has to apologize."

He puts the truck in gear before driving away. I don't think I have anything to say sorry for, but it might get her talking. We might not end up having a heart-to-heart. Actually, I fully expect her to decline to come with us no matter if I apologize or not. If I show up without her, Chase will bust my balls.

"Gemma," I call as soon as I come through the front door. "Chase is waiting at the diner."

Gemma wanders from the living room, facing me but staring at my shoulder. "Have fun."

She turns toward the stairs to retreat. I jolt forward, my fingers brushing her arm. An electric shock rolls up my skin and she jerks around. I stare at my palm, expecting a mark to be left behind. Gemma's wide-eyed gaze finds mine, then her face shutters and all the emotion drains away.

"Did you need something?" she asks, her voice so monotone it physically hurts.

"I want you to come with." I hold my breath. An apology is still dancing on the tip of my tongue.

She tilts her head. "Why?"

"Because I like spending time with you," I say as desperation bleeds into my tone.

She nods slowly, staring at my shoulder again. Her phone buzzes and her head drops.

"Okay. Let me get my shoes."

I breathe a sigh of relief as I grab my keys. Even if she's still holding me at arm's length, at least we're making progress. It's a start. My muscles relax and my resolve to mend whatever is broken within Gemma solidifies.

# Bending Over for Bigfoot

## Gemma

Numbness has been my constant companion since my conversation with Slade. The only way I've kept my shit together is by repeating his words in my mind over and over. If I kept going or, goddess forbid, took the next step, I'd ruin Slade's relationship with his friend. I may be a big girl who can make my own decisions, but I'm not an asshole. Intentionally hurting my brother isn't something I'd do.

Not to mention Slade's assessment of me cut deep. He knows Jake better than I do. I didn't think Jake cared about my randomness, but it might explain his attitude toward me. My heart hurts every time I think about it.

I sigh as he rushes out the front door. I stuff every emotion down, layering apathy over them all and hope for the best. It's the only way I'll get through these next couple weeks.

I slip on my sandals before following Jake, who's already in the truck waiting for me. I can't bring myself to hurry. Chase probably doesn't even want me to come. I haven't seen him since Jake forgot me in town. My cheeks flush, wondering if Jake told Chase about my meltdown.

Did they laugh at me thinking Jake was dead? Did they crack jokes, imagining me sobbing as I walked down the street? Did Jake mention how I grilled him in the middle of the woods? Each question stabs at my confidence. I've spent too long caring about what other people thought. As I grew older, I got over it, but after talking with Slade, all my past insecurities have reared their heads and sent me spiraling.

"Buckle up," Jake grunts as he starts the truck.

I do, then stare out the window as he pulls around and points us toward town.

Jake clears his throat. "I talked to Slade."

My lungs seize and I curl my hands into fists, wheezing, "Oh?"

"I'm sorry," he whispers.

My mind scrambles, trying to figure out what he's apologizing for. We haven't exactly been interacting the last few days. And when we do, I keep things civil, never diving below the surface. I have no idea what he could possibly think he's done wrong, but I don't want to ask him. If I question him, then I'll be forced to have a conversation and I don't know if I have it in me.

"Okay," I mumble.

He sighs and I peek at him from the corner of my eye. He looks miserable. I press my lips together, afraid to ask what's wrong. I don't want him thinking I care for him. It will only complicate things later. But it hurts my heart.

I dig my nails into my palms. "Everything okay?"

"No. It's not." He doesn't elaborate, instead squeezing the steering wheel as if he's resisting the urge to rip it right off.

"Is Chase okay?"

"No, he's not. But he will be eventually. I'm more concerned with what's going on with you."

"Nothing is going on with me." My words are rushed and unconvincing, even to my own ears.

He huffs, then pulls over just as we crest the hill. The town's small main street spreads out before us, yet it feels like a million miles away. He throws the truck into park and turns in his seat.

"You want to try that again?" he asks, raising an eyebrow.

I stare at Chase's truck sitting in front of the diner. Is he inside the restaurant waiting for us? Or is he sequestered in his vehicle, too afraid of facing Tess by himself?

"Chase is waiting. We should get going. Of if you'd rather go alone, that's fine as well. I can get myself something to eat at the cabin."

"For fuck's sake, Gemma. Stop shutting me out. Slade told me what he said to you."

I flinch, closing my eyes. Of course Slade talked to him. Jake is his friend and Slade wouldn't see anything wrong with sharing his observations. I'm not so sure Jake was laughing. Not with the way he's acting now.

"I don't know what you want me to say," I whisper as my throat tightens. I really do not want to cry in front of this man.

"Just talk to me," he pleads.

Slowly, I swivel my head until our gazes meet. "What exactly would you like to talk about?"

"Anything. Just stop pretending like we're not..." He swallows, his Adam's apple bobbing. "He was wrong, Gemma. Slade doesn't know what the fuck he's talking about."

I tilt my head, wondering what part Slade revealed to him. I'm sure my brother wasn't worried about Jake wanting to get involved with me romantically. Slade probably thinks I'd be the one pursuing his friend. When he told me all those years ago his friends wouldn't be into me, I assumed it was because I was younger. I didn't realize someone like me meant awkward.

"His delivery might not have been the best, but he was right, Jake. I have a hard time connecting with other people. It's part of the reason I haven't found a place to settle down. Nothing feels like home. I'm not everyone's cup of tea and that's okay."

He gives me a look. "You don't really believe his bullshit, do you?"

I sigh, wondering how far I could make it if I made a run for it before Jake caught up with me. Shifting would give me the advantage. Then he'd probably spot me, and it would be high school all over again. I doubt Jake will let this go.

"Why do you care so much? You barely tolerate my presence half the time. You spent two weeks waffling between ignoring me and hitting on me. Then you told me I was too clingy—" I suck in a breath as he rears back. "And now that I'm aware of my behavior and striving to fix things, you're still not satisfied. So, what exactly do you want from me, Jake?"

"I never said you were clingy," he growls, nostrils flaring. "And we talked about the other shit. Your 'behavior' is part of why I—"

He shakes his head and squeezes his eyes shut. Rolling his neck, he shudders, then presses a fist to his chest, right over his heart. A rumble overhead has me glancing out the window. I don't know what's happening to him, but he's not just stopping himself from blurting something out.

"Jake? What's wrong?" I unbuckle and scoot closer to him, my hand hovering between us. I'm afraid to touch him in case I make things worse.

A flash of lightning illuminates the darkening sky. Silently, I count as I wait for the thunder to rumble around us all while I watch Jake. His mouth parts as he tips his head back. When his eyes meet mine, I shiver. It's as if something ancient rests within the green depths, spearing me in place, and I freeze.

He blinks and it's gone, leaving an emptiness in its wake. "We should go. Chase is probably wondering where we are."

"Are you okay?" I ask as he faces forward again. I don't even have my seatbelt on before he takes off. I fumble with the clip as we hit a pothole.

"I'm fine. Must be coming down with something. Please be nice to Chase. He's had a hard few days. And stop lying. It's not a good look on you."

My mouth drops open, and I jut my chin out. I shouldn't be surprised he's turning on me.

"I'm not lying. But if you can't be civil, I'd rather go home." The word slips out before I can stop it. Jake's cabin isn't home, as much as I wish it was.

"I want you there. And I want you to be yourself. Not this impostor you think everyone wants to see. If you keep it up..."

I huff, lip curling. "You'll what? Yell at me again? Or try to force yourself to be nice to me?"

He slams on the brakes again and the seatbelt cuts into my shoulder. We're close enough to town that people are probably watching now. The gossip mill will be flying if he keeps it up. Marcy will swoop in, attempting to comfort Jake in his time of need. A heavy weight settles on my chest.

"I don't have to force anything with you. Ignoring you was the hardest thing I've ever done. Don't even get me started on resisting you. Slade might not approve of us getting involved, but despite him, I would if I could," he snarls, then his head drops. "But I can't for reasons that have nothing to do with you. I don't want you leaving here thinking you did anything wrong."

He eases the truck forward again, not waiting for my rebuttal. Not that I have one. It's probably the most honest he's ever been. It kills me I can't give him the same honesty. Jake isn't the type to take change well. Revealing I'm a shifter might send him over the edge. Not that it's an option, since he clearly has some demons he's fighting. Or he just enjoys being alone so much he can't imagine sharing his world with someone else.

"What are you going to tell them?" I ask as he pulls into a spot next to Chase's truck.

I lean forward, watching Chase as he scrolls through his phone in the front seat. When he looks up, he doesn't wave. His usual grin is nowhere to be found. Whatever is going on with him is more than just sickness. Maybe he's fighting the same demons Jake is. He nods to me before going back to his screen.

"Tell who?" Jake asks, turning tired eyes toward me.

"When I leave, people are going to ask where I've gone. When I'm coming back. They'll ask what happened. I'm just wondering what you're going to say. You can make me the bad guy if that makes it easier. Although, then you'll have Marcy trying to comfort you." I should stop talking, but the words won't stop.

"You could just say we're doing things long distance. You don't share a lot about yourself anyway, so it should be easy to fend off any questions."

"Gemma, stop. I dragged you into this mess and I shouldn't have. I'm not going to use you as a scapegoat too. Everyone will just forget about it after a while," Jake says.

I snort, cracking the first smile I have in days. "In this tiny town? Good fucking luck. They'll be talking about this for years. Unless Chase suddenly turns into a cat in the middle of main street or something."

The image of Chase shifting into a house cat filters across my mind, and I giggle. I may not sense other shifters like Slade, but the idea that Chase is one, much less a cat shifter, is funny.

It takes me a bit to realize Jake isn't laughing. He's scowling. Once again, I've put my foot in my mouth somehow. I've made him uncomfortable with my disconcerting words. Jake pushes from the truck and slams the door behind him. I follow slowly, resolved to keep my damn mouth shut.

It feels like no matter how much we talk, we never get anywhere. Two weeks. That's all I need to survive. Then I can leave this town behind. Maybe my mother was right and the only place I belong is where I grew up. When I left Moon Cove, it didn't feel like home, but it might be the only place left I can run to. My heart aches at the thought.

I sigh, trailing after Jake and Chase as they make their way into the diner. Neither of them pays me any mind as I slide into the booth at the back. Jake's eyes dart between the two seats before he finally settles next to Chase and another bolt of pain hits me. I duck my head, resigning myself to wading my way through the rest of my time here alone. Then I'll tuck my tail between my legs and move home.

# Lost in the Woods

## Jake

Four days later and I'm still thinking about our conversation in the truck. It didn't go the way I thought it would. Nothing goes the way I think it will when it comes to Gemma. When I almost slipped and threw out the L-word, I was rendered speechless, just like when she told me to shut up. It was as if I didn't have control over my own body.

I don't know what the goddess handed me, but I'm starting to think Gemma's not entirely human. Whenever the thought crosses my mind, I'm reminded of all the very human things she does, and I dismiss the idea until the next time I think back on it.

Dinner was a disaster. There's no other way to describe it. Chase barely spoke two words and kept shooting wary glances at Gemma. Not that she noticed. She spent the majority of the time with her chin tucked to her chest, even when she was eating. Conversation was stilted. Most of the time I was the only one speaking, which isn't my strong suit. When Chase swiped a full glass of water off the table for no fucking reason, I figured it was time to go. Chase drove away without a backward glance.

The drive home was more of us studiously ignoring the elephant in the room and each other. Every time we have an honest conversation it's like we take one step forward and two steps back. I thought explaining to her that I can't be involved with her, but it had nothing to do with her, would help. It didn't do anything other than throw more obstacles in our way.

I'm still pissed she told me to throw her under the bus when ending our fake relationship. Honestly, I don't feel like we're doing very well at selling it, anyway. If I were watching us, I wouldn't assume we were dating. I'd think we were strangers or coworkers who didn't particularly like each other. I certainly feel like I'm an acquaintance who was forced into a project with her nowadays.

She doesn't come down for meals. She doesn't start conversations. She hasn't asked to borrow a book in a week. Last night, she offered to sleep on the couch. I didn't take it well.

A cold wind whips through the air, ruffling my hair. I shouldn't be up this high in a tree while it's blowing this hard, but the lights need to be strung. The farther I go down the trail into the woods, the more the beast inside me rages against the cage I've shoved him in. He wants out. And he's not going to let me forget it until I shift. The new moon is only a few days away, but isn't far behind Samhain. I'm kicking myself for not shifting earlier.

"Jake! It's getting dark. Either you come down and take me back to the cabin or I'm walking," Gemma yells from the start of the trail. Her voice carries along the wind, floating past me to disappear into the trees.

I sigh, knocking my forehead against the trunk. We're running out of time to get this done. The college kids who are now counselors are set to arrive in just a few days to help us finish up. Based on the clouds overhead, they might not get here in time. If a storm blows through, we might not be able to have the festival at all.

"Alright, I'm leaving unless you're dead from falling out of a tree," she bellows.

I roll my eyes. "I'm coming, just hold your horses."

I lean back to make sure she can't see me before sliding down the trunk. Wrapping the lights around the tree, I secure the end so they won't get damaged if the wind picks up even more. When I'm finished, I make my way to her, leaves crunching under my boots. In the last week, we've lost half the canopy overhead and I suspect the rest will litter the ground by Samhain.

I'm not particularly fond of this time of year. Without the extra cover, it's hard to hide when I'm shifted. It's part of the reason I live so far up the mountain. Less chance of someone happening upon me. Being spotted usually results in viral videos and vans filled with supernatural chasers touting their documentary credentials like they're saving the planet. At best, it's annoying. At worst, it's exposure I can't afford.

"I don't own any horses to hold," Gemma deadpans as she comes into view.

She pivots, stomping toward the truck. The wind howls as it weaves through the forest, and I glance over my shoulder. When I turn back, she's inside the cab and buckling like she sprinted the hundred yards. I didn't realize she was in that much of a hurry. All day she's been grouchy and on edge.

"You going to tell me what your problem is or are we going to ignore this, too?" I snap as I slam my door.

"I'm not ignoring anything. I'm doing my job. One I'm not getting paid for, I'll add," she snaps back.

I grit my teeth, holding in my comeback. I can't help but assume this is because she saw my spreadsheet. Gemma never mentioned having a shortage of cash. She did lose her job before she got here, though.

"Didn't realize you wanted to be compensated. What's the going rate for room and board nowadays?" I sneer, focusing on the road instead of looking at her like I want.

She makes a noise in the back of her throat, and the air around us thickens. We're almost to the cabin when she huffs, waving her hands around.

"I don't want your fucking money," she says, wrinkling her nose. "I'm just in a shit mood. It has nothing to do with you. I'm sorry."

I nod, but I'm not sure she's being entirely truthful. I pull in front of the cabin, the lights illuminating the front porch.

"Do you want to talk about it?"

"No. I..." She wraps her arms around herself as if she'll break into a million pieces if she doesn't physically hold herself together.

"Gemma, please," I whisper.

She peers out the window at the trees swaying under the force of the wind. After a whole minute, I wonder if I should ask again, but I'm sure she's warring with herself. Pushing her might make her shut down even more.

"I don't want to go back. My mother keeps texting me, asking when I'm coming home. Slade's texts are updates on their festival, as if I even care. My sister won't stop messaging me that it would be a terrible idea for me to come back. It's just a lot. And my stomach hurts. It's fine. It's nothing you need to worry about." She waves her hand, then leans her head against the window.

"You don't have to go back if you don't want to," I say, and she snorts. "If you need money to set up somewhere else—"

"Money isn't the problem. I've moved at least a dozen times since college and nothing fits. It's just hard. Maybe I should become a recluse like you. I like my own company. I could read all day and freelance or something." She huffs as she meets my eyes. "Sorry. This isn't your problem. I'm just going to go to bed."

She swings open the door before I can stop her.

"You don't want dinner?" I call after her as she rushes up the stairs.

She lifts a hand over her shoulder but doesn't answer. Dark clouds cover the sky, swallowing the landscape in shadows. The new moon is only a few days away, leaving a sliver behind. Not that I can see it right now, but I can feel it in my bones. I wanted to hold out until after Gemma left, but I don't know if that will be possible. I'm determined to get through Samhain through sheer force of will.

I hurry after Gemma, hoping to convince her to eat something. If I can get her to the table, I might be able to keep her talking. I may not have answers, but I can listen. Which might be all she needs.

Regardless of our future, I want to be here for her as long as she stays. I'm determined to squeeze as many memories as I can from this. They're the only things I'll have to carry with me in the years to come. I doubt I'll find someone else like her.

I shove the door closed as the wind fights me and glance around the space. She couldn't have gone far. Searching the first floor doesn't take long. Once I get upstairs, I find the bathroom dark and my bedroom door closed. Knocking on the wood gently, I listen for any movement.

"Gemma?" I murmur.

"I'm just tired, Jake. I'm going to sleep."

I sigh, resting my forehead against the door. I'll check on her after I've started a fire. Maybe a nap is all she needs. The aroma of a home-cooked meal might lure her downstairs, too.

I fuss around for the next two hours—stoking the flames in the fireplace, tidying up my office, and finally starting dinner. There's no sound from upstairs and hasn't been since a branch hit the bedroom window an hour ago. I almost went to investigate but didn't want to disturb her. The more time passes, the tenser my muscles become. Not to mention the pulse of pain in my chest is back, surging with every one of my heartbeats.

It's as if a thread is wrapped around my heart, cinching tighter with each passing minute. I've never felt something like this before. It must have something to do with being a shifter, but I don't even have someone I can call to ask.

My parents disappeared into the forest long ago, confident they'd given me the knowledge to make it on my own. I've never wished they were here more than in the last month. I could use some sound advice both in dealing with Gemma and the strange sensations plaguing me as of late.

I creep up the stairs, knocking on the door again. "Gemma? I've got dinner ready."

A profound silence echoes from the other side of the door. Usually, I can hear her soft breath as she slumbers, but not tonight. Panic takes over and I twist the knob. I growl at the handle, then slam my shoulder into the door, splintering the wood. I expect a shout or squeal, yet it's nothing but more silence.

The bed sits untouched, her book lying innocently on the nightstand as it waits for her to continue reading. Clothes spill from her bags, so at least she didn't sneak out to run away. Unless she didn't care if she left them behind. I shake my head, looking for clues to where she could have gone.

A chill seeps into the room despite the fire roaring downstairs. Prowling toward the window, I find it cracked and wind whistles through the small gap. I shove it open, then lean out. Freezing rain pelts my face as I squint into the storm that's blown in. From the looks of it, things are only going to get worse.

"Gemma," I bellow, but the screaming wind carries my voice away.

I slam the window shut and set about combing the house again. No use freezing my ass off if she's hidden in some corner. It doesn't take me long and before I know it, I'm pulling on my boots and the winter jacket I dug out of the closet earlier in the week. I scribble a note and leave it on the table next to the rapidly cooling food.

Flinging open the front door, I find her car right where she left it. It hasn't moved in weeks. My truck sits next to it, the windshield frosted with ice. Nothing moves other than the branches. I stumble back through the house and grab a small survival kit from my office.

Rushing out the back door, I stutter to a stop on the back porch. If I didn't know any better, I'd think a freight train was fifty feet away, the gusts are so loud. Gemma wouldn't go out in weather like this. Not without a very good reason. Unless she left before it started, assuming she could get back in time before the storm blew in. The thought sends a chill down my spine.

I rip off my clothes until I'm naked and shivering. I coax the beast within me forward, transforming on the back porch. Closing my eyes, magic swirls through the air, wrapping around me before spearing into my chest.

Fur sprouts from my pores, covering my body within a matter of seconds until I'm protected from the elements. I flex my fingers, now covered in thick pads of dark skin. Shifting so quickly leaves me dizzy, but the need to save Gemma urges me on. I squint into the shadows as sleet obscures my view.

My eyes flash from one blink to the next and I can finally see into the trees. It's still not ideal, but at least the night vision will help me spot her. Icicles hang from my fingertips already.

Gripping the survival kit, I hope it's enough to help her if she's injured. I shake the snow from my coat before rushing toward the tree line, then following it around the house.

There's still no sign of her. I retreat to the backyard, searching for any sign of where she went. It's not until I'm ten feet into the woods that I find her shoe slowly being buried in the snow. Ice floods through my veins and a growl rumbles through my chest.

I need to find her. However long it takes, I'll find her. And then I'll convince her she belongs with me.

# Naked and Afraid

## Gemma

Going out to shift right before a massive snowstorm wasn't the best decision. I couldn't wait any longer, though. I put it off, thinking everything would be fine and now I'm reaping the consequences.

I feel bad for snapping at Jake, then lying to him about the reason. I couldn't very well tell him I've been riding on a razor thin line for the past two days. By the time we got home, I was liable to shift right in the middle of the living room. Guilt rolls through me and I shove it away.

Hopefully Jake bought my stomachache and won't come searching for me. I doubt he will, since we've been silently dancing around each other. Even more so since the disastrous dinner with Chase.

Whatever I did to piss him off isn't clear. But his treatment of me had me on edge the whole time. He kept glaring at me and my inner shifter rose to the occasion, attempting to protect me. I'm glad Jake got us out of there when he did, or I was liable to bite Chase's head off.

I sniff the air to orient myself in the storm. Stumbling back to the cabin would not be great. He probably has a shotgun he uses on stray coyotes or wolves. It wouldn't be the first time I was shot at, but it would hurt that he was the one trying to kill me.

Shaking off the ice clinging to my coat, I gingerly step over the trickle of a stream. The air is thinner up here and I huff, my breath fogging in front of my muzzle before blowing away in a gust. I stretch, sticking my hindquarters in the air to ease the ache in my muscles.

As good as it feels to be shifted, something keeps pulling me back down the mountain. An impulse or instinct I can't pinpoint tugs me toward the cabin—toward Jake. The farther I run, the harder it gets to keep going.

Thankfully, I don't have to be out for long. But every time my chest seizes, I wonder if the goddess is trying to tell me something. Could he be hurt? Or panicked? Maybe he discovered I was gone. I should have moved my car to make it look like I just went into town. He probably would have come after me then. Actually, he would have caught me as soon as I started the car. For a human, he has uncanny hearing.

A roar rings out over the howling of the wind, and I whip my head toward the noise. Even with my night vision, I can barely make out anything beyond ten feet. I lope toward the sound, snow coating my paws. It's heavy, sticky, and hard to move through. I bound over a fallen log as another bellowing growl overtakes the night.

Usually, I wouldn't engage in this form, but the animal sounds like they're in pain. I can't leave them to fend for themselves when I'm capable of helping. My thoughts drift back to the buck we came across.

As I allow my wolf to take over, I spend the minutes wondering what happened to the deer. Hopefully, he was able to deal with the lopsided antlers. He won't shed them for another couple months and dealing with them in the winter won't be easy.

A grumbling wail bounces off the trunks, then cuts off abruptly. I pick up my pace, practically sprinting by the time I reach a clearing. Prowling around the outskirts, I search for the source. I sniff the air, picking up a scent laced with blood that has my muscles clenching.

*Jake.*

No way he came out into the forest to look for me. It would be a death wish for a human. The animal I heard before must have attacked him—the same one

I was set on saving. Even if he attempts to hurt me, not knowing that I'm *me*, I won't leave him out here. As much as I don't want to reveal I'm a shifter, I can't run. I've been doing that enough. I shake my head, then start searching.

A metallic scent weaves its way around the one I've grown so used to over the past few weeks. I follow the trail, dancing back when I spot him. A splatter of crimson stains the light dusting of snow next to his head. A trickle of blood tracks from his temple to his ear.

It's not until I'm sniffing around the injury I realize he's naked. Completely fucking nude. If I wasn't shifted, I probably would have noticed earlier. Why the hell is he naked in the forest during a snowstorm? If he was coming to save me, wouldn't he have gotten dressed? It's not like remnants of fabric are left behind when he was attacked. *If* he was attacked. The lack of torn clothing hanging from his body leaves me with more questions. I doubt I'll be getting answers any time soon. If ever.

Pacing around him, I sniff at his body, searching for more injuries. I whine when reach his ankle twisted at an odd angle. Toes are not supposed to point that way.

*What the hell is going on?*

I don't know what to do. If he had a coat, I could drag him somewhere. I'm a lot stronger when I'm shifted. Biting him while naked, then dragging him who knows how far would definitely do more harm than good, even if he is heading straight for hypothermia. If he was awake, I doubt he'd follow me out of the woods. I do look like a wolf right now. And I really don't want to shift in front of him. He'd probably try to run away screaming and hurt himself more.

I nudge his cheek with my nose, and his head lolls to the side. Nipping at his ribs has no effect either. I'll have to drag him in human form, which is going to be fucking cold, not to mention exhausting. I'm not as strong while human, but even as a wolf, I'd struggle with his large frame. Leaving him would be cruel even if I went to get help.

Bounding away, I scramble around for an area protected from the wind and snow. A dip in the ground, a hollowed-out tree, or a cave would do. Actually, a cave would be perfect. I could start a fire maybe, to warm him up. Except I have nothing to start a fire. A growl rumbles through me in frustration.

I wish I would have grabbed one of Jake's survival kits before venturing into the woods. Not that I thought I'd need it. Now I'm kicking myself.

Just when I'm about to give up, I stumble upon a dark smudge ahead. Not thirty feet away from Jake's prone body is exactly what we need—a cave. Brush covers the entrance, and I latch onto the larger branches and drag them away a little. I rush back to Jake and brace myself.

My wolf isn't ready to retreat, but she whines when I glance at Jake's face, his lips turning a concerning bluish color. She's just as worried about him as I am. My shift is slower than I'd like as my wolf retreats to cower deep within, howling and whimpering as she urges me to help him.

A wave of dizziness hits me, and I almost collapse on top of his body. Then the cold douses me like I jumped into a frozen lake and my muscles lock up. I really wish I would have kept my clothes with me instead of leaving them in a tree not far from the cabin. They've probably blown away by now.

A string of curses falls from my lips as I fit my hands under his shoulders and drag him toward the mouth of the cave. Even with my added strength, it's a struggle. He's too tall and beefy to make this an easy task. I'm slightly terrified I'm doing more damage, but I keep going.

The sweat covering my skin freezes as I carry him, stopping several times to catch my breath. We finally make it over the threshold, and I halt. I should have checked if there were any other animals in here. The last thing I need is to protect an unconscious, naked, six-foot seven-inch lumberjack of a man from a bear. I can't partially shift like Kira, so I set Jake down and venture into the blackness. I huff out a sigh of relief when I find it empty and hurry back to Jake.

Tucking him as far into the cave as I can, panic overwhelms me. I push it down deep. I don't have time to freak out. There are more important things to do first. Then I can come back and fuss over him. Rushing back to the entrance, I shift and warmth seeps into my skin.

I drag the brush toward the cave again to block the opening. I'm almost done when I catch Jake's scent, not from behind me, but from the clearing. I pray to the goddess it's his clothes. When I investigate, I find the second-best thing—a survival kit. It's small, but knowing Jake, it has something we need. I snatch it up with my teeth and bound back for the cave.

Shifting again, I rip open the kit and find a glow stick. I crack it, a cry of triumph leaving me. A tin falls out for starting a fire, along with a mess of other items, including an emergency blanket. Unfurling it, I drape it over Jake's shivering body. Usually I'd be worried about him trembling so much, but in the brief time Jake and I weren't tiptoeing around each other, he taught me some things about surviving in the woods.

"Come on, Jake. Open your eyes."

I finally have the good sense to check his pulse. It's strong. At least I think it is. His ankle is still the wrong way, his toes pointing toward his other foot. I don't want it to start healing without straightening. I've done this often enough with my siblings to know what I'm doing unless he has internal damage. Waiting any longer could hurt more than it helps.

Shuffling down to his feet, I run my trembling hands along his calf, then get it over with. I ease the foot straight, then grab the bandage and wrap it around his ankle. It's the best I can do at the moment. He didn't even flinch while I did it. My entire body is shivering by the time I'm done, but I push through the pain to search the small cave.

"What the hell, Jake. Were you heading here when you hurt yourself?"

He obviously doesn't answer. It makes me feel better to talk to him, though. There's a makeshift fire waiting to be lit in the corner of the cave, complete with a smoke hole funneled into the stone above our heads. I wonder how many of these hidden spots he has tucked away in the mountain.

With the fire starter from the kit, it's actually pretty easy to get the flames going. I add a few logs to it from the pile he's left stacked along the back wall, then settle next to his still shaking body.

I watch his chest rise and fall as the storm howls outside our slowly warming den. Hopefully by the time the sun rises, the weather will calm down and I can go get help. There's no way I can drag him through the forest—shifter or not. I wish we were back at his house, eating dinner. I wish we were bickering about books. I wish we were ignoring each other still. At least then he'd be safe in the cabin, instead of slowly freezing to death with his chance of survival hanging solely on me. A choked sob leaves me, and I clamp my mouth shut.

"Please wake up," I plead, brushing my fingers over his parted lips.

They still have a touch of blue to them. I resist the urge to kiss him in the hopes of waking him up. Every time we've come close, some disaster has befallen us. In the morning, I might try it, just to see what happens. I'd rather our first kiss not happen when he was unconscious, but some things can't be helped.

Cuddling into his side, I attempt to slide under the silver emergency blanket. It slips, exposing his arm, and I give up. I won't last like this, with only the heat from the fire to keep me on this side of the living. There isn't enough wood to last more than a few hours. With Jake's body blocking most of the warmth, I won't survive without shifting.

I sigh, then press a kiss to his forehead before retreating closer to the entrance and get it over with. Hopefully, he doesn't freak out when he wakes up to find a wolf cuddled up next to him. Maybe I can still keep the truth from him. I don't know how I'll be able to leave now, though.

I've studiously ignored the growing realization of how I feel about Jake in light of the crisis in front of me. As I shrink, limbs elongating along with my face, I can't hide from the truth any longer. Somehow Jake and I are connected and to dismiss that thread between us would be detrimental to both of us. Is it love? I don't know. But I'm done fighting whatever the goddess has in store for us.

I curl up close to his side and his arm wraps around me, fingers digging into my fur. He sighs in his sleep. As much as I fight it, I end up following him into a deep slumber, my dreams filled with heartache and death.

# It's Not Gonna Fit

## Jake

I groan before I even open my eyes. My head pulses, my ankle throbs, and I'm cold. The last thing I recall was racing through the trees, tracking Gemma's scent. My foot hit a divot in the ground, twisting my entire leg around, and I went down hard. I must have hit my head because it's nothingness after that. At one point I swore Gemma was scolding me, but then warmth seeped into my side like a fur blanket was tossed around carelessly and I was too weak to cover myself.

The warmth must have been me, since I've shifted, fur covering my body again. I remember him retreating when I hit my head and my vision darkened. I don't know how long I was naked in the snow, but I'm sure my inner sasquatch took over to speed up the healing process. Based on the various aches plaguing my body, the work isn't done yet. At least the storm blew itself out. I'm not ridiculously cold and my fur is dry.

*Gemma*, my mind whispers, and my eyes fly open.

I struggle to sit, but a weight holds me down. When I glance down, intending to shove whatever sits on my chest off, I freeze. A slumbering Gemma is sprawled across me, one hand resting on my heart and her leg tucked between mine. I must be more hurt than I thought if I didn't notice her. I lift the corner of the blanket, then drop it, staring at the ceiling with wide eyes. She's completely

193

naked. I can't see anything with the emergency blanket draped over us, thankfully. Her scent fills my pores, and my cock hardens against her thigh. This is not the time to get horny, but with her I can't help it.

I close my eyes, focusing on shifting back, but my beast refuses to be forced into his cage. I'm not proud of myself, but I panic. With my brain foggy and crucial memories missing, I have no idea what she saw.

Does she know I'm a sasquatch? It's not possible. If she did, she would have run away, not cuddled closer. Did she see me shift? Probably not. Again, running and screaming would occur. I don't know if I can handle her rejection.

I ease her off me, but she digs her fingers into my fur, tugging and pulling, and I swallow a groan. It's been too long since I've been with a woman and my feelings overwhelm me. I've never experienced it in this form. I still don't want to wake her, so I try to untangle our legs. Every time I slide hers away and move to her hands, she throws her knee back between mine. I move her hand and move to her leg and her fingers worm back into my fur. Rinse and repeat.

The more she wiggles, the harder I get. I need to remedy this situation before it gets out of hand. My stomach flips as she rubs her body against mine. She's locked away in dreamland or maybe in a hellscape. I don't know what happened after I was knocked out. I must have hit my head pretty fucking hard.

"Jake?" Gemma murmurs, her voice still groggy from sleep.

"Go back to sleep." It's the only thing I can think to say.

Maybe she'll roll over and I can leave the cave to shift. If I do it here, she'll definitely wake up. She'll definitely notice. And she'll definitely freak out. I'll save her from that if I can.

Last night, I was determined to convince her to stay. I needed her with me, safe and sound. In the early morning light filtering through the entrance, I realize that all the obstacles standing in our way yesterday are still here today. They didn't magically go away because she was in danger. I wish I could go back to assuming I was merely attracted to her instead of falling for her. Then when she walks away, it won't hurt so much.

Gemma gasps, bolting upright. Her eyes glance down at her naked body, and I stare at the ceiling. She snatches the emergency blanket and wraps it around her, leaving me uncovered, and she gasps again. I may be covered in fur, but it doesn't hide my raging hard-on. Maybe she won't notice since it's still hidden by massive amounts of hair. Her gaze travels down and I roll away from her, stopping just short of the smoldering fire she must have started.

"You're...you...you're a...holy shit," she stammers.

I scramble toward the entrance, hitting my head on the ceiling. The blow has me swaying, then crashing on my side into pure white snow. It cushions my fall just enough to not do more damage, but I groan nonetheless. Gemma calls my name, concern lining her voice, but that won't last. I didn't think I'd be the one running. She is naked, though.

Sitting up, I lean against a fallen tree trunk next to the cave. I can't leave her here to fend for herself. I also can't shift. Not only will I be naked, I'll also freeze my balls off. At least she has a blanket. She must have found the survival kit I grabbed.

"Jake? Please tell me you didn't run away," Gemma says, her voice coming closer.

"You should put your clothes on," I say, closing my eyes.

She sighs, stopping in the mouth of the cave. I can just make out her pink toes peeking around the corner. She'll lose them if she needs to walk through the foot of snow the sky dumped last night.

"Problem is, I don't have my clothes," she mumbles.

I clear my throat. "Tell me you didn't use them to start the fire."

"I did not use them to start the fire," she states with conviction. I don't believe her.

"I'm going to go get someone to rescue you. I'll stay away from the cabin until you're gone." My throat closes when I finish getting the words out.

"Why can't you rescue me?" She makes a sound in the back of her throat. "Wait, no. I don't need anyone to rescue me."

I huff, shaking my head as I gaze out at the transformed landscape. "Gemma, you're stuck in a cave halfway up the mountain, completely naked. You definitely need rescuing. But also, I know you don't want *me* to rescue you."

She snorts. "Why not? Because you're a sasquatch? Well, I've got news for you, honey."

Her voice trails off, probably the implication of her words finally settling in. I'll wait for her to come to the conclusion she's better off staying here while I go get help. Chase will most likely come for her as long as he hasn't shifted yet. If he has, then I'll have to call someone in.

There's shuffling within the cave, then a rustle of magic tinging the air. I glance down, wondering if I just didn't notice shifting back, but my fur is still intact, blowing slightly in the breeze. A wolf pads from the den, light brown eyes regarding me warily. My jaw drops as I peer at the dark fur, the exact color of Gemma's hair.

I scowl, though she probably can't tell. "You've got to be fucking kidding me."

The wolf's head tilts. If she could raise an eyebrow right now, I'm sure she would. I lift my hand, then drop it back to my side. I'd rather not lose my hand because I touched her without permission. Our instincts run closer to our animalistic sides when shifted. Our.

*Our.*

The truth hits me hard. Both of us in our other forms, staring at each other in the hopes that they won't run away. That we won't be rejected. What I assumed was the obstacle we could never get past was never truly an obstacle at all. She's a shifter.

She whines, nudging me with her nose, and I swallow hard before running my fingers through her fur. Her body shudders as she cuddles closer to my side, her snout bumping my chest. Ducking, I bury my face in her neck, wrapping my arms around her. Something within me slots into place as I hold her. It's a feeling I don't recognize and that terrifies me.

Gemma nips at my thigh, then throws her head toward the cave. We need to talk, and we can't do that while she's shifted. The nerves hit me again as I follow her. Sasquatch shifters are so rare, maybe she doesn't understand the ostracization from the community. Maybe she doesn't fully comprehend why I live so far from civilization.

I avert my gaze when she shifts, waiting for the crinkle of the blanket before I look up. As she settles against the back of the cave, I throw another log on the fire, coaxing the embers until a flame catches on the bark. The contents from the kit are scattered about, so I gather them up to give my hands something to do. It isn't easy to zip it with my fur getting in the way. Gemma's fingers slip between mine, closing it effortlessly.

"I can't shift right now," I say, staring at the tiny package.

"Are you still hurt?" she whispers.

"Not really, but there's only one blanket." I peek at her as I smirk.

She bites her lip, clutching the sheet with one hand. "So, you're a shifter…"

"Apparently I'm not the only one. You want to explain how you thought it was a good idea to go out in the middle of a snowstorm?"

She huffs, sitting against the wall again. "You know how it is. I waited too long. I'm guessing my pathetic attempt at a stomachache didn't throw you off?"

"It was more the morose look on your face when you lied about going home." I close my eyes, wondering why I'm picking a fight.

"Don't start, Jake. We can finally have an honest conversation and you're not going to snap at me while we have it." She presses her lips together and I nod. "Good. Now, what attacked you?"

"Only thing that attacked me was a hole in the ground," I admit ruefully.

She shakes her head, confusion flooding her flushed face. "But you were…roaring."

"I was frustrated I couldn't find you. I thought you were hurt."

"You thought I was dead," she whispers, eyes taking a faraway look, remembering when she went through the same emotions for me.

The vise around my heart squeezes and my hands tremble. "What happened after?"

I barely register the story she tells me I'm so overwhelmed with the truth. She isn't running. She isn't upset. She hasn't even mentioned anything about the fact I haven't shifted back. It's as if she doesn't even notice.

"I'm a sasquatch shifter," I blurt out, interrupting her story about starting the fire.

Her eyes widen and she purses her lips. "Uh, I'm aware, seeing as how you're sitting in front of me as a sasquatch."

"That's it?"

"Should there be more?"

I scowl, tugging the hair on my thighs. "Most people—"

"When exactly did I become 'most people'? Because last I checked, I was your fake girlfriend. And unexpected house guest. And your haunted house assistant. And—"

I hold up my hand to stop her tirade. She smirks, crossing her arms. The blanket slips and she yelps, tugging it over her body again.

"Sorry, forgot I was naked, and you probably don't want to see that." She laughs nervously as she avoids my eyes.

It takes me all of ten seconds to decide. I shift, shoving my other form down. The process usually takes me longer, but I'm so desperate to be human again it happens in the blink of an eye. Magic rushes through the air, swirling around us before dissipating.

"Better? Now we're both naked." My legs splay in front of me, and I can barely lift my hands.

There's no way I'll be able to cover myself, but that's the least of my worries. I suck in a deep breath, trying to ease the dizziness in my head.

"Seriously? You're going to hurt yourself more," she scolds as she crawls toward me.

I lick my lips, tipping my head back to stare at the ceiling. She left the blanket behind. While shifters are used to being naked around each other, it's still uncouth to have a boner in front of them. Gemma's a temptation I can't refuse. Her hand brushes my arm and I shudder.

"Are you okay? What hurts?" she murmurs, fingertips trailing along my chest and up to my neck.

*My cock. Want to make it better with a kiss?* I choke at the thought.

"What is it? Is it your head?" Her fingers continue their quest over my body, and I groan.

"Sweetheart, you have to stop or I'm going to end up hauling you into my lap."

She freezes, barely breathing, and I resist the urge to open my eyes. I bite my lip, holding my breath while I wait for her to retreat.

"Let me help you then," she whispers, her breath coasting over my lips.

Her leg swings over mine as she settles on my thighs. I groan, my hands gripping her hips. She leans her forehead against my chest, and I bury my face into her hair, breathing her in. She runs her palms up my bare chest, then links her fingers behind my neck. Nothing could have prepared me for the feel of her in my arms. I tug her forward until we fit together, my cock trapped between our bodies. Her wetness slides against me and I swear I get even harder. Her breath hitches and I freeze.

She gasps, fingers digging into my skin. "Wait."

# Don't Mind All the Hair—It's Worth It

## Gemma

Jake's entire body tenses the moment the word leaves my mouth. Then his hands drop from my skin and his head tips back. I didn't want him to stop. I just wanted him to wait.

I scramble, sitting up with my hands resting on his shoulders. "No, don't. I just...dammit."

There's been a lot thrown at me in the last hour and I don't know how to process it all. The fact that he's a shifter and I had no idea—not even an inkling —blows my mind. The only thing standing in our way now is my brother. And my insecurities. Those are rearing their ugly heads, whispering that I'm not enough for him.

I sigh, tucking my chin to my chest all while taking the easy way out. "Are you sure we should be doing this in a cave?"

"What exactly are we doing?" he asks gruffly, and a blush spreads across my face.

I grimace as the flush travels down my neck and to my chest and I push back. Jake's hands land on my hips again, holding me in place.

"Are you hiding from me or staring at my cock?" he whispers in my ear.

I wasn't before, but now I can't see anything but his massive length. My mouth waters all while nerves dance in my stomach.

"That's not going to fit," I mutter.

He chuckles. "It'll fit, sweetheart."

He tips my chin up with his knuckle and the thread between us hums. His hand cups my face as his lips brush mine. We both freeze, waiting for something to go wrong.

"I think we're in the clear," I say softly, and he covers my mouth with his.

My eyes fall closed, giving into the sensation of something finally going right. His hand slips around, gripping my neck as he angles my head to deepen the kiss. I lick at his lips, and he opens, tongue sliding against mine.

A bolt hits me, robbing me of breath, and I rip my mouth from his. Panting, I find the emotions flaming through me mirrored on his face. The thread I thought was merely attraction solidifies and morphs. I fall into his eyes as one word echoes through my mind—*mate.*

"That explains a lot," he breathes and the bond linking us together shivers as if it's a sentient being.

I don't know who moves first, but we crash together in a whirlwind of lips and tongues. His hands roam across my flesh, and I rub my center along his cock, coating him with my wetness. As I rock my hips against him, I'm hit with the overwhelming urge to bite him. The mating bond shimmers between us, egging me on, but I know it's too soon.

"Ride me, Gemma. I've waited too long to feel your pussy clinging to my cock."

His arm wraps around my waist as I lift myself. He grips the base, lining up with my core. A flash of nerves hits me, but they're washed away by the mating bond.

"Relax for me, sweetheart. You can take it all. You're made for me and I for you."

I shudder as I sink down, stretching around his thick cock. It's nothing like I've ever felt before. I half expect the skies to open up, a choir to start singing, and the goddess herself to strut into the cave.

Instead, the fire flares, our mingled moans echo around the cave, and the bond between us cements itself deep within my soul. It's familiar, yet not, like a long-lost memory found in a stranger. A lyric to a song never heard before that resonates through history. A random choice that changes the trajectory of the world. It's perfectly imperfect.

Jake melds my body to his when I'm fully seated, pulsing around him.

"Perfection. I knew you'd be fucking perfection," he breathes.

He kisses me slowly, drawing out the pleasure, and I whimper. I don't know how long I can last like this. I need more—more of him.

"Jake," I whine. "Please."

His fingers dig into my hips, and he lifts me until only the tip remains and I spasm around him. I plunge onto him, impaling myself on his cock. Magic swirls around us as we move. It pulses in time with our heartbeats, which have synced, as the bond between us falls into place.

"Mine," he grunts with every thrust of his hips.

He reaches around, gripping my ass, his fingers burrowing into my flesh. I don't know why I ever worried he wouldn't find me attractive. His hands run over my body, then cup my breasts. His mouth descends on my nipple, sucking on the tight bud. I throw my head back, my hips stuttering as desire shoots through me.

"More," I whimper, holding his head in place.

He growls, and he wraps his arm around my waist. Before my brain can catch up, he's on his back, gripping my hips as he thrusts into me. Bracing my hands on his stomach, I let go, shuddering my way through my orgasm.

"That's it, sweetheart. Let me hear how much you love me inside you."

I collapse, stars flashing behind my lids as my pussy clenches around him over and over. I knew Jake had a dirty mouth. How could he not with the books he reads? But I didn't expect it to affect me to this degree. He could make me come with words alone. Whether that's a mate thing or a him thing, I don't know. And I don't particularly care. He slows, rolling his hips to draw out my pleasure.

"You didn't go," I mumble into his damp chest.

He chuckles, brushing my hair from my forehead, then pressing a kiss to my skin.

"I'm not done with you, mate," he grunts.

The title sends a thrill through me, and I clench around him. He grunts, wrapping his arms around me and kicking up his hips. There's a crinkling sound I should investigate, but there's a weightlessness to my body I'm not sure I can pull myself from. I squeal when he rolls and I cling to him. He grins, tucking the blanket under my head.

"I'd wait until we're home, but I can't wait to claim you, Gemma," he says.

He grits his teeth when I wrap my ankles around his hips, forcing him deeper. I let my knees fall open and he sits back, his gaze raking over me and leaving flames of desire in their wake. When his eyes reach where we're joined, I glance down. He's right. We're made for each other, fitting together perfectly.

His hips pull back slowly, and my eyes roll to the back of my head. When he sinks back in, a guttural moan leaves me, more animal than human. He repeats the move again and again until I'm coiled so tight the slightest touch will have me detonating around him.

"Faster," I gasp. "Harder."

He growls in response, doing exactly what my body is begging for. He tips his head back, a growl building in his chest. I cup my breasts, arching my back as he completely consumes me.

"Come for me, sweetheart," he snarls through gritted teeth.

His fingers dip to my clit, circling the tight bud once, and I explode. He bellows my name as he comes. Yanking me up, our bodies fit together, and he sinks his teeth into my neck.

"Do it," he pants as he laps at the mark he's left behind.

I bite him over his heart, never breaking the surface, but it's enough. The mating bond snaps fully into place and another orgasm rips through me. He holds me as I shudder, pressing kisses to my neck, shoulder, face, then back to the mark that claims me as his. Tears fill my eyes as emotions batter my senses.

"Shh, sweetheart. I got you. Always."

The cabin hasn't changed in the twelve hours we've been gone, but something is different. Both our clothes were soaked by the time we gathered them up. He tugged me upstairs to change as soon as we made it through the back door. Now we're settled on the couch, and I have no idea what we're supposed to do.

Jake can't seem to keep his eyes off me. The only reason I know is because I'm the same with him. We keep stealing glances at each other until I blush and look away. We're linked through our fingers, neither of us daring to let go. I'm terrified he'll disappear—a cruel joke from the goddess.

Jake fills my soul, though that should be impossible. He's what I've been missing as I've skipped from city to city, never fully growing roots. It's as if the goddess was laughing at me from afar, nudging me ever closer to my fate. To my mate. It's hard to trust all that.

"Are you sure your feet are okay? What about your head?" I ask for the third time.

The man did haul me onto his back as if I weighed nothing, then walked the entire way back from the cave. I'd traveled farther than I thought last night. He must have carried me at least ten miles, the emergency blanket tucked around me as I buried my face into his fur. I could have shifted, but my wolf refused to come out. She was too busy basking in the realization we found our mate.

After ten minutes of silence, he started talking. At first the words were stilted, like he was drawing on some deep reserve to open up about being a sasquatch shifter. The more he spoke, the easier it seemed to become. Soon he was telling me about his parents, growing up, how he started the camp with only five campers. With every new revelation, the bond between us thickened.

Then came the questions. What were my siblings like? What was it like to still have my parents in my life? Where did I go to college? Why didn't I study art like I wanted to? In any other circumstance, it would have felt like an interrogation. With my mate it was easy, his enthusiasm feeding my soul in a way I hadn't felt in...ever.

No one had cared enough about me to ask what my dirtiest fantasy was. Or if I ever regretted not going home. I knew when I answered that question, he wouldn't judge me. He wouldn't pounce on my weakness and tell me to just go back. We connected more in those ten miles than in the weeks we spent together tiptoeing around each other while we kept our secrets locked away.

"My feet don't hurt, Gemma. My head doesn't either. Stop worrying. Plus, you'd sense if I was hurt," he grumbles, finally getting annoyed at my worry.

"I forgot. I never paid attention when everyone was talking about fated mates. I just assumed I'd never find mine," I say, attempting to tug my fingers from his.

He pulls me onto his lap, and I straddle him, resting my hands on his broad shoulders. I press my lips together, staring at his left ear.

"Just because we're mates doesn't mean we're not going to be the same people, Gemma."

"I don't know what that means."

He sighs, shaking his head. His hands cup my face, forcing my gaze to his. "It means I'm still a grumpy bastard that doesn't like anyone but you. And you're still—"

"Choose your next words wisely, sir." I cross my arms, my eyebrow popping up.

He grins. "You're still going to snap at me when I'm being an asshat. We're not going to instantly be the perfect couple. We'll fight and nag and get frustrated with each other. The bond merely makes it possible for us to find each other. And then find our way back when we get lost."

He pulls me down, lips brushing mine in an apology. Sliding my hands up his chest, I shiver at the feel of him hardening underneath me. My fingers twist into the hair at the nape of his neck, tugging the strands, and forcing a groan from him.

He tips his head back as his hands fall to my hips, helping me rock into him. "Woman, you're going to be the death of me."

"What a way to go, though," I say, giggling when he growls, the sound reverberating through me. I'd be wet from that alone if I wasn't already horny.

"As much as I'd like to fuck you on every surface of this cabin, we have to go."

"What? Why?"

"Because Chase texted me. He's going through something, and he needs...h elp," he says before licking the mark he left on my neck.

I slide off his lap, disappointment crashing through me. I didn't think we'd end up spending every second together and I don't want to keep him from his friend, but it hurts that he's leaving not even four hours after we figured out we were mates. My mark throbs and I rub at it, huffing.

"What's wrong?" Jake calls from the small foyer.

"Nothing. I'm just going to have to invest in more scarves," I grumble.

He leans around the corner, a questioning look on his face. I shake my head, waving him away. I'll be disappointed when he leaves. Making him feel like shit right as he walks out the door isn't fair.

"Why more scarves, Gemma." It's a demand, not a question.

I gesture to my neck. "I'd rather not everyone see what they'll assume is a hickey every time I go into town."

"Not a problem, sweetheart. Only other shifters can see mating marks," he says as he disappears around the corner again.

I'm going to have to call someone so I'm not relying on Jake for the ins and outs of being mated. It's embarrassing. Retreating to the bookcases, I scan the titles without really seeing them. I'm waiting for the door to close behind him, leaving me alone. Now is not the time to get clingy. Jake doesn't *do* clingy. He does alone. He does solitary existence. He does lone wolf.

*What if he never wanted a mate to begin with? Maybe he only claimed me because the bond took over and he lost his head.*

I shake my head, resigning myself to spending however long fielding off the doubts bouncing around my mind. I create a to-do list, starting with showering, followed by wallowing, doubting my self-worth, and ending with getting the fuck over it.

When Jake gets backs, I'll ask him what he wants—really wants. It's a conversation we should have had before we kissed, before we slept together. Before we marked each other. The one thing I'm certain of is breaking a mating bond ranges from painful at best to deadly at worst. I'll take that risk if it makes him happy. As long as he gets what he truly wants, then I'll live with the consequences.

The door shuts and my heart cracks. If he rejects me, I don't know if I'll ever be whole again.

# Big Shifts Happen

## Jake

I wait in the truck for ten minutes, but the door remains shut. I don't know what's taking her so long. My mating mark pulses, leaving a burning sensation behind. Pressing my fist to it, I lean over the steering wheel. I may know about fated mates, but I don't understand the feelings that come with having one. I chalked up the twinges and aches to the bond settling, but now I'm not so sure.

Stomping through the door, I search for Gemma, finding her exactly where I left her in front of the bookcase. Her shoulders slumped, hands flexing by her sides, she must not have heard me come in. Her body heaves once, but she sucks in a deep breath. Shit.

"Gemma?"

Her spine snaps straight, chin tucking to her chest. "Did you forget something?"

Tears in her voice. Sorrow in her tone. Somewhere between the couch and the door, I fucked up.

"Yeah, you," I say gently, coming up behind her. The familiar scent of her fills my pores, calming the racing of my heart.

She angles her face away, sniffing. "What exactly did you need from me?"

"You were supposed to get in the truck, Gemma. Is that why you're crying? Because you thought I didn't want you to come with?" I slide in front of her, ducking to see her eyes, but she drops her head.

"It's nothing. I don't think it's a good idea for me to go. Chase wasn't exactly happy you brought me with last time," she whispers.

I shake my head, sliding my hand to her side to keep her from dashing away. "Gemma, look at me."

She finally meets my gaze and I huff. Her red-rimmed eyes hold a hint of defiance in them, daring me to comment. Her cheek twitches as if she's biting it.

"I don't want to be the one who tells you what's going on with Chase. That's his business. But I think you can help. And I don't know what was up at the diner. He's the one who told me to invite you in the first place. I don't think it had anything to do with you, though." I say it as calmly as possible, wanting to give her time, but we need to get going. Chase texted me while we were still in the cave, and I don't know where he is now since he isn't answering his phone.

She nods slowly. "Okay, but if he wants me to leave, I'm shifting and comi ng...back here."

"Home, sweetheart. It's okay to call it home," I tell her as my brows drop.

"We'll talk about it when we get back. There's probably a lot we need to discuss."

She pulls away from me and my palms itch to reel her to me once more. I let her go, though, tracking her as she stumbles, knocking her knee into the arm of the couch. It slides at least six inches before coming to a stop and she mutters a curse as she pushes it into place.

"Are you sure we shouldn't talk about it now? I don't want to ignore you anymore, Gemma." I hold my breath, hoping she just tells me what's wrong.

"Later. It's not that big of a deal. Just what's going to happen in the next few days."

She's lying. I don't know how, but I can feel it in my bones. Maybe it's the bond or the fact she's skirted around the truth the entire time she's been here. Either way, I doubt I'll get it out of her right now. I follow her out the door, hoping this doesn't bite me in the ass.

The ride to Chase's is silent, nothing like our walk from the forest. My giddiness at finding my mate, at learning that it was Gemma, flowed through me the entire time I carried her. How we broke down to this stillness between us, I don't know. By the time we're pulling into Chase's driveway, I've thought of a dozen more things I want to know, but never asked. I'll give her time and then coax her into telling me what's going through her mind.

"Why don't you stay here while I go check on him," I mutter and her head whips toward me.

"You're telling me you didn't ask if it was okay I come? Dammit Jake, you can't just..." She runs her fingers through her hair, gripping the strands. "You shouldn't have brought me. And you certainly shouldn't have made that decision as an afterthought."

"An after—Gemma I didn't invite you as an afterthought. Or because you were crying. This wasn't a consolation prize. I just wanted you with me," I snarl. "Just get out. If he doesn't want you here, we'll leave. Simple as that."

I shove from the truck, slamming the door behind me. As I round the hood, the metal screeches, announcing her departure. I should fix the hinges on her side.

"Simple as that? What the fuck, Jake?"

I stop, pulling in a calming breath before turning to face her. "You're my priority, Gemma. If you're uncomfortable, then we leave. Not you. Us. That's how it's going to be. And Chase will just have to understand."

"What exactly am I understanding?" Chase asks, fatigue weighing his voice down.

I spin again to address my best friend. I'm going to get dizzy if I keep this up. And after my head injury, that probably won't be good. I open my mouth to explain, but I realize I don't know how. Not without revealing their secrets. I don't know who to encourage to go first. I should have come up with a plan.

Just when I've made up my mind, Chase glances over my shoulder at Gemma, still standing next to the truck. His face morphs to one of disgust, and he hisses at her.

"Chase," I warn, side-stepping to block his view of her.

It doesn't help. He crouches, his head tilting as he eyes her. Glancing over my shoulder, I wave her back, but she doesn't notice. Her wide eyes are fixed on Chase. Magic ripples through the air and my nostrils flare.

As Chase shifts, I bound to Gemma, covering her with my body. I've never witnessed someone's first shift and I have no idea what will happen. My father never told me about this. He probably assumed I'd never see it.

"He's a shifter?" Gemma gasps as she clings to me.

"Goddess-made. It's his first time." I grunt when a concussion of air hits my back, knocking the wind out of me.

"Move, Jake. We need to see if he's okay." She pushes at my chest, and I spin, still guarding her.

Before us, a golden cougar crouches where Chase once stood. There's a predatory edge in his blue eyes as his head bobs and weaves. Why he's fixated on Gemma, I can't fathom, but Chase seems determined to get to her.

"Oh shit. Jake, I'm a wolf. He's a cougar. Sure, we wouldn't normally meet in the wild, but they do *not* mix."

"What the hell does that mean?"

"There's a reason the saying is 'fighting like cats and dogs.' It's not just a cute little cliché. Plus, your first shift you're at the basest form of your animal. I doubt he even realizes who I am," she whispers frantically as Chase prowls toward us.

"Really wish I had a spray bottle right about now," I mutter. I can practically hear her rolling her eyes.

"Talk to him. Before he tries to maul me. Or I'm forced to shift and defend myself."

I clear my throat and the cougar eyes me. "Listen Chase. You're not going anywhere near Gemma right now. You're going to go deal with your shift and then come back and apologize for hissing at her."

The cougar licks its lips, probably fantasizing what her blood will taste like. Gemma snorts, resting her forehead against my back.

"Got any other ideas?" I ask, holding my hands up.

"Other than you getting out of the way? Or me shifting, which might make it worse?" she says, her voice muffled by my shirt. "Nope."

Fear rolls through me, followed closely by the protectiveness I've only felt for Gemma. I was so oblivious to the bond, but it was right there in front of me. Of course, I'd be protective of my mate. Chase might be my best friend, but I won't let him hurt her. I shuffle forward, keeping my body between them.

I shift, using the magic still hanging in the air to speed up the process of sprouting hair all over my body. My muscles stretch, and my arms lengthen until I'm no longer fully human. Chase halts his stalking and his nose twitches as he sniffs me. A cougar might not mingle with a wolf well, but his inner beast probably won't know what to make of me. I'm banking on being the bigger predator.

Gemma's fingers slide through my fur, gripping the hair to keep me close. I'm not going to fight him. Even if I was, I wouldn't leave her unprotected while I do it.

"Go. Meet us at the cabin when you're ready to shift back." I point toward the trees.

The cat gives us a disdainful look, then leaps toward the forest, disappearing into the shadows within seconds. Relief floods me and I sag.

"Are we really going back to the cabin instead of waiting here for him?" Gemma asks as I face her.

"I'd rather your scent not be all over his house if he comes back still in animal form. No reason to rile him up more right now."

She nods, eyes fixed on where Chase vanished. Her lip sneaks between her teeth and I reach to tug it out, then remember I'm still shifted and drop my hand.

"Are you afraid to—Never mind. Let's go." The pain is back in her voice.

I almost wish Chase would appear again to distract her from whatever insecurities are cropping up in her mind. It's the only explanation I can think of for why she's acting this way. She swings open the door and it hits me. As she climbs in, I glance at my dark brown palms. They're leathery, padded, and scarred. Rushing forward, I stop her from closing the door, almost ripping it clean off.

"I'm not afraid to touch you. I didn't think you'd want me to like this," I say, the words tumbling out. I hold up my hand so she can tell what exactly I'm talking about.

Her finger traces over my palm as she examines the skin. A soft smile overtakes her mouth, and she tugs my hand closer until I'm cupping her face.

"You're soft. And fluffy." She ruffles the hair on my chest. "And you kept me warm while in the middle of a snowstorm. Don't know why I would want to change anything about you."

My chest swells with something I've never felt before—pride. If Gemma accepts me for who I am, why would I keep fixating on it being a problem? From now on, I'll just have to take her lead and stop creating issues that don't exist.

"You really were made for me," I say gruffly, and she grins.

I glance down and grimace, my hand dropping to my side. With Chase ambushing us with spontaneous shifting, I didn't have time to undress before I shifted myself. Now I don't have any clothes, since they've disintegrated. I used to think magic made them vanish, but my mother corrected me pretty quickly. I heard her giggling as she told my father. Gazing at Gemma, I can only hope we end up with the same love as them.

"Are you coming?" she calls, hanging out the window.

"Gotta grab something first. Put up the window and stay in the truck." I wait until she's listened, even if it is with an eye roll thrown in.

Dashing into Chase's house, I grab an extra jacket from his front closet. I snatch a pair of sweats from the back of his couch, hoping he's not particularly attached to them. I close my eyes, slowly shifting back. The hair retreats under my skin, fingers shorten, and the pads on my palms melt into human skin.

Huffing, I slip into the gray sweatpants, slinging them low on my hips. No use choking my cock just to make them fit. They're four inches too short, but they'll get me home and that's all I need. As soon as I step outside, flinging the coat around my shoulder, I catch Gemma's eye. She covers her mouth as she stares like a deer in headlights at me.

Scowling, I climb into the truck. "Go ahead and laugh. It's better than driving home naked."

"I'm not laughing," she says, her voice muffled by her hand. Her shoulders shake as she steals glances at me.

"If you're good, I'll let you take them off when we get home."

Her peals of laughter ring through the air all the way back to the cabin.

# He's Not Just a Furry

## Gemma

"Jake, the kids are coming," I shout over my shoulder, giddiness invading my pores.

I bounce on the balls of my feet as headlights flash up the road. The setting sun splashes reds and oranges across the sky, lighting the remaining leaves in a myriad of colors. The last week has been a whirlwind of getting the rest of the haunted house set up and learning about each other. And a lot of reenacting scenes from the books Jake owns. I grin, hoping no one wants to eat at the dining table anytime soon. I'll end up giggling the entire time.

Spinning around, I search for Jake's broad frame, finding him at the start of the haunted trail, bellowing at the counselors deeper in the woods. They know what they're doing, but Jake's been worried they'll forget. They won't. All of them seem like they would do anything for Jake. One girl even told me he saved her. Not literally, but in all the ways that counted. I knew the camp was important to Jake in a way I doubt I'd ever fully understand, but after watching the young adults interact with Jake, I realize it's so much more.

Turning back, I freeze when I see the truck pulling off to the side of the driveway. It's not the kids coming like I thought. Chase hops out and I ease back. He doesn't look like he's about to attack me, but I'd really rather not get into an altercation with him while there's a bunch of other people around. I'd rather not fight with him at all.

If I'm going to stay in Whispering Pines, I need to at least be in the same space as him. If I'm going to stay with Jake, I definitely have to be able to be around Chase. I won't make Jake choose. Chase never showed up after he shifted back. Plus, he's been avoiding Jake's attempts to reach out. Jake hasn't said anything, but I can tell it hurts him.

"Gemma, stop. Please," Chase calls, and I realize I've been slowly backing away.

"This isn't exactly the place, Chase."

"I'm better. I swear I didn't realize what I was doing." He holds his hands out, blue eyes pleading with me to understand.

I sigh, then peer into the rapidly darkening night. We're far enough away from everyone they won't overhear, but the kids will be here soon. There's no rumble of cars or headlights bumping up the road, though. At least I don't have to explain to him I'm a shifter. At least, I hope he read Jake's messages informing him he didn't have to hide from me.

"Did you read Jake's messages?" I ask, narrowing my gaze.

He nods. "I just couldn't answer. I didn't know how. I wasn't exactly in my right mind and then everything with you and…"

"I get it. I remember my first time and it wasn't fun. I'm pretty sure I bit my sister." I give him an awkward smile as his eyes widen.

"You bit your sister?"

"Oh yeah. She deserved it, though." I smirk and my muscles relax when he tucks his hands in his pockets.

"So, you know about this stuff?" He winces, shaking his head.

"Yeah, except I was born a shifter. I get this might be a little much being an adult. It was bad enough as a teenager. And you don't have to feel bad about the whole stalking me thing. It'll get easier once you level out," I say, wrapping my arms around my waist.

He looks lost, like his entire world has shifted beneath his feet. "Level out?"

"Your animal side and human side will learn to work together instead of shoving each other out of the way for dominance. It'll be a shitty couple of months each time you shift, but it gets better. Promise." I scan his face as he processes what I've said. It's a lot to come to terms with and I don't blame him for being a little off.

He runs his fingers through his blond hair, swallowing hard. "I just feel like there's a lot of shit I don't understand."

"You'll figure it out. You sticking around? Jake would probably like that you're here."

He nods, glancing over my shoulder, and a familiar grin spreads across his face. I follow his gaze and almost burst out laughing. Jake lumbers toward us in full Bigfoot costume. He pulls off the head and tucks it under his arm.

"You could have just shifted and given them the full experience," I say, giggling.

Jake's face transforms when he smirks, a twinkle in his eyes. "Thought that might get awkward since Bigfoot doesn't wear pants."

He tucks my hair behind my ear, then turns to Chase. "You good?"

Chase nods, then glances at me, and I smile. "Yeah, we're good. You need any help?"

Jake gestures him toward the lodge and they take off. They're halfway across the grounds when Jake whips back around and jogs back to me.

"What's wrong?" I frantically search around for whatever I missed.

He doesn't answer, just slides his arm around my waist and kisses me hard before grinning and hustling back to Chase. Since we woke up in the cave, he's opened up, smiling and laughing more. When we do go into town, he's his usual surly self, but that's okay.

Sometimes I worry this is all a dream and I'll wake up with Nigel looking down at me in the warehouse. It seems too good to be true. Yet every time I catch Jake smiling at me, I'm reminded how real it is. His presence is a cool balm on my tattered nerves, soothing my insecurities with a soft touch.

The arriving kids consume all my thoughts and I barely see Jake for the next four hours. The littles loved the haunted house, complete with a bouncy obstacle course at the end. Jake's roars filter through the air, followed by laughter and shouts from the teenagers. Families traveled from far and wide to attend, which is all I wanted. As much as Jake said he was roped into this, he's thrown himself into planning everything, making sure it goes off without a hitch.

The last counselor leaves, their taillights glowing through the night. Main Street is still in full swing, though I'm not sure what they have planned down there. With all the work around here, there hasn't been time to even wonder about the other events.

My feet ache and I'm about ready to curl up for a nap in the hammock Jake refuses to take down. Jake disappeared down the trail ten minutes ago, probably making sure nothing was left behind.

I collapse into the hammock, sending it swinging. The stars sway overhead, and my muscles relax. A twig snaps and I roll my head toward the noise. Jake appears, holding the Bigfoot mask, but his elongated face is covered in hair.

"Give up on dressing up as Bigfoot and just decided to go for the real thing?" I call out.

"You should go down the trail, get the full experience," he says as he drops the mask.

Nervous anticipation bubbles in my stomach, and I roll off the hammock. He tracks my movements as I advance on him. Resting my hands on his chest, I lean close, tipping my head up.

"Are you going to chase me?" I bite my lip, a thrill crawling up my spine.

His lips brush the shell of my ear. "Run, little wolf."

I spin around and his hand lands on my ass. Squealing, I take off for the trail. Leaves crunch under my feet as I push myself faster as he howls behind me. Glancing over my shoulder, I can barely make out his outline as he gives me a head start. Jake never took me down the trail, having me focus on the lodge. I wonder if he had this planned all along.

With only Christmas lights illuminating the path, I almost miss the turnoff leading deeper into the forest. Laughter bubbles up within me, and I clamp my lips together. He won't have any trouble finding me, but the thrill has heat building in my stomach. I'm sure this was scarier when people were jumping out at them, but I only have one surprise coming and I can't fucking wait.

I almost lie down in the middle of the trail as a sacrifice to him. I think better of it when his bellow echoes through the night. Could I shift and see how long it takes for him to find me then? Sure, but what's the fun in that? The bond tethering us together shivers, the sensation running through me, and I stumble.

Bracing my hand on a tree, I lean over to catch my breath. As a wolf, I can run for hours. Apparently not so much when I'm a human. Tipping my head back, I pull in a lungful of air, letting the scent of pine and leaves fill me up. I missed this. Not my hometown, not my family—just being in nature. I missed being able to witness the stars journey across the sky and the changing of seasons. The city bled my soul dry.

A rustling behind me has me shooting up and I yelp. I got so distracted I forgot he was chasing me. His chuckle echoes through the night and I take off again. As his heavy footsteps get nearer, I weave into the trees, dodging trunks and jumping over heavy brush.

"The woods won't hide you, little wolf," he calls in a singsong voice.

My heart pounds in my chest, wetness gathering between my legs as I run. When I can't hear him anymore, I slow, then duck behind a tree. Resting against the rough bark, I peek around the trunk. The silent forest is the only indication that he's near. I cover my mouth as my nostrils flare. I wish I could partially shift like Jake. Then at least I'd be able to see into the dark and probably smell him coming.

"Gotcha," Jake rumbles and I shriek, spinning back.

His body traps mine against the tree, his hips the only thing holding me up. I don't bother resisting when he dips his head and nuzzles my neck.

"Do you know what you smell like, sweetheart?" he murmurs, and I shake my head, running my fingers through his fur.

A growl rolls up his throat, dousing me with desire. "You smell like you're mine."

I whimper, knees buckling, and his long fingers grip my hip, keeping me upright. He presses his lips to my jaw, down my neck until he reaches the collar of my shirt. He huffs, leaning away as he eyes the material as if it has personally offended him.

His deep green eyes meet mine and I swear he smirks. Alarm runs through me, riding the crest of yearning. Before I can react, he grips my shirt and rips it from collar to hem. My bra is next, shredded remnants of it scattering at our feet. His long finger toys with the waistline of my leggings as he scans my body.

I narrow my eyes. "You wouldn't."

Within five seconds my pants are in tatters, leaving me shivering in a pair of lace panties and a shirt he's turned into a coat, the two sides flapping in the cool breeze. I don't know if I'm trembling from anticipation or the cold. Clearly it's the former since fire races through my veins.

"Mine," he whispers before his teeth sink into the mating mark.

I moan, melting into him. His soft fur tickles my skin and I wrap my leg around his thigh. He's too tall for me to reach his waist, but that doesn't mean I don't try. He chuckles as I stand on my tiptoes. Finally, he puts me out of my misery and lifts me with an arm around my waist. His mouth is everywhere, as I lock my ankles around him. I rub against him as his lips wrap around my nipple.

Arching my back, my fingers spear into his hair and I hold him there as pleasure rolls through my body. My head digs into the tree and I use the pain to center myself. Magic pings around us, leaving my skin flushed.

"Jake," I groan, frustration building in my chest.

He unhooks my ankles, setting my feet on the ground. I shiver when he steps away, and I launch into his arms.

He catches me with a grunt, hands gripping my ass. "Gemma, let me shift," he says with a chuckle.

"No." I pout, sticking my bottom lip out. He leans forward and nips at it. "I want you like this."

He's shaking his head before I've finished talking. "Not a good idea, sweetheart. I can't even kiss you like this."

"Then shift your head, silly. Please," I plead, locking my hands around his neck.

He sighs, then tucks my head against his chest. His body trembles and I squeeze my eyes shut while he partially shifts. Peeking up at him, a sharp laugh escapes me, and I slam my hand over my mouth. He scowls, fingers digging into my flesh.

"You're head's so small." I bite my lip, then pull his mouth to mine.

My back slams against the tree as he takes control, devouring me as his tongue duels with mine. I moan into his mouth, rocking against him. He rips his mouth from mine, glancing down as he holds me.

"Wrap those pretty little fingers around my cock, Gemma."

I dive my hand between us, expecting him to be covered in more hair down there. To my surprise, my questing fingers brush against smooth skin. As I grip him, he groans, and I realize he's a lot bigger in this form. He licks my mark, nibbling at the skin, but for once it doesn't distract me.

"You're definitely not going to fit," I whisper.

His hand wraps around my throat and a shudder rolls through me. "We've been through this already, sweetheart. It'll fit."

"I really don't think so."

"Let me in. I want to see that pretty little pussy choking my cock," he growls.

He reaches down, covering my hand with his own and guiding him to my entrance. I pant, eyes fixed on the tip disappearing into me.

"Relax," he breathes before licking the mating mark once more.

I shudder as he slips deeper. Gasping, my eyes roll back in my head. Nothing could have prepared me for the sensation of him sinking into me like this. Our bond hums and I swear it vibrates my clit. When he's fully seated, he pauses, waiting for me to adjust. It doesn't take long before I'm whimpering.

"Please," I whine, trying to create friction.

"Please what?" he asks, nibbling at my ear.

"Claim me," I wheeze, throwing my head back.

His large hands grip my waist, holding me in place while he thrusts into me. There is no buildup, no slow and steady. This is primal, hard and fast. Within seconds, I'm riding the edge of an orgasm, pleading with him with every breath.

"Howl for me, little wolf," he grunts.

I sail into oblivion, following his demands as a primal noise echoes into the night. He rolls his hips, sending shock waves through my system. Running my fingers through the hair on his chest, I tug on the strands, searching for the mark I left on him. The urge to bite him overwhelms me, and I lean forward. A hand on my forehead stops me. His leathery palm pushes me back against the tree.

"Don't want to do that, sweetheart. You'll end up with a mouthful and not the good kind."

He kisses me, cutting off my protest. He's right, but I won't admit that. I clench around him, and he grunts while I smile.

"I'm not sure you're ready for round two," he murmurs against my lips.

"Try me."

He lifts me, his cock slipping out of me, and I snarl as he sets me on my feet. Stepping back, he shifts to fully human. At least his head fits his frame again, but I didn't exactly mind the warmth.

"I wanted to..." I don't know how to finish my sentence without sounding petulant, so I snap my mouth shut.

"Unless you want a little one running around in nine months, it's better this way," he murmurs, cupping my face and pressing our bodies together.

I lean back, trying to focus on his words instead of his hands running over my body. "What?"

"Sasquatch shifters only reproduce when they're shifted. It's why there aren't many of us anymore. Usually, they never tell their partners they're shifters and they don't have any children as a result." He kisses me softly. "We'll talk about it later, though."

He deepens the kiss, igniting the fire in my belly again. As his hands skim down my sides, I pull my mouth away from his and press my lips to his mating mark. He sucks in a sharp breath, his fingers threading through my hair.

"On your knees, Gemma," he says gruffly.

My mouth waters as I glance down at his length. A bolt of desire shoots through me as I lick my lips. My shirt flutters around my body when I sink to my knees and peek up at him. His hand cups my chin, tilting my head back.

He smirk, raising an eyebrow. "Not in the middle of the forest, sweetheart."

He steps around my body, then drops to his knees behind me. My skin tingles in anticipation and I close my eyes. I jump when his hand slides up my back under my shirt., then pushes me onto all fours. I swallow hard, glancing over my shoulder.

"Perfect," he whispers, eyes fixed on my ass.

His fingers dip between my legs, caressing me. I clench around them when he slips two into my core. My head drops and a low moan erupts from my throat as I push back. He builds me up slowly, whispering words of encouragement as my movements become frantic.

My stomach coils tighter and I teeter on the edge. My cries turn to a moan when he pulls from me, then thrusts into me, filling me up. He grips my hips, nails digging into my skin as he surges into me. My fingers find my clit as his hips stutter. Circling the sensitive bud, I spasm around him as he roars my name. He collapses, barely catching himself from smothering me.

"Gemma," he sighs, over and over as our hearts and breathing slow to normal.

We untangle and he pulls me to my feet. I grimace, wrinkling my nose when I glance down. My clothes are in tatters, barely covering anything, and Jake is completely naked. Good thing we're close to the cabin and can walk home. I close my eyes, smiling at the thought.

Jake's arms wrap around me, and I tuck my face into his chest. "You ready to go home?"

I nod, no longer afraid of the future. I'm exactly where I'm meant to be.

# Big Feet-Bigger Heart

## Gemma

**Epilogue-Two Months Later**

It's snowing. Again. I'm not surprised since it's been snowing non-stop for weeks. I wouldn't care either except it's winter solstice. A cheery fire warms the living room and the scent of pine fills the air. After weeks of bugging Jake, he finally put up a tree in the corner. A lone present complete with a red bow rests underneath. My vision blurs while I stare at the bright wrapping paper.

We didn't talk about exchanging presents and now I'm wondering if I should have just let it go. Bringing it up seemed too bold, regardless of the fact we're fated mates. Neither of us has brought up the L-word.

Everything moves faster in a shifter relationship, but it still feels too soon. At least that's what I tell myself every time it crosses my mind. In reality, I don't think Jake is ready. I don't know if he ever will be unless I force the issue and I'm not about to do that.

Which is why getting him a solstice gift might have been too much. He clearly didn't get me anything. I didn't expect him to, but it still hurts. I sigh, tipping my head back on the couch to stare at the shadows dancing across the ceiling. With only the fire and lights on the tree illuminating the space, I can't exactly read. I still have a book sitting next to me. I've only made it a fraction of the way through his library.

Shoving to my feet, I groan. My journey into the woods yesterday was fun, but I may have overdone it. My inner wolf took over, excited by the fluffy snow covering the ground. She ran farther than normal, leaving us tired and sore by the time we got home.

I gaze out the window, searching the tree line for any sign of Jake. He said he'd be back by nightfall, yet the sun set almost an hour ago and he isn't home. Before I knew he was a sasquatch shifter I would have been worried. Now I'm just annoyed. He probably got caught up with Chase. They've been hanging out a lot lately. Today was no different.

I straighten, an ache in my chest hitting me hard. I haven't felt it since Jake and I discovered we were mates. Jake has grown more distant the longer I'm here. We had several weeks of bliss before he started disappearing to Chase's. At first, I assumed it was due to his friend becoming a shifter. Now I wonder if it's something else.

Shaking my head, I dismiss the thought. I'm not the insecure woman I was a few months ago. I'm more grounded than I've ever been before. I'll just talk to Jake about it when he comes back.

The back door swings open, banging against the wall, and I jump. Hurrying back to the couch, I sink down and grab the book. It's still too dark to read, but I'll pretend anyway.

"Gemma? You awake?" Jake calls from the hallway, and I roll my eyes.

It's barely six in the evening. Unless he thinks I was napping all day, which isn't out of the question. After I shift, I usually end up groggy the next morning. Jake said it was because I don't shift enough. We've been shifting together more, but it hasn't made a difference yet.

"Gemma?"

I glance over my shoulder as he rounds the corner, attempting to school my face into one of serenity. His face is covered by a thick beard now. If it gets too cold in the bedroom, he wakes up with hair covering his chest, arms, and legs. I swear it's like he shifts randomly while he sleeps.

A flutter of nerves dance in my stomach at the thought of confronting him. I wish I could just live in the bubble of happiness we've had for the last two months. If he's having second thoughts, I'd rather know now. I'd rather not tuck my tail between my legs and run home. Especially since I told Slade I was staying in Whispering Pines.

"What are you doing?" he asks, setting his boots by the front door.

I fix my eyes on the page instead of staring at him. "Reading. How's Chase?"

He collapses on the couch next to me, tipping his head back. "Not great. He's not adjusting well. I'm not exactly the best at explaining shit. Plus, I didn't grow up in a shifter community like you."

"Maybe he should go to one," I murmur.

He sighs, closing his eyes. "Go where?"

"To a shifter community. There's probably a couple around here if he needs to stay close for work."

Jake snorts, rolling his head to face me. "He doesn't work. He helps me with the camp and lives off his inheritance. Said he didn't want to waste his time making rich men richer. Built his house out by the lake and has lived there ever since."

"Well, then nothing is standing in his way of going to find some other shifters who might help him. I'd offer, but I doubt he'll want me around," I say, turning the page. Not that I've read even a single word.

"He just doesn't want to put you out."

That's the line Jake always feeds me every time I offer to go with him. I don't blame him. It's not his fault that Chase doesn't want to be around me. I'm sure he's afraid of spontaneously shifting again. Maybe that's why Jake has been distant. It can't be easy having his best friend and his mate at odds with one another.

We sit in silence for several minutes while the fire crackles in the hearth. Methodically, I turn the pages, never fully concentrating on the words. I'll have to find where I was before and reread it, but that's fine. When I can't take it anymore, I pull in a deep breath.

"I was thinking of going home." I wince as soon as I say it, and he stiffens.

"What does that mean?" He tries to be nonchalant, but tension bleeds into his tone.

"Haven't been home in a while. Thought I'd go before we're snowed in."

He leans forward, resting his elbows on his knees. "There a reason you decided this so suddenly?"

"It's not sudden. I told you two weeks ago I was considering going back. Plus, Kira said our mother has been lamenting about how I'm never home." I swallow hard, finally setting the book on my lap.

He hangs his head. I don't know why he's acting like this is the end of the world. Then again, I am ignoring my heart seizing in my chest at the thought of leaving. I don't even know if it'd be forever or just for a visit. I could be back in a couple weeks.

He rubs his hands over his face. "Why haven't you been back?"

"Um, well, I was a late bloomer. I didn't shift until I was in high school. It was a point of contention amongst my siblings. You know how Moon Cove is with the festivals and people coming in to 'catch' a supernatural creature. The residents thought it was a great money maker, so they had the teenagers go out and shift so the cameras could spot them. Honestly, it's terrifying." I wipe my sweaty palms on my leggings, hoping he doesn't notice how nervous I am.

"What does that have to do with you being a late bloomer?"

"Because I wasn't allowed to participate. They had to pick up the slack, and they didn't think that was fair. So, they made me be the one who shifted for Samhain even though I'd only shifted once before. It would have been fine. I mean, I was nervous as hell, but I could have gotten through it. Until Alissa decided to trick me."

"Your sister? You never told me how many siblings you have. Or all their names." He glances at me, but quickly drops his head again.

"Alister, Sloane, Slade, Kira, Alissa, and Eli." I rattle them off like I have a thousand times before. He whips his head around, eyes widening. "Yeah, it's a lot."

"Where do you fit in the lineup?"

"After Kira, before Alissa. Anyways—" I pull out the word, hoping he won't interrupt again. It's hard enough to get this story out.

He gives me a sheepish look before saying, "Sorry."

"Alissa was always the main instigator in things. She thought it was hilarious to jump out and scare people. Most of it was harmless until my first shift for the docuseries crew in town for Samhain. She told me the wrong time to be ready for the cameras. Then someone slipped a note in my locker at school. I thought it was from a boy I liked. He wanted to meet me in the woods on the other side of the lake. When I got there..." My cheeks heat just remembering the humiliation.

"Did he stand you up?"

I let out a sharp laugh. "I wish he would have. No, half of my class was out there with the boy, who was front and center. For some reason, I still didn't get it. That was until they started throwing stuff at me."

"Stuff?"

I huff, wondering if I should have just kept this story to myself. "Rotten food, pinecones, dirt clumps. It wasn't exactly a fun experience. Then Alissa came strolling in and informed me I was late. No time to get cleaned up. Then my mom started calling, then Kira, all while Alissa and the others were laughing and jeering at me while I ran toward the set up in the middle of the forest."

"How old was Alissa?" he asks gruffly.

"Does that matter? She was old enough to know better. Found out later she wanted the boy I was crushing on." I snort, shaking my head. "Turns out I was almost late, and the cameras caught me before I shifted. They knew something was wrong when a wolf suddenly appeared without a gangly teenager running from the trees and screaming for her life. They accused the town of staging it all for clout. They lost a lot of money and it was my fault. At least, that's what everyone said. I spent the rest of high school keeping my head down, then left. I haven't been back since. It was a long time ago."

He pushes from the couch, then stomps toward the kitchen. My eyes catch on the present under the tree, and I bite my cheek. I thought it would be funny, but I shouldn't have bought it. I thought the goddess guided me here. It was fate leading me to where I was supposed to be. With the way Jake has been acting, I'm wondering if I'm merely stuck in the same cycle I was before.

"I talked to Slade," he calls with his head stuck in the fridge. "Finally asked him why he didn't say anything about being a shifter."

"What'd he say?" I don't really care. I want to talk about why he's keeping me at a distance.

"He didn't want to out me and make things awkward. Oh, and he sent you here on a hunch. Said the moon guided him."

"What the hell is that supposed to mean?" I push to my feet. My hands flutter at my sides before I sink onto the couch sideways. I don't want to follow him around like a lost puppy.

"No idea. You going to tell me why you're talking about going back to Moon Cove? And why you were sitting in the dark pretending to read?" He closes the fridge, then leans against the counter and crosses his arms.

"You going to tell me why you keep disappearing off to Chase's every day? Or why you keep dipping from conversations? Or how about the fact you never answered me when I asked about celebrating winter solstice?" I snap, jumping to my feet.

Shit, now I'm standing and I have nowhere to put my hands. I wrap them around my waist and tip my chin up. He nods sharply, tracking my movements as if I'm going to dash out the front door. He forgot I'm not the one who runs away.

"I told you Chase isn't doing well. He's not exactly adjusting," he says slowly. "Do you expect me to let him muddle his way through this shit?"

He's put me in an impossible position. Of course I don't want him to abandon Chase, but he's not the only one suffering. I won't make him choose between us. That's not fair.

"No, I don't. But I also expected when you weren't with him, you'd actually be here. The only time you pay me any attention is when we're shifted. Just because we're fated doesn't mean..." I glance away to hide the sheen in my eyes.

The tug on the bond between us is the only warning I have before he vaults over the couch. I stumble back as it tips backward, his body crashing to the ground with it. He groans, curling into a ball.

"What the hell," I whisper, peeking over the furniture. "Did you honestly think that was a faster way of getting over here?"

"I didn't think it would fall over." His muffled words hold more embarrassment than pain, thankfully.

Crouching next to him, I pat his arm. He rolls onto his back, dark green eyes finding mine. The bond shimmers between us, but I no longer understand where it's leading me. His palm cups my cheek and I duck my head.

"I'm sorry. I can't...I don't..." His hand drops as he wipes it across his face.

Sitting back on my heels, I swallow once. Twice. "It's fine. We tried at least."

"No, I just don't know how to say what I want." He props himself on his elbow, his other hand digging into his pocket.

He pulls a small box out and I fall onto my ass, shock flooding me. "Oh no. Jake, absolutely not."

A grin spreads across his face. "I'm not proposing, sweetheart. But I did get you a solstice gift. I wanted to get you something special. That's why I've been going into town more. I swear Paul was about to throw me out, I was hanging around the store for so long waiting for it to come in."

I don't reach for the jewelry box, though I can't pull my eyes away from it. "Why haven't you been talking to me when you are here?"

"Nervous," he grunts, proffering the gift.

When I still don't take it, he huffs, then sits up. The lid creaks as he opens it, revealing a necklace.

"Are those moonstones?" I whisper.

"I figured it was appropriate. Slade helped me get in touch with a jeweler in Moon Cove. I don't know how, but she said it's made with magic, so it won't break when you shift." He blushes, fingers brushing the wire pendant.

Two trees, one white and the other black, intertwine with one another. Moonstones make up the buds of the dark tree.

"What are the dark gems?"

"Black diamonds. Happy solstice, Gemma."

A tear drops onto my hand as I reach for the box. I blink rapidly, sniffing. "I'm sorry. I should have just said something."

"So, you like it?"

Leaning over his outstretched hand, I kiss him hard. He falls back from the force, and I go with him. His arm wraps around my waist, sealing our bodies together. I sigh as his tongue sweeps along my lips, and he takes full advantage. Every time we collide, all my worries fall away, melting into the bond between us. I struggle to remember why I ever doubted him.

His head thumps against the floor as he pulls away. "Every fucking time."

"What?"

A smile plays on his lips, his eyes softening when they meet mine. "Every time I kiss you, I feel like I'm home. I'm right where I'm supposed to be."

I rub my nose along his jaw, his beard tickling my skin, and I shiver. He's been growing it out and I can't tell whether I love or hate it. It's fluffy, just like when he shifts. He sits up, pushing me onto my knees. Biting my lip, I try to contain my giggle while he struggles with the clasp on the necklace.

"Need some help?" I ask, tilting my head.

"No. I can get it. If my fingers can make you come in under two minutes, I can open a fucking necklace," he mumbles. I chuckle, his tone so at odd with his words.

After a few minutes, he cries out in triumph, gesturing for me to turn around. It takes him another minute to secure it, but eventually it settles on my chest. The wire warms and my mating mark pulses. Or maybe that's the gems. Either way, it glows in the soft light from the fire. I spin, glancing up at him, and he swallows hard.

"Does it look okay?" My fingers brush the necklace and another bolt of heat flows to my mark.

"No. You're radiant. She said it would glow if it was meant for you. That the goddess approved," he whispers, his fingers trailing down my arm before tangling our fingers together.

He tugs me closer, brushing his lips against mine. My eyes flutter closed, giving myself into the pleasure he's building within me. I keep waiting for it to diminish, or settle, but every kiss is like the first time.

"I have a present for you," I murmur.

"It'll keep. I've got another to give you first."

I pull back, raising an eyebrow. The smirk spreading across his face should warn me, but I'm still caught off guard when he tugs me to my feet. Guiding me to the thick rug in front of the fireplace, I glance under the tree, searching for another box. Mine is the only one still there.

"Where is it?" I ask as his hand lands on my shoulder.

Slowly, he eases me onto my back, and I swivel my head from side to side, still looking for something I missed. I yelp when he hooks his fingers into my waistband.

"Up," he grunts, tugging on the fabric.

I lift my hips before I've fully processed what he's doing. Before I know it, he's flinging my pants toward the overturned couch.

"Jake, what are you...oh." I moan, eyes rolling to the back of my head when he licks me from core to clit. "I...What..."

I can't pull in a full breath. He swirls his tongue, devouring me as I try to complete a sentence. A growl rumbles from him, vibrating between my legs, and I shiver.

"Do you mind? I'm trying to give you your gift, sweetheart."

His head drops again and he nips at my inner thigh, making me yelp. His lips press to the mark I'm sure he's left behind and his beard tickles the sensitive skin. I giggle as my legs clamp around his head, trapping him between my thighs. He growls once more, the sound vibrating my clit, and another moan leaves me.

Jake wraps his arms around my legs, fingers digging into my skin. My knees fall to the sides, giving him full access. I pull the tie from his hair and wind my fingers through the strands, tugging them with each pass of his tongue over my clit. Every time he slows just a little more, and I swear he's doing it on purpose. A whine leaves me when I'm teetering on the edge, and he pulls away.

"Something wrong?" he hums, licking me again, and I shudder.

"I don't recall asking for edging as a gift," I gasp, throwing my head back on the rug.

He chuckles, pressing a kiss to my center, then glances up at me. "Would you like to give me your gift?"

I raise an eyebrow. "Stop looking at my mouth like that. Your gift is under the tree."

His eyes dart to the package and the corner of his mouth tips up. "Can I open it now?"

He doesn't wait for an answer before scrambling toward it on all fours. I launch myself at his back, wrapping my arms around his chest and my legs around his waist. Peals of laughter ring throughout the room as he hauls me along with him. His fingers brush against the shiny paper and I sink my teeth into his neck. Instantly he drops to his stomach, taking me down with him. His muscles ripple and he groans.

"You play dirty, sweetheart."

"Be a good boy and finish what you started, and I won't have to play dirty," I murmur in his ear.

He snarls, flipping over, and I'm suddenly on my back with him hovering over me. My stomach flips in anticipation as his mouth skims over my jaw, then he seals our lips together. He grinds his hips into mine and I yelp. He pulls back and I glare at him.

"Take your pants off. Zippers hurt," I huff when he grins.

My fingers tremble as they grasp at the button. He bats my hands away, then stands to shove them down his legs. His shirt follows close behind and I drop my own onto the pile. He tugs me to my feet, melding our bodies together, but we don't exactly match up. I giggle when he stoops, expecting him to kiss me again. Instead, he tips me over his shoulder, and I let out a shriek.

"Jake," I giggle, and his hand slides up my thigh, leaving goosebumps in its wake.

He spins around several times, searching for a place to set me down. The couch is still tipped over. The oversize chair won't hold both of us. He takes one step toward the kitchen, and I let out a sound of protest.

"Not the table. My shoulder blades can't take it." There's still laughter tinging my voice, and he pinches my inner thigh.

He drops me to my feet, and I grin up at him as the bond between us shivers, making my breath catch. Planting my hands on my hips, I tilt my head. The second a smirk overtakes his face, I realize I've made a mistake.

His hand lands on my shoulder and guides me to my knees. My tongue darts out, then I pull my bottom lip between my teeth. Glancing up at his broad frame, my mouth waters. His cock bobs in front of me and I lean forward.

He steps away and I pout while he chuckles. "Sweetheart, I've waited long enough. You can wake me up in the morning with that sweet mouth wrapped around my cock."

A shudder rolls through me and I wrap my arms around my waist, curling my body around them. Every time he says something like that, I feel like I've been transported into one of the books behind him. I'm pretty sure he's learned everything from those stories. It's the best and worst since I don't think I hold up to the fictional women in them.

Jake drops to his knees in front of me, tucking his knuckle under my chin. When our eyes meet, a shockwave of desire splits the air between us. His arm wraps around me, pulling me on top of him as he lies back. I settle my hands on his chest as he runs his palms along my skin. Fire flows through my veins, igniting a flame within my belly. I rock against him, sliding my wetness along his length. He groans, fingers digging into my waist.

He lifts me and I sink onto him, my legs trembling as he fills me up. It's still a stretch, and I pause while I adjust to his size. No matter how many times we join, it's like the first time. A rush of pleasure ripples through me, and the bond anchors deeper within me. My mark pulses and need flows through me. I need his mouth, his hands, his everything.

Slowly, he rolls his hips, sending a spasm through me, and he grunts. He does it again, but it's not enough. It's never enough. A whine leaves me as I try to take over. He huffs, then rolls us, the fluffy rug tickling my neck.

"Faster," I gasp, hooking my ankles behind his back and forcing him deeper.

The vein in his jaw ticks as he grits his teeth. His eyes flash between human and shifter as he thrusts into me. Each surge sends another pulse down the bond, another bolt of bliss resonating within my chest. My nails dig into his skin as my climax looms just out of reach. Then his hand drops between my legs, fingers circling my clit, and I explode.

A low groan leaves me as I tip my head back. Jake doesn't slow as he eases me through my orgasm and I collapse, my body weightless as he roars out his own release.

Our panting fills the room, and his hands skim along my back as I cling to him. He murmurs words I can't make out, but it doesn't matter. He says the same thing every time. Just my name over and over, spoken like a prayer to the goddess, thanking her for bringing us together. These moments are my favorite. There are no doubts, no insecurities or worries. It's just us—fated mates bound together as we should be.

"I'll never get used to this," he murmurs into my hair.

Folding my hands on his chest, I rest my chin on them as I gaze at his face. "Like the first time, every time."

He smiles, brushing hair from my forehead. He cups my cheek and I close my eyes, relishing the feeling of still being joined.

"You know I love you, right?"

My eyes fly open, and I suck in a sharp breath. "What?"

I heard him, but I didn't expect those words to come so soon. He grins, fingering the pendant of my necklace.

"Probably not the most romantic way to tell you, huh?" Fear flashes in his eyes before his gaze darts away.

"Did you mean it?" I whisper.

His arms tighten around me. "With everything in me."

I sigh, swallowing hard. "I love you, too."

"You don't have to—"

"Do not interrupt me," I snarl, and his gaze snaps to mine. "I have for a while, but I wasn't going to push you. I thought you'd only want me around because we were fated."

He's shaking his head before I've even finished. I swallow the groan wanting to escape as I sit up. He's still deep inside me and the move makes me quiver around him. He helps me off him and I curl into his side.

"I love you, Gemma. Not because we're fated. Not because of magic or the goddess or anything else. I love you for worming your way in. For calling me on my shit. For showing me I'm worth something. You're everything I was too afraid to hope for." He presses a kiss to my head as I sniff.

"Do you want to open your gift now?" I should tell him why I love him too, but I've cried enough tonight. We'll have plenty of time to share those things later when I won't fall apart.

He reaches his hand under the tree and snatches up the package. I sit up, spinning to lean against the overturned couch. Tucking my knees to my chest,

I wrap my arms around my legs. He settles next to me, shaking the box, then glances at me. I rub my palm along his beard.

"Did you ever think of shaving this?" I ask, and he raises an eyebrow. "I'm just saying, I usually like a clean-shaven man."

It takes everything in me to not laugh. The shock in his eyes followed quickly by a scowl almost do me in.

"I didn't realize that," he mutters, turning the gift over in his large hands.

I wave my hand lazily around. "We'll talk about it later. Open your present."

I bite my lip as he rips at the paper, completely forgetting my question. There's a giddiness to him I've never seen before. No, I have. It was there when he was convincing me to ride the zipline. It was there when the campers were piling on top of him in his Bigfoot costume. It's there when he holds me.

"Dog clippers?" He shoots me a confused look.

I press my lips together, holding back another giggle. "I told you I like a man clean-shaven."

His eyes narrow and I burst into laughter. Jake growls as he lunges for me. I shriek as he throws me over his shoulder once again and takes off for the stairs, the dog clippers lying forgotten on the floor. As he hauls me upstairs, a flash of bright white light temporarily blinds me. When my vision clears, a single white feather rests under the tree, illuminated by the magic within. A peace rolls over me as I know I've finally found a place to call home.

# Thank You

**Thank you so much for reading Jake and Gemma's story!**

Ready for another adventure?
Check out the other works available by Emilia Abraham
If you'd like to hear about the other stories that have been living in my head, sign up for my
newsletter (including extra scenes & epilogues), visit my website, or follow me on social media
visit:
emiliaabraham.com

Special Thanks:

K.B. Barrett Designs-Cover Artist and Formatter
Emily Michel-Editor
Erenee-Beta Reader
Krysten-Omega Readers

# Other Works

**Also by E. Abraham:**

Shadows of Synd:

Under the Shadows: Book 1

Between the Shadows: Novella

Running From Shadows: Book 2

Becoming Shadows: Book 3

Shadows Within Us: Book 4

Ruins of Rima:

Spin-off Series

Chasing Darkness: Book 1

Charmed by Darkness (Winter 2023)

Available on Newsletter:

Extra Scenes/Bridging Epilogues

Also by Emilia Abraham:

Stuck at Sundown

# About the Author

After many years of dreaming of becoming a full-time writer, Emilia Abraham took the
leap, bringing her words to print. From sweet contemporary romance to spicy why
choose and everything in between, she focuses on the happily ever after.

Emilia lives in the Upper Midwest with her husband (who's probably sick of listening to
her expound on fictional men) and three kids (who try to steal her post-it notes). When
she's not writing, she enjoys reading, playing video games, and consuming copious
amounts of energy drinks.